WHAT'S LEFT OF ME

KRISTEN GRANATA

To Jasmine, Carrie, Janae, Jennifer, and Chelsea, Thank you for sharing your stories with me and allowing me to share them with the world.

This book is for every woman who's fighting a secret battle. You are not alone.

AUTHOR'S NOTE

I started writing this story after a friend of mine lost her baby when she was eight months pregnant.

I realized that I had nothing to say, nothing to offer that could make it "better" for her. As a writer, words are my thing, so I feel helpless when they fall short.

Whenever someone experiences something that I haven't, I try to put myself in their shoes. How would I feel? How would I react? What would I do? But it's not the same.

It's easy to make judgments from where we stand, not truly knowing or understanding what it's like. (And even when we've gone through something similar, we each handle it differently.) So, I decided to talk with women who've been through the themes I wanted to cover.

This story contains topics that may be sensitive for some readers. I hope that I've handled them realistically, yet delicately enough so that the triggers aren't too overwhelming for you.

ONE

CALLIE

I'M NOT GETTING out of bed today.

This is an amazing mattress. Just the right amount of firm-to-soft ratio. This comforter rocks too. It's puffy but not suffocating. These sheets are a high thread count. Breathable. I did good when I picked these out. I could stay here all day. Don't need to go grocery shopping. Who needs to eat when you have a mattress like this? Laundry? Pffft. I won't need clothes if I stay in bed. This is the perfect solution to all of life's problems.

But what is that awful smell?

A long, wet tongue slides across my cheek, and I groan. "Go back to sleep, Maverick."

With my eyelids still closed, I reach out and smooth my fingers through my retriever's fluffy fur. His tongue makes another pass over my cheek, and again, I'm hit with a blast of that stench.

My nose scrunches as my head jerks up off the pillow. "Maverick, did you eat your poop again?"

His head dips down, and he rests it on top of his front paws.

"Don't give me those eyes! They're not going to work on me this time."

He leaps off the bed and bounds into the hallway, tail swatting from left to right as he waits for me at the top of the stairs.

Guess I'm getting out of bed.

I flip the comforter off my body, swing my legs to the side of the mattress, and jam my feet into my plush white slippers.

Once I'm vertical, my head throbs like someone dropped an anvil on it. I grip onto the cool iron bannister and take my time down the spiral staircase. Maverick waits at the bottom, his body thrashing like a shark from the momentum of his tail.

"You are way too awake for me right now, bud."

He *woofs* in response and prances into the kitchen ahead of me.

When I stagger into the kitchen, sunlight streams through the windows, reflecting off the marble countertop and searing my retinas. I yank the cord on the blinds and bury my face in the crook of my elbow, hissing like Dracula.

Maverick plops down at my feet, nuzzling my ankle with his wet nose. We both jump when we hear the creak of the front door, and then he takes off into the foyer.

Paul strides into the kitchen, saturated in sweat from his morning run, and I hold my breath until his lips curve up into a smile.

"Good morning, gorgeous."

Relief washes over me. "Morning. How was your run?"

Paul snatches a water bottle from the refrigerator and twists off the cap. "Four miles today."

His royal-blue Under Armour T-shirt clings to his broad chest, the muscles in his biceps flexing with his movements. His blond strands are damp and disheveled, and his skin glows with a golden sheen.

I lift an eyebrow. "How is it that you look this sexy after a four-mile run?"

He grins. "How is it that you look this sexy when you just woke up?"

I huff out a sardonic laugh, knowing damn well I resemble the Crypt Keeper at the moment.

Paul leans in with puckered lips, but I make an X with my forearms in front of my face. "The poop-eating bandit got me. You might want to stay back."

He looks down at Maverick, and as if he knows we're talking about him, Maverick ducks around the corner of the island.

"You're nasty, dog."

"I'll call the vet today. Maybe they'll know how to deter him from eating his own feces."

Paul leans his hip against the counter. "I think all dogs eat their own crap."

"We have to watch him better when he's out back. Stop it before he can get to it." I walk around the island so I can start on breakfast. "I read something once that said dogs eat their poop when they're lacking vitamins in their diet. Was it an article? Maybe Josie told me. I don't know; I can't remember. Either way—"

I stop moving and snap my fingers in front of Paul's face. "Are you even listening to me?"

Paul shakes his head, his eyes roving over my body. "I haven't heard one word since you stood up in those silky shorts."

I smile and set a frying pan on top of the stove. "Please. This isn't anything you haven't seen before."

"Yet it never gets old." He closes the distance between us and stands behind me, trailing his hands up my arms.

I hum at his light touch, welcoming it. "Let's hope you always think that."

"I know I will." He tilts my head to the side and presses his lips to my neck. One of his hands slips under my camisole, cupping my breast, while he tugs my shorts down with the other.

My head falls back against his shoulder, and a long exhale leaves my parted lips. "Don't you have a meeting?"

"Just means we'll have to be quick." His fingers slide between my thighs and press inside me while his thumb rubs circles on my clit at the same time.

My legs quiver, and I reach forward to grip the edge of the counter. Paul gives my back a gentle push until my chest is pressed against the cool marble, and then he slides his length inside me.

"I love you," he whispers at my ear, gripping my hips, pumping in and out of me in long, controlled strokes.

I arch my back to meet each of his thrusts, and his fingers return to my clit as he drives into me faster, harder, deeper. I moan, writhing against his hand, and his pace quickens.

I can feel the pleasure mounting in my core, the steady build like a rising wave. Soon, it crashes over me. I cry out as the spasms rack through my body. Paul goes under too, grunting as his hot liquid fills me.

He holds me there, pressing soft kisses to my shoulder, my neck, my temple. "This is what I've missed. I'm so glad we can finally get back to how things used to be."

"Me too."

And that's my halfhearted truth.

I should relish in this feeling, the closeness, his gentle love, but my mind crawls toward the analytical place it always goes to, calculating the date, the time, the exact location in my cycle. My fingers itch to reach for my phone and click on the fertility app out of habit, but for the first time in three years, I don't.

And after last night, I never will again.

With a pat on my backside, Paul pulls away and tucks himself back into his running shorts. "I'm hitting the shower."

My eyes linger on his wide back and confident swagger as he leaves the room with his head held high, free from the anxious thoughts that plague me.

Guilt squeezes my chest when I think about everything that I've put him through over the past few years. The stress, the doctor's appointments, all my tears.

No more.

Paul's right. We need to get back to the way we used to be. Back before I became obsessed with starting a family. Before I plunged into depression and dragged him down with me. Before the people we were when we got married turned into strangers.

It's time to put it to rest.

And it's up to me to do it.

I can be better.

I can find happiness again.

I straighten my camisole, pull up my shorts, and start gathering the ingredients I need for breakfast.

The kitchen is my favorite room in this entire house. Beautiful marble countertops; tall, white cabinets; stainless steel appliances. Paul had the contractor create it based off of my exact vision. He says it's because he loves me so much. I say it's because he needs me to cook for him because Paul could burn water.

Sometimes it feels like I'm living someone else's life, like this is all a dream. Living in a mansion in Orange County, California, married to the Adonis that is my husband, not having to get up and work 9-5 every day. I'm very fortunate to have everything I could ever need at my fingertips.

I didn't grow up with all this. I came from an average, middle-class family. But when I met Paul in college, everything changed. We've been together for nine years now, and I'm still not used to this lifestyle. I don't think I ever will be.

As I scoop the egg-white-and-spinach omelet with hash browns into the glass container, Paul struts back into the kitchen, dressed to perfection in his navy suit. I hand him his lunch bag, his breakfast, and his coffee mug.

He presses his lips to the top of my head. "Thanks, gorgeous. I'll see you tonight."

"Have a good day."

"Be good, poop breath," he calls over his shoulder.

Maverick barely lifts his head from where he's sprawled out by the back door, bathing in the sunspot.

The dog-life of Riley.

When I hear the click of the front door, a long exhale whooshes out of me. I want to walk upstairs and climb right back into bed, but if I'm going to make things better, I have to start by looking the part. So instead, I drag myself up the stairs and into the bathroom.

It's been a while since I've cared about my appearance. Been a while since I've cared about anything other than becoming a mother.

Fake it 'til you make it, they say.

Flipping on the lights, I shimmy out of my pajama shorts and tear the camisole over my head. I suck in a sharp breath when my eyes land on my reflection in the mirror for the first time this morning. My stomach clenches at the sight of the dark-purple splotches along my left bicep, memories of last night flooding my vision.

Damn you, Maverick. I wanted to stay in bed today.

I blink away the hot tears before they get the chance to brim over, quick to replace the weak emotion with logic.

Paul drank too much last night, and everything we've been holding in for the last three years came to a head.

It was my fault.

I shouldn't have let things get to that point.

I shouldn't have spoken up.

I'll do better.

It won't happen again.

Needing a plan rather than wallowing in self-pity, I examine the span of the bruising and mentally scour through my wardrobe for the right sweater. Hopefully, today will be brisk enough to wear one without drawing attention to myself. Even if the weather's hot, I could get away with wearing one of my cardigans with three-quarter-length sleeves. Shouldn't be too conspicuous.

Deep breath in through the nose, and out through the mouth.

Maverick.

California king bed.

Walk-in closet.

Dream kitchen.

Yard with a pool.

Mercedes.

"I'm fine," I tell my reflection. "Everything's fine."

I twist the lever in the shower and step under the waterfall, letting the warm water cascade over my skin. By the time I lather and rinse, the urge to cry is gone and I can breathe easy again.

Wrapping the towel around myself, I swing open the bathroom door and head to my closet. My pale-yellow sweater covers the mess on my arm, and I leave it unbuttoned over my white-and-yellow floral maxi dress. I spend thirty minutes lining my eyelids, curling my lashes, and passing the flatiron over my blond waves, taming it the way I know Paul prefers it.

With my armor in place, I square my shoulders in the mirror and heave a sigh. "Good as new."

At the sound of my sandals clunking down the stairs, my overeager dog gallops toward the front door.

"Ready for your walk, Mav?"

He *woofs* and spins in a circle.

I'm clipping his leash onto his collar when a loud *boom* echoes outside. My shoulders jolt, and Maverick jumps to scratch at the door, barking like a madman.

"Are we starting with the fireworks already?"

The Fourth of July isn't for another week. Plus, it's nine o'clock in the morning.

I push the sheer cream curtain aside and peer out the window. A white pickup truck rolls to a stop in front of Josie's house across the street. Well, there are visible areas of white paint—the truck was white at *one* time—surrounded by burnt-orange rust spots eating away at the metal. The bed of the truck is covered by a blue tarp, securing the contents underneath with a yellow bungee cord. Thick, black smoke billows from the exhaust pipe, trailing all the way down the block.

The truck pops again as it idles, sending Maverick into another barking fit.

"All right, bud. Enough." I reach down to pat his head, keeping my nose glued to the windowpane.

The driver's door swings open, and a man steps out. A navy-blue baseball cap sits on his head, pulled down low over his eyes. His plain white T-shirt, which looks more like an undershirt, is wrinkled and smudged with brown stains. His jeans are ripped—not the kind of rips people pay for—and equally as filthy as his shirt. He strides around the front bumper and up the walkway that leads to Josie's backyard.

"He must be the new landscaper."

Maverick cocks his head to the side as if he's listening to me.

Josie's Lexus isn't in her driveway, so I find it strange that she'd give a stranger the passcode to get in through her back gate. Maybe she left it unlocked for him before she left. Seems odd, but we've been desperate to find a new landscaping company after one of the workers from our old company got caught having an affair with Mrs. Nelson down the street. If Josie found someone dependable, I'm going to need his card. Paul will be thrilled. Our shrubs need trimming, and weeds are beginning to poke up through the pavers in our driveway.

"Come on, bud." I snatch my sunglasses off the entryway table and lead Maverick out the front door.

Once we cross the wide street, Maverick pulls ahead of me, his nose to the ground, sniffing his way up the path of pavers. The iron gate is ajar, and Maverick continues pulling me through the opening into the backyard.

The layout is like mine. Same-sized rectangular inground pool, similar patio furniture. But Josie's yard is full of life, whereas mine has barely been touched. Squirt guns, skateboard ramps, and balls from every sport litter her grass. It's obvious that a family lives here.

Josie often complains of the mess, but I'd give anything to step on a Lego block belonging to *my* child.

The landscaper is standing in front of the pool house with his back to me, one hand on his hip while the other tips the neck of a brown glass bottle into his mouth.

So much for finding a reliable landscaper.

I stop a few feet behind him, wrapping Maverick's leash around my hand a few times to keep him from pulling me any further.

"Don't think you should be drinking on the job, sir."

The man spins around and blasts me with a scowl that sends a shiver down my spine. Under the brim of his hat, I spot a deep, disgruntled crease that lies between his dark brows. His prominent, unshaven jaw pops, clenching, as if he's gritting through physical pain while he glares at me with piercing steel-blue eyes.

The hairs on my arms lift in a whoosh of awareness, and fear slices into me.

I shouldn't have come back here alone.

Maverick's tail thumps against my leg as he leans forward to get to the stranger, clearly unfazed by the potential danger I've put us in.

"I ... I'm sorry." I pull Maverick back. "I didn't mean to startle you. I live across the street."

Great idea. Tell the nice murderer where you live.

He doesn't respond. Doesn't introduce himself. He just keeps hitting me with that unwavering glacial stare. It's too much, too powerful to withstand, so I lower my gaze and take in the rest of him.

Strong shoulders span wide, adding to his towering height. His shirt is taut around his upper-body. The muscles in his arms are well-defined striations, more than just swollen biceps and triceps. He's carved from stone, detailed and unforgiving. A work of art that people travel from all over to stand in front of in admiration.

This man is beautiful.

Then again, that's probably what every woman said about Ted Bundy right before he killed them.

I should leave. Flee back to the safety of my home.

But I'm frozen, sucked in by the enigmatic energy surging around him like a tornado of rage and agony.

And I'm standing right in his path.

I swallow, my throat thick with apprehension. "I, uh, we're in need of a new landscaper. I saw you come back here and figured I'd come ask for your card." I swallow again, my gaze flicking to the beer bottle glinting in the sunlight. "It's a little early to be drinking, don't you think? I mean, you shouldn't be impaired while operating heavy machinery. Don't want to lose a foot in the lawn mower."

I choke out a laugh, desperate to make light of the situation, but it comes out strangled and strained.

The man doesn't laugh with me. He doesn't crack a smile. Not sure his facial muscles would know how if he tried to. One massive hand is curled at his side, as if he's gripping the leash on his composure, his self-control ready to snap.

"You've got some nerve coming back here like this." The man's voice is gruff with a sharp edge, like he gargles with a throatful of razors every morning.

My eyebrows lift in a flash of irritation. "Me? I'm a potential customer. One who wants to pay you for your landscaping services. Or I did, before I caught you getting drunk on the job."

Why am I arguing with the scary man?

He folds his arms over his chest, accentuating the corded muscles in his forearms. "And you assume I'm a landscaper because why?"

"Your truck, for one." I wave my arm in front of him. "You're too dirty to be pool maintenance. If you were a roofer, you'd have a ladder." I shrug like it's simple addition. "And this isn't your backyard, so unless you're here to rob the place ..." My fingers touch my lips. "Oh, God. You're not here to rob them, are you?"

He edges closer, the look of disgust twisting his features—the look he's directing at *me*.

I lift my chin and try not to flinch.

I've learned that flinching only makes it worse.

Maverick strains against his leash, his eager nose in the air, wide eyes begging the stranger to pet him. I have to use both hands to tug him back.

Some guard dog you are, Mav! This man is about to kill me, and you're trying to sniff his crotch and make friends.

The man points his index finger at me, revulsion rolling off his tongue with each syllable. "You self-righteous, pretentious little princess."

My mouth falls open, and my stomach bottoms out.

"You stand there in your designer clothes, your shoes that cost more than a month's rent, scrutinizing everyone behind your ridiculous fucking sunglasses, and you're gonna judge *me*?" He shakes his head. "My clothes are dirty because I work my ass off. My truck's a piece of shit because I have more important things to pay for. And I'm a grown-ass man, so I'll drink whenever the fuck I feel like drinking. All you rich motherfuckers act like you're better than people like me, but I know the sickening truth. I can lay my head down at night with a clear conscience because I'm not living a lie. I'd rather look ugly on the outside than be ugly on the inside like you."

His words pack a physical punch, hitting way too close to home. A tremor rips through me, and before I can stop it, a tear escapes from under my sunglasses.

It's time to go.

"I'm sorry." I whip around and bolt out of the backyard, dragging Maverick behind me.

My legs carry me across the grass as fast as my wedges will allow. I bunch my dress in my fist, hiking it up over my knees so my strides are longer.

When I reach my house, I slam the door closed behind me and press my back against it. My chest heaves as I gasp for air, my heart racing. A sob gurgles in my throat, but I swallow it down.

Maverick.

California king bed.

Walk-in closet.

Dream kitchen.

Yard with a pool.

Mercedes.

Maverick whimpers, nudging me with his cold nose. I sink down to the floor and fling my arms around him, burying my face in the comfort of his soft fur.

"It's okay, Mav. I'm okay."

Everything's okay.

I shouldn't have confronted him like that.

It's my fault for making him so angry.

My speeding pulse returns to normal after a few minutes of deep breathing, and I push off the floor. Maverick follows me into the kitchen as I swipe my purse and my car keys off the counter.

"Sorry, bud. You gotta stay here. I'm running to the store. Making a special dinner for your dad tonight."

I kiss the top of his head, and then I'm back out the door, head down, without so much as a glance at the pickup truck out front.

~

"Mmm. So good, babe."

My lips spread into a smile. "Figured I'd surprise you with your favorite dish tonight."

Paul's hand slides across the cherry wood table, and he entwines our fingers. "I love it. Thank you."

"How was your day?"

He tugs on his tie, loosening it, before popping his collar and slipping the loop over his head. "Good. Meeting went well. I think Haarburger's going to sign with us."

"That's great."

He dabs the corner of his mouth with his napkin. "How was therapy?"

"It went well."

His Adam's apple bobs up and down. "Did you, uh, tell her what we talked about last night?"

"I told her about our decision to stop trying to have kids. She thinks it's good that we're on the same page, that we're able to move on together."

"Not what I was referring to, Cal."

"Oh."

He's asking if I told her about the bruises he left on my arm.

I look down at my spaghetti. "No, I didn't mention it."

"Good." He sets his fork down beside his plate. "Because I meant what I said last night. It won't happen again."

I nod, unsure of what he wants me to say to that. It wasn't the first time he put his hands on me, nor was it the first time he promised that it won't happen again. I want to call him out on that. I want to ask him why he feels the need to hurt me in order to get his point across. I want to ask him why he can't control his temper. I want to ask him what happened to the sweet man I met in college. I want to ask him to get some help.

But sometimes, silence is easier than navigating around all the egg shells lying at my feet.

He picks his fork back up. "Did you call the vet?"

"I did. They said to watch him when he's in the backyard so he doesn't get the opportunity to eat his poop." I lift my goblet to my lips and take a long sip.

"Did you ask why he's doing this?"

My stomach coils. "The, uh, the doctor said it could be due to anxiety."

"Anxiety. Like you."

"Yeah. He asked if we've been stressed, because dogs can pick up on our feelings."

Recognition flashes across Paul's face, his light-brown eyes hardening. "So what did you tell him?"

"I told him everything's fine, of course. He said we could put Maverick on a low dose of anxiety medication, but I said that won't be necessary. We'll just watch him better when he's outside. Won't happen again if we keep an eye on him." I force a smile and clasp my hands together. "Ready for dessert?"

He shakes his head and pushes his chair back as he stands. "I'm going to change. Got some e-mails to send out."

"Of course. I'll get this all cleaned up."

He's gone before the sentence leaves my lips.

Could've gone worse, I suppose.

I release a sigh and begin stacking our plates.

While I rinse off the dishes in the sink, I gaze out the window into the darkened yard. The pool house at the far end elicits the memory of the bizarre encounter in Josie's backyard this morning.

I've tried not to think about the rude stranger all day, but my mind keeps drifting back to him. Back to what he'd said.

He was right. I'd judged him by his appearance and made an assumption based on it. Shouldn't have been that big of a deal, though. He could've laughed it off like a silly misunderstanding. He didn't need to go off on me like he did. People judge books by their covers all the time.

Hell, he did the same thing with me, didn't he? He lumped me in with the wealthy people in this neighborhood, pointing out my expensive clothes and accessories, calling me a fake without knowing anything about me. I could call him a jerk and chalk it up to him being mean.

But his words carry weight.

I *am* a fake.

I *am* living a lie.

Who was that man, and how did he read me so easily?

More importantly, does Josie know that someone was in her yard today?

I dry my hands on a dishtowel and dig through my purse to find my phone. Before I can tap out a text, I spot one already waiting in my inbox. When I click on it and read the words that pop up on the screen, my hand clamps over my mouth.

JOSIE: So I heard you met my brother this morning.

TWO

CALLIE

No white truck.

My shoulders lower, and I expel a relieved breath as I lock my door behind me.

I'd almost said *no* when Josie asked me to come over. Between the idea of putting on a swimsuit and the encounter I'd had with her brother yesterday, it was a recipe for disaster.

But Josie is my best friend, and I can't hide from her forever. It's already been a few weeks since I've seen her, and I don't doubt that she'd make good on her threat to knock down my door if I didn't come by today.

When I step onto Josie's monogrammed welcome mat, the door swings open before my finger makes it to the doorbell.

"Why aren't you in your bathing suit?"

I glance down at my teal dress to avoid looking into Josie's demanding gaze as I lie. "I don't feel like swimming today."

She plants her hand on her hip. "Why the hell not?"

I pop a nonchalant shoulder and step inside her foyer. "Just not in the mood."

Her suspicious eyes narrow. "Well, the heathens are out back, so we're sitting poolside until the twins wake up." She waves her arm and leads the way to her kitchen.

The *heathens* she's referring to are her children: Brandon, Miles, Lucas, and Serenity. Brandon is on the cusp of becoming a teenager, Miles not far behind him. The twins are two years old and living proof that birth control is only 99.7% effective.

Josie hadn't been prepared for another child, let alone twins. But she took it in stride, like she does with everything. Josie is a force. Strong. Outspoken. Hardworking. A loving wife. And the best mother to those kids. She's a fierce friend too.

Which is why I do my damndest to keep my truth from her when I have to.

"Grab that pitcher." She gestures to the carafe filled with lemonade on the granite countertop as she lifts a large veggie platter. "Nothing but healthy snacks for these little fuckers today."

I chuckle and slide open the glass door for her. "Let me know how that goes."

"Oh, it's gonna go." Josie saunters to the large, teak patio table and sets the platter down. "The boys think they can live off of Flamin' Hot Cheetos all summer, but they've got another thing coming."

"Hey!" Brandon shouts. "Cheetos are orange, just like carrots. Totally healthy."

Josie raises her eyebrow at me. "Do you see what I'm dealing with?"

I shake my head. "Brandon, you're going to need a better argument than that."

His shoulders slump. "I'll work on it."

"Your hair looks so good natural like this." Josie twirls a lock of my hair around her finger. "You should wear it curly more often."

"Thanks." I tuck the strand behind my ear. "Paul likes it better straight."

"Callie! Watch this!" Miles charges full-speed toward the inground pool, his dark curls bouncing in the wind. When he gets to the edge of the pool, he hurtles himself into the air, tucking his chin to his chest, and does a somersault into the water.

I clap when his head emerges. "Woo! That was awesome, Miles!"

"What score do you give me?"

I tap my index finger against my chin. "Hmm. Dismount was solid. A little shaky on the flip toward the end, though. I give it a nine."

He gives me a solemn nod, taking my feedback as seriously as if he were in a competition. I suppose with his big brother watching, he is.

"Keep your knees tight to your chest next time, and it'll be flawless."

A grin brightens his face as he hoists himself out of the pool. "I'm gonna practice."

My heart swells. I love Josie's kids as if they were my own.

My own.

Something I'll never have.

I shake off the pang of jealousy and set myself straight. There's no room for that here. Only love.

"Now, if *I'd* told him that?" Josie says, lowering herself into a lounge chair. "He would've told me to fuck off."

"He would not! You're the only one with a potty mouth in this house."

"Dan's waiting for the day one of them repeats me." She waggles her eyebrows. "I am too. He promised he'd spank me instead of them."

I throw my head back and laugh. "You're sick."

The synchronized wail of toddlers awakening from their naps crackles through the baby monitor.

"God damnit! I just sat down."

I hold my palm up and rocket out of my chair. "I'll get them."

Josie collapses back against the red cushion. "Thank you. You're the real MVP, Callie."

"Mom," Brandon drags out in a whine. "I told you, nobody says that anymore."

I smirk as I pad into the house.

Lucas and Serenity's cries get louder as I jog up the winding

17

stairs. Once they hear the crack of their bedroom door opening, they fall silent, peering through the slats in their cribs.

"I thought Mommy was going to get you guys outta these baby cribs."

"Lucas not a baby!" Lucas shouts.

I smile as I reach into his crib and hoist him out. "No, you are a big boy, aren't you?"

"Lucas big boy!" His chunky, bare legs wrap around my hip as I bounce him.

Serenity watches me from her crib, big brown eyes taking it all in. She and Lucas are like night and day. Lucas is a ball of energy. Loud, headstrong, demanding all of your attention. He gets that from his mother. But Serenity hangs back. Timid. The observer.

Lifting Lucas above my shoulders, I press my nose to his diaper-clad bottom.

He giggles. "Poopy."

"Yep." My nose scrunches. "Definitely poopy."

I lay him on the changing table and breathe through my mouth while I clean him up.

"Did you sleep good, Lucas?"

"No sleep! No tired!"

I laugh, snapping his onesie back together and plunking him down in front of his oak toy chest.

His sister raises her arms, reaching out for me, knowing her time has come.

"And how about you, sweet Serenity?" I wrap my arms around her, inhaling her perfect toddler scent. "Did you sleep good?"

She nods, sticking her thumb into her mouth.

When I lay her on the pad, I wiggle my fingertips on her belly, and she squirms, grinning around her thumb.

I don't mind changing diapers. I know it'd feel different if I had my own kids. Kids are exhausting, and it's common to take mundane tasks for granted when you have to do them every day. When they come easy.

But after what I've been through? I'd savor every smelly poopy diaper.

I always thought I'd have a family of my own by now. Always pictured a different life for myself and Paul. But the things we dream about aren't always in the cards for us. They become nightmares, haunting us, reminding us of what we'll never have, no matter how hard we try.

"All clean." I scoop Serenity back into my arms and hug her close, just for a minute longer.

Her tiny fingers curl around a lock of my hair as she rests her head against my shoulder. "Pretty hair."

I twirl one of her dark ringlets. "You have pretty hair too."

Lucas stands, banging his palm against the door. "Hungry! Go eat!"

"Okay, tiny tyrant. Let's go eat."

I balance Serenity on one hip while I clutch Lucas against the other. Lucas starts bellowing, "Go eat! Go eat!" and by the time we get down to the pool, all three of us are chanting.

"There are my babies!" Josie spreads her arms wide, and Lucas lunges out of my arms, dive-bombing for his mother.

Serenity waves but stays content in my arms. Her gaze is pulled in the direction of the splashes coming from the pool several feet away, and she points when she spots her older brothers.

"You can swim after you eat lunch." I sit with her in my lap. "You hungry?"

She nods, popping her thumb out of her mouth.

"So," Josie starts, handing Lucas a carrot to munch on. "Want to tell me about what happened with my brother yesterday?"

I groan, squeezing my eyes shut. "I'm so embarrassed."

"Don't be. Cole is the one who should be embarrassed."

I shift Serenity on my lap as I break apart pieces of turkey for her. "What did he say, exactly?"

"He said you thought he was the landscaper, and that set him off." She shrugs. "He's a man of few words. Figured you'd give me more."

"I thought you'd found a new landscaper when I saw the beat-up truck out front and caught him walking into your backyard. I came back here to see if he had a business card. Then, I saw him drinking." I shake my head. "I shouldn't have approached him like that. I feel so stupid."

Josie scoffs. "You did nothing wrong. I saw the way he looked when I got home. I would've assumed the same as you."

I lift a shoulder and let it fall. "I feel bad. He seemed so ... angry."

"He's going through a lot right now." Her eyes roam over Lucas' face, the corners of her mouth tugging down. "He's really not an asshole. You just caught him at a bad time."

A heaviness settles in my chest when I recall his rigid body, muscles wound up tight, his eyes mirroring a raging storm.

What happened to him?

"You never talk about him," I say. "We've been friends for five years, and I don't think you've said his name once."

"We had a fight after my dad passed. Cole said some awful things to me after the funeral. He resents me for not being there often enough when our parents got sick."

"You were on bedrest with Miles, and Brandon was only one. It wasn't like you chose not to be there."

She nods, though it's clear she doesn't agree.

"Why is he here now, after all this time?" I ask.

"His ex-wife and her filthy-rich parents took everything in their divorce. He needs a place to stay, so he'll be living in our pool house for a while."

I cringe. "And I basically told him he looked homeless. Great. Way to go, Callie."

"Way go, Callie!" Lucas shouts.

Josie chuckles. "It's fine. Forget about it. I'll tell you what. Why don't you and Paul come over for dinner tonight? You can get to know Cole, and then you won't feel so awkward about things. It'll clear the air."

I chew my bottom lip. "I'm not sure that's a good idea."

"Why not? You guys haven't been over in a while. I'm starting to think you've found another couple to double-date with."

I laugh. "We haven't. I just ... Paul's on a cleanse, so no alcohol for him until the Fourth."

She lifts an eyebrow. "We have water and iced tea, you know."

"Yeah, but I don't want to make you go out of your way, cooking something healthy especially for him. We'll be here next week for your Fourth of July party."

"Pool! Lucas swim now!"

Josie sets Lucas down on the grass and shimmies a pool diaper up his legs. "You have to stop referring to yourself in the third person, Lucas. It's only cute for so long, and you're pushing the limit."

She tosses me a bottle of sunscreen. "You do Serenity, and I'll wrangle this bull."

"Lucas no screen! Lucas no screen!" He attempts to make a run for it, but Josie lifts him up onto the chair.

"Lucas needs screen, so hold still."

"No hold still!"

"You're like a parrot who talks back, you know that?"

I stifle a laugh and squirt sunscreen into my palm. Serenity sits still for me, calm, watching her brother as he throws a fit.

"Hey, Lucas," I call over my shoulder. "If you don't put sunscreen on, you will get a boo-boo. Did you know that?"

His eyebrows dip low as he looks at me, disbelief written across his adorable, chubby face. "Lucas gets boo-boo?"

I nod. "It's true. The sun can burn, like fire. The sunscreen protects you."

His eyes go wide, and his body stills. "Fire burn."

"Good one, Callie," Josie whispers. "See, this is why I keep you around."

I wink. "Okay, my sweet Serenity. You ready to swim?"

She grins, fisting my sweater as I hoist her into my arms. When I set her down on the grass by the pool, she pulls my sweater down with her.

Josie gasps. "Callie, your arm!"

My heart leaps into my throat, and I yank my sweater back over my shoulders. "Oh, you know how easily I bruise."

She jerks Lucas into her arms and closes the gap between us in two strides with her long legs. "That's not just a little bruise.

What happened? Is that why you didn't want to go swimming today?"

I swat her hand away as she goes for my sweater. "Paul got a little rough the other night." I lower my voice. "During sex. Let's not make a big deal out of it."

A wary look flashes across Josie's face. "Like the good kind of rough?"

I nod, pushing my lips into a smile. "Paul didn't realize how hard he was grabbing onto me."

"Damn, Callie." A relieved breath rushes out of her lips. "You're freakier than me."

I huff out a laugh. "Hardly."

"Come on, Serenity." Brandon slaps his palms onto the concrete. "Come swim with your big brother."

Serenity cranes her neck to look up at her mother. "I swim?"

"Yes, my girl." Josie kneels down and kisses her forehead. "You swim with Brandon."

I gather my dress around my knees and sit by the edge of the pool, letting my feet dip into the cool water. Josie brings Lucas in by the shallow end, and all conversation about my bruises are forgotten.

I love swimming. Paul had our pool installed when we first moved into our house. We both had visions of splashing in it with our children and having their friends over for barbecues and pool parties.

Now, we just throw money down the drain every year for the upkeep.

At three o'clock, I help Josie clean up and get ready to head back to my house.

"Thanks for a fun day." I wrap my arms around Josie's shoulders and give her a squeeze.

She holds me out in front of her, her dark eyes bouncing between mine. "You know you can tell me anything, right?"

"Of course."

"And you know I'd help you with anything, no matter what it was?"

I offer her a reassuring nod.

Her gaze lingers on me for another moment longer, and then her face breaks into a smile. "Good. Talk soon!"

Once I'm out the front door, I release the breath I've been holding.

That was close. *Too* close.

I'll have to be more careful.

If Josie finds out, there's no way she'll keep my secret.

Eager to get home and away from my friend's prying eyes, I scurry down the path with my head down—which is why I don't see anything coming when I slam into someone. My sunglasses fly off my face and clatter onto the concrete.

"I'm so sorry. I—" My spine stiffens when my eyes land on the victim I collided with, like I'm a helpless bystander on the shoreline, watching the swell of an incoming tidal wave. Nowhere to run, nowhere to take cover.

Cole crouches down and plucks my frames off the ground. Then he stands to his full height and examines my lenses. He's wearing the same filthy outfit and fitted hat that he had on yesterday. That intense energy rolls off of him as he looks into my eyes, and it seizes my lungs. Being near him is like being zapped with an electrical current.

He holds out my sunglasses. "Don't look like they're scratched, princess."

Princess?

"It's fine. They're ridiculous anyway, remember?" I snatch my glasses back and try to maneuver around him.

"Wait."

His hand shoots out for my wrist, but I jerk my arm back, gasping as I recoil at the sudden contact.

"Whoa." He holds his palms up on either side of his head. "Not gonna hurt you."

I avert my eyes to my feet, cheeks flaming, embarrassed that he caught me off guard. "What do you want?"

He heaves a sigh, his big shoulders rising and falling. "I owe you an apology. My sister told me you're a friend of hers. I shouldn't have spoken to you that way."

I should accept the apology and move on. But his attitude provokes something within me, something that should be ignored, remain in its place. Something that knows better than to enter into confrontation.

Something that only gets me into trouble.

"You're sorry because I'm friends with your sister? Or because what you said was rude and hurtful?"

His jaw clenches, the muscles working under his skin. "Both."

"Because it was, you know." My eyes flick up to his. "Rude and hurtful."

"Which is why I'm apologizing," he grits out.

"But you meant what you said yesterday, didn't you? I mean, you wouldn't have said it if you didn't mean it."

His head jerks back. "You judged me by my appearance the same way I judged you. I don't hear an apology coming out of *your* mouth."

"That was a misunderstanding. Some random man traipses into my friend's backyard, covered in dirt. Who else would I have assumed it was?"

"You know what they say about assuming, princess. It's very unbecoming on you."

I scoff, setting a hand on my hip. "You're the one assuming things about people's lives you know nothing about."

"So, you're telling me those sunglasses weren't a couple hundred dollars?" He gestures to my sandals. "Those shoes weren't the same price as a car payment? I know people like you better than you think."

My finger jabs the air between us. "Why don't you worry about your own damn problems instead of worrying about what I spend my money on?"

He raises his arm, and I duck behind my forearm on instinct.

"Shit," he mutters, merely reaching up to adjust the brim of his hat. "Why are you so jumpy?"

"I'm not jumpy. You're jumpy!"

The corner of his mouth twitches, and his eyes sparkle with amusement. "Good one."

A frustrated growl creeps into my throat. This man is infuriating. "Just ... leave me alone. Apology accepted." I wave my hand as I step around him. "Whatever."

I stomp across the street, every nerve in my body tingling, heat scorching my insides.

Josie was wrong about her brother.

That guy's an asshole.

THREE

COLE

I AM IN HELL.

I'm in hell, and the devil is a tiny blond woman who lives across the street.

The woman who walked into my sister's yard yesterday like she owned the place, looking down her perfectly shaped nose at me as if I were the hired help.

Fucking rich people.

My skin crawls being here, living amongst the fakes and the self-righteous. It's the reason I left New York, yet here I am, living in a pool house, for God's sake. My sister has become one of *those* people.

"Uncle Cole! Uncle Cole! Watch this flip!"

I stop walking across the yard to watch my nephew run and fling himself into the pool.

I tip my chin. "Nice, Miles."

"Thanks! Callie gave me some pointers, and now my flip is perfect. She gave me a ten!"

And she gave me a headache.

"That's great." I jerk my head toward the pool house. "Gonna go shower now."

Brandon jogs alongside me. "Are you coming over for dinner tonight?"

I hike a noncommittal shoulder. "Don't know."

"Please come! Please, Uncle Cole."

I want to tell him no. I want to tell him I'll never be a part of his family, of his life, because it's too painful for me to witness. It makes everything worse, makes me remember, and all I want is to forget.

But I make the mistake of looking into the kid's eyes, wide and full of hope. The kind of innocence that can only belong to a pure, happy soul. One not desecrated by the vileness of the world.

To add insult to injury, my sister trudges across the lawn with a twin on each hip. Lucas' ranting about something, tiny fists balled in the air. He's like a drunk caveman, shouting in two-word demands.

But it's his sister who has the bile churning in my gut, threatening to spill over. I try to tear my gaze away from her, but I'm a masochist. Her round, brown eyes capture me in an instant, dragging me down into the depths of despair where all my hopes and dreams now float like bodies in the water.

Serenity rests her head of curls on Josie's shoulder, lips around her thumb, watching me.

I almost puke when her fingers wiggle, waving at me in that wary but curious way she has about her.

How am I supposed to stay here?

How am I supposed to bear this?

I gnash my teeth together and swallow around the lump in my throat.

Just need to get my feet back on the ground.

Then, I'm out of here.

"I'm making Mom's lasagna tonight," Josie says. "Kids would love to spend time with their uncle."

Guilt-trip Josie. That'll be her new name.

"I'll see."

She scoffs. "What else are you doing? You need to eat, Cole."

"Cole, eat! Cole, eat!"

Serenity giggles at the tiny caveman. The fluttery sound of her laughter is equivalent to a grenade going off in my chest cavity.

"You should teach your kid how to speak in full sentences."

Josie lifts an eyebrow. "His Uncle Cole can teach him how. Tonight. At dinner."

"Yeah!" Brandon pumps his fist in the air. "Uncle Cole's coming to dinner."

I glare at my sister.

She winks. "And clean yourself up. You look like the landscaper."

Damn that blond she-devil.

"No!" The scream tears from my mouth, my soul crying out in terror.

I jolt upright, chest heaving, gasping for air.

A nightmare.

It was a nightmare.

If only it were just a nightmare.

I swing my legs out of bed and plant my feet on the cool tile floor, my head dropping between my shoulders. Pressing my fingertips to my temples, I make small circles while I gulp my breaths down.

I knew being here would make the nightmares worse. I expected as much.

Dinner with my sister and her family tonight was another reminder of the life I'll never have.

The life I almost had.

So close I held it in my hands.

But I took it for granted.

Had to pay the price.

Was my own damn fault.

Pushing off the king-size mattress, I head to the stainless steel fridge and swipe two bottles off the bottom shelf before returning to bed. I pop the top off one and set the other on the side table beside me on standby. The cool liquid slides down my throat, soothing my insides as it sloshes into the pit of my stomach.

If only the blond devil could see me now, double-fisting at close to two o'clock in the morning.

My lips curl into a smirk as I allow my thoughts to drift.

Callie Kingston came into Josie's backyard yesterday like a blinding ray of sunlight. Pin-straight hair, not a shiny strand out of place. Killer curves wrapped in that tight, yellow dress. Everything about her screamed perfection. Money. Luxury. Look but don't touch.

Everything I despise.

But today, when she practically tried to run through me, she seemed different. Off. Her mask had slipped, revealing something else entirely.

Wild, golden waves cascaded down her back, a slight frizz to them, like she'd been sweating in the sun all day. (The girl was wearing a cardigan in the middle of summer—I broke a sweat just looking at her.) Without the ginormous sunglasses in the way, I was able to catch a glimpse of her stunning emerald irises.

But it isn't her obvious outer beauty that has me thinking about her in the middle of the night.

Something flashed in those eyes of hers, something worldly. Like she'd seen too much, experienced more than someone her age should have. She was so deep in thought that she didn't even see me standing there in the middle of the walkway. As if whatever was on her mind consumed her.

I know the kinds of secrets that lurk behind the closed doors of the wealthy. Know how they can eat you alive from the inside until there is nothing left but a shell of yourself. Rotting flesh and bone for the vultures to pick apart.

What's your secret, princess?

I polish off my second beer, and my stomach rumbles. I had two bites of lasagna at dinner. Lost my appetite after Serenity tried to wrap her fingers around my thumb when I reached for the bread basket. The gentle affection seared my skin, a branding iron on top of a gaping wound.

I couldn't stand the jealousy that coursed through me when I saw the interactions between Josie and Dan. The love and adoration that poured from their hearts nearly drowned me, not because they didn't deserve it—my sister deserves everything good in this world—but didn't I deserve it too?

I did once.

What's left for me now?

My empty stomach growls again. Since I'll likely be up the rest of the night—always am after a nightmare—I shove my feet into my sneakers and head across the yard to Josie's house.

I punch the code into the alarm pad and slide open the glass door. Expecting everyone to be asleep, I'm surprised to find Josie, Dan, and Lucas sitting on stools at the granite island in the kitchen.

"Come to join the party?" Dan tips his *World's Best Dad* mug in my direction.

"Didn't know there was one."

"Lucas here can't sleep." Josie presses her lips to the top of his head. "Think he had a nightmare."

Lucas whimpers and nuzzles his nose against her neck.

"That makes two of us." I gesture to the stainless-steel fridge. "Mind if I make something to eat?"

Dan waves a hand. "Knock yourself out, brother."

"So, anyway," Josie says, continuing the conversation I barged in on, "Serenity pulled down her sweater, and there were all these bruises on her arm."

Dan's head cocks to the side. "Bruises?"

Josie runs her index finger from her shoulder to her elbow. "Like someone had grabbed her too hard."

"What did she say about it?"

Josie's eyes roll. "She lied. She claimed Paul got rough during sex."

"Could be true." Dan hikes a shoulder. "Paul hasn't complained about their lack of sex in a while. Maybe things are back to normal between them."

I'm about to carry my plate of cold lasagna back to the pool house, skulk out of the kitchen before anyone notices I'm gone.

"Cole, sit. We're talking about your new friend from across the street."

I stifle a groan. "Not really one for gossip, Josie."

"It's not gossip. Callie's my best friend, and I'm worried." She kicks out the stool beside her. "I could use an unbiased opinion."

Blowing out a sigh, I drop onto the stool and shove a forkful of lasagna into my mouth.

Josie's voice lowers. "I think Callie's husband is hitting her."

My jaw stops moving, and I immediately think back to our encounter earlier. The woman flinched every time I moved.

Like she expected it.

Like she was used to someone raising his hands to her.

Not my business.

I shovel another bite into my mouth. "Bruises don't mean she's getting abused."

Dan nods. "I've never seen Paul with a temper. He's so even-keeled."

Josie shakes her head while she rocks Lucas. "Those are the most likely suspects. The ones you'd never believe could do such a thing. You didn't see her arm. Something's wrong. I feel it in my gut."

"Have you seen bruises on her before?"

Why am I entertaining this?

"No. But it's strange that she's always covered up. If I had a body like hers, untainted by four kids, I'd be flaunting it all over this place."

Dan chuckles. "Would you ever ask her? There's no way I could ask Paul something like that."

Josie's mouth tugs downward. "She won't tell me the truth. She lied to my face today."

"Nothing you can do if she doesn't want you to know." I wipe my mouth on a napkin and toss it onto my plate. "Penny's family went to great lengths to hide anything that would tarnish their reputation."

Josie's hand clamps over mine. "I'm sorry you had to go through that."

I shake my head. "Not your fault."

Nobody's but my own.

I push back and carry my plate to the sink.

"Feels like it is," she says.

My head jerks around to look at my sister, confusion etched onto my face.

"I wasn't there for you. Not enough. It kills me that you had to endure something like that by yourself."

Grief twists my stomach. "I'm glad I was alone. Glad Mom and Dad weren't there to witness that."

Dan nods like he understands, but he doesn't have a fucking clue. Nice guy and all, but he's never known suffering a day in his life.

The kind that obliterates joy.

Shattering any morsel of hope.

Extinguishing the sun for all eternity.

I glance over my shoulder as I move for the door, watching as Josie kisses Lucas's head, Dan rubbing his back in soothing circles.

A family.

One last look to twist the knife in deeper.

FOUR

COLE

Six Years Ago

TODAY STARTED like any other day.

Almost ended like any other day too.

I was on my way home from the construction site, counting down the seconds until I could scrub the dirt and sawdust off of me.

Then, my phone buzzed from my tool belt on the passenger seat.

I answered it with my car's Bluetooth. "Yes, Mom. I'm coming tonight."

"Oh, good!" her cheery voice boomed through the speakers. "I need you to pick up that bread from that place near your apartment. La Vida ... La Dolce ... La Vida Loca ..."

I grinned as I made a quick U-turn. "La Dolce Vita."

"Yes! That's the one. They have the best bread."

"How many loaves do you want?"

"Two should be fine."

"I'll get three. You can freeze whatever's left."

"Good idea. My boy's so smart."

I chuckled and shook my head. "See you in a bit, Mom."

"Drive safe!"

Every Thursday since my sister moved out to California with her fiancé, I ate dinner with my parents.

Tonight was a regular, run-of-the-mill Thursday night.

But tonight, I had to make a pitstop for bread.

The silver bell on the door clanged when I walked into the bakery. My mouth watered when the sweet, sugary aroma wafted up my nostrils. After a long, scorching day of working outside, I couldn't wait to have a beer and a heaping plate of Mom's lasagna with some of this bread.

A brunette with a tiny frame stood in front of me in line. My eyes lingered on the swell of her ass in her tight pencil skirt, the way the curtain of her dark hair shone under the fluorescent lights, the way her heels accentuated her calves.

I hadn't even seen her face, and I was already intrigued.

Her red fingernail tapped on the glass display case. "I'll take two loaves of the sesame bread, please."

Her voice was a melody, a song I wanted to learn all the words to. My body hummed along to it, inched closer so I could hear it better.

She shifted to the cash register, and when I stepped forward, she turned her head toward me.

My heart stalled in my chest, popping and sputtering, forgetting how to beat.

Big, brown eyes blinked up at me with long lashes fanned out around them. Her nose was perfect, small and slightly turned up at the tip. Her pouty, full lips were covered in a pink-tinted gloss.

The whole world tilted on its axis.

She stole the breath right from my lungs.

She was the most beautiful woman I'd ever seen.

The woman's cheeks flushed, and her eyes averted to the ground before flicking back up to mine. "Thank you."

I tilted my head to the side. "What?"

"You said I was the most beautiful woman you'd ever seen."

"Shit," I muttered. "I said that out loud?"

She giggled, and Cupid shot my heart with another arrow. "Yeah, you did."

I stepped closer, her fresh, flowery scent intoxicating my senses, luring me in. "Sorry. My mouth gets ahead of my brain sometimes."

"Don't be sorry." She fidgeted with the strap of her purse. "I don't mind."

My heart kicked back to life, a jackhammer in my chest. "I'm Cole."

I extended my hand but yanked it back when I realized how filthy it was, covered in dirt from the day's work. "Shit, sorry."

She shook her head, her hair swishing around her shoulders. "Stop apologizing, Cole. You look like you've had a long day at work. Nothing wrong with that."

"Miss," the cashier called. "Here's your bread."

The brunette turned away from me to hand the cashier her credit card, and it felt like all the warmth left the store. Like nothing would be the same again without her deep, dark eyes on me. Like everything in my life would always be less than if she wasn't with me.

I had to know her name. Had to kiss those lips. Had to wrap my arms around her, hold her close.

After she paid, she spun around and gazed up at me. "Well, Cole. It was nice to meet you."

"You didn't tell me your name."

"Penelope." She blushed again. "My friends call me Penny."

Penny.

My lucky Penny.

"Sir, can I help you?" the cashier asked.

Keeping my eyes on Penny, I said, "Can I have three loaves of sesame bread, please?"

"Sorry, sir. We're all out."

Penny's head whipped around. "But I just bought some."

"You took the last of it. We're closing in twenty minutes."

Penny looked down at her white shopping bag and back up at me. "You can have one of my loaves. One's better than none."

Sorry, Mom.

I shook my head. "No, no. Don't worry about it. You bought it, fair and square."

Her cheeks pushed up as she smiled, and I vowed right then and there to keep that smile on her face.

"Penny, would you like to have dinner with me?"

Her lips parted, and I had to hold myself back from claiming them as my own.

"It doesn't have to be tonight, if you're busy. Maybe tomorrow? Or Saturday? Whenever you're free."

She tucked a strand of hair behind her ear. "I'm free tomorrow night."

Tomorrow.

My spirits soared.

From that moment on, my life was never the same.

That was the moment I let a woman steal my bread—and my heart.

FIVE

CALLIE

"Happy Fourth of July!"

"Happy Fourth of July, Miles." I place my bowl of homemade potato salad on Josie's patio table.

"Callie, you have to watch my flip! I've been practicing."

"I can't wait. Let me see if your mom needs help first. I'll be back out in a few, and then I'm all yours."

"Okay! Hey, Paul, want to watch me?"

Paul slides his sunglasses on and rubs the palms of his hands together. "Let's see this flip I've been hearing about."

I grin as I make my way inside.

"Oh, thank God you're here." Josie shoves Serenity at me when I step into the kitchen. "Take her. I still have to cut the vegetables, clean the chicken, mix the dip, and Lucas literally just shit up his entire back."

I choke out a laugh. "Go. We'll handle the kitchen. Isn't that right, my sweet Serenity?"

Josie scurries into the hallway, holding Lucas out in front of her at arm's length.

I spin in a circle, and Serenity giggles, flinging her arms around my neck.

"You look so beautiful in that dress. Are you going to stay up for the fireworks later?"

She nods emphatically. "Fire go boom."

"Yes, it does. Now, let's see. Where does Mommy keep her cutting board?"

"Cabinet to your left."

I gasp, my head snapping in the direction of the deep voice.

"God. How long have you been lurking in the corner?"

Cole shrugs. "Since you walked in."

"You scared me."

"Like I told you, you're jumpy."

I roll my eyes and rummage through the tall, white cabinets for the cutting board. When I stand, Cole is at my side, invading the space I'm standing in. He gives me a gentle nudge with his elbow, and it's not in the domineering way I'm accustomed to.

"I'll chop. You can make the dip."

I blink up at him, curiosity piquing my interest. He isn't wearing his hat today, so his face is on full display. Hard lines and sharp angles, his chiseled jaw flexes like he's thinking about something that's pissing him off. His eyebrows slant downward, pinched together in the middle. Thick, chestnut hair sits in an overgrown, messy pile on his head.

Though he smells like fabric softener, his fitted gray T-shirt is wrinkly. He's dirt-free, but he's still unshaven, still rough around the edges. It's a half-assed attempt to look presentable for the party, yet he's incredibly handsome.

Makes me wonder how good he'd look if he put in a full-assed effort.

Cole tilts his head, and the full weight of his steel gaze bears down on me. "What?"

"You look clean today."

Oh my God. Did I really just say that out loud?

"I mean *nice*. You look nice." I clear my throat. "Gray is a good color on you."

"Had to clean up." His eyes narrow. "Heard the princess was coming."

My top lip curls at the nickname he keeps tossing at me as an insult.

Jerk.

Plopping Serenity on the counter, I pour the packet of onion mix into a bowl with sour cream and stir. Her little hand wraps around the top of the spoon to help me. She observes Cole over my shoulder, leery eyes watching to see what he does, like she doesn't trust him.

Smart kid.

Josie saunters back into the kitchen with a clean Lucas attached to her hip. "Need a damn hazmat suit every time I change this kid's diaper."

I chuckle. "Not surprising with how much he eats."

The loud melody of the doorbell echoes in the room.

"Party!" Lucas shouts.

Josie carries him into the foyer, and I'm relieved that guests are starting to arrive. The awkward tension between me and Cole is palpable, to say the least.

Josie returns with a couple who she first introduces to her brother. They shake hands, and then it's my turn.

"Callie, this is Dan's co-worker, Jeff, and this is his wife, Brenda."

"It's nice to meet you." I extend my hand to Brenda, and she shakes it with a bright smile.

With bleach-blond hair and a fit body, she's much younger than Jeff, which is a common thing here in Orange County.

Jeff hoists their baby carrier onto the counter with a grunt. "Gonna pull my back out one of these days. This thing weighs a ton."

I peer inside at the sleeping infant who's mostly covered by a blue blanket. "Oh, my goodness. He is absolutely precious."

"That's just 'cause he's sleeping." Jeff chuckles. "Don't let him fool you. The kid can scream his head off."

Brenda nods, running her pink acrylic fingernails through her loose waves. "We barely got any sleep last night. Our nanny had the night off for the holiday, and I could *not* get him to stop crying."

"She's talking about me, not Braxton." Jeff's round belly shakes as he cracks himself up.

"Josie, I don't know how you do it without a nanny." Brenda turns to me. "Do you have one?"

I shake my head, my stomach twisting as I prepare for the inevitable next question.

"How many children do you have?"

"None." I offer her a smile and return to stirring the dip.

Please stop talking to me, Brenda.

Clueless Brenda waves her hand and continues. "Well, when you start a family, get yourself a nanny. Makes life so much easier. Carlita does *everything* for us."

My grip on the spoon tightens.

What's the point of having children if you're not going to raise them or take care of them? I couldn't imagine pawning my own kids off on someone else.

Then again, I don't have my own kids. Therefore, I don't get to have an opinion about them. Something people often remind me of, which is why I keep my opinions to myself.

I'm mixing the dip so aggressively the bowl topples over and clatters to the floor, flinging dip onto my dress, the cabinets, and the floor.

"Crap." My cheeks burn, and I drop to my knees to start cleaning the mess.

Cole crouches beside me. "Why don't you go get cleaned up?" He touches my hand, his voice gentle. "Go upstairs. Take a minute."

I nod, keeping my head down, and then I bolt out of the kitchen. I take the stairs two at a time, my airways constricting, heart thrashing in my chest.

In the bathroom, I rest my shaking hands on the marble countertop, letting my head fall forward. I squeeze my eyes shut and try to speak louder than the thoughts screaming in my mind.

"Maverick. California king bed. Walk-in closet. Dream kitchen. Yard with a pool. Mercedes."

I'm fine.

Everything's fine.

It's not Brenda's or Jeff's fault. They don't know my situation. My heartache. Most people don't realize they're being insensitive. They don't know they're taking what they have for granted, because they can't fathom not having everything they want. But some of us don't get to have the things that are supposed to come naturally for us.

Some of us are broken.

I have to appreciate the things I do have. "Maverick. California king bed. Walk-in closet. Dream kitchen. Yard with a pool. Mercedes."

I slip my sweater off and twist the chrome knob on the faucet, rinsing off the clumps of dip under the cold stream. I use a handful of wadded toilet paper to wipe the splatters off my dress, but there's no salvaging the oil stains.

I swing open the bathroom door and let out a yelp. "Jesus, Cole. You need to start wearing a bell."

"Just came to see if you're okay."

"Yeah, I'm fine. Just clumsy."

He arches a brow. "You should've just thrown the dip on Brenda and her geriatric husband instead of on yourself."

I roll my lips together and stifle a laugh. "That's not nice."

He pops an unapologetic shoulder. "Never said I was."

"Yet you're here, checking on me."

He doesn't respond to that. His gaze moves to my arm, trailing down my bruised skin. The muscles in his jaw pop, and then his eyes flick back to mine. But he doesn't ask what happened. The way he's looking at me is as if he already knows the answer.

I push past him and make a beeline for Josie's walk-in closet to look for something I can change into.

Cole follows me in, as if he's not finished scrutinizing me with that intense stare.

I sigh after flipping through several hangers. "Josie's too tall. None of her dresses will fit me. I should run home and change."

"Or you could just stay in the dress you're wearing."

My nose scrunches. "And stay in a stained outfit all day?"

"Just a few stains, princess."

I rest my hand on my hip. "Look, if you came up here to judge me, then you can go back downstairs."

"That's not why I came up here."

"Then why did you?"

His teeth grind together, arctic eyes boring into mine.

"Awesome. More scowling." I roll my eyes and brush by him to return to the bathroom.

He stops me, clasping my hand. "Callie, please wait."

I look down at our joined hands, noting the difference in the way this man touches me versus my own husband.

Paul grips my bicep, forceful and hard, to keep me where he wants me.

Cole clasps my hand, asking me to stay.

And it makes me want to.

"I came to check on you because you looked upset, and you shouldn't let entitled assholes like them upset you."

When was the last time someone cared that I was upset?

"I'm fine." I slip my hand out of his and head back to the bathroom.

I soak the corner of a hand towel with cold water and attempt to scrub the stains out of my dress again—just to prove a point.

I'm no princess.

Cole reappears in the doorway and leans against the doorframe. "What was that you were saying before you came out of the bathroom?"

I glance up at his reflection in the oval mirror. "What?"

"Sounded like you were talking to yourself when I came upstairs."

Heat creeps across my chest and onto my neck. "It's an exercise. Something I do when I feel anxious."

"Maverick, dream kitchen ..." His chin tips. "What does it all mean?"

"Why, so you can use it to mock me?"

"I wouldn't do that."

His eyes offer a silent plea. The man looks tormented, desperate for something. Like he *needs* to hear this.

"When I started having panic attacks last year, my therapist told me to run through a list of all the things I'm grateful for. I think about what makes me happy, what I'm fortunate to have."

"And that helps?"

I shrug and drop the towel onto the counter. "It takes my mind off of whatever's stressing me in the moment. Plus, it puts things in perspective. When things seem bad, when I feel like I'm spiraling, I remind myself of the things I love."

Cole lifts an eyebrow. "What about your husband?"

"What about him?" Paul's voice has both me and Cole whirling around.

He steps through the doorway, making Josie's enormous bathroom suddenly feel small and crowded, shifting the energy.

Quick to explain myself, I wave my arm in front of my dress. "Spilled onion dip on myself like a klutz."

Paul presses his lips to my temple, eyes locked on Cole in the mirror. "That's my clumsy girl."

"This is Josie's brother, Cole. He's staying with them for a while."

Paul snakes one arm around my waist and reaches out to Cole with the other. "Good to meet you."

Cole glares at his hand like it's poison, his body language that of a coiled rattlesnake. A warning.

Then, like he snaps out of a spell, he clasps Paul's hand and gives it a firm shake. "Likewise."

The two are so visually different, their contrasting colors and tones like black and white. Paul's groomed golden hair versus Cole's unruly coffee-colored tresses. Paul's warm eyes, light brown like a rich honey, while Cole's steel-blue orbs are cold and piercing. They're both tall with athletic statures, but Cole is hard, lean muscle, whereas Paul's muscles are bulkier.

On the outside, Paul seems like the friendly, more charming of the two. But I've seen what lurks beneath the surface. Appearances can be deceiving, which makes me wonder what's really underneath Cole's surly exterior.

Why am I comparing the two?

"Let's get back downstairs." I turn to Paul and hold my arms out wide. "Do I look totally stupid?"

He shakes his head, eyes flicking to my arm. "Just put your sweater back on."

Of course.

Cover up the imperfections so no one sees.

Cole is gone by the time Paul and I exit the bathroom. We head out to the backyard where more of Josie's guests have gathered, but Cole is nowhere to be found.

"There they are." Dan waves us over to the barbecue, sporting his *Kiss the Cook* apron. "One cheeseburger, medium-well for the lovely Callie Kingston, and one for the weirdo she's married to who likes his meat still mooing on the plate."

Paul claps him on the back. "Says the weirdo who eats dried-out hockey pucks."

I smile as I take the paper plate. "Thanks, Dan. Can I get you another beer?"

"I'm all good. Go eat. Enjoy the party."

Paul stays with Dan while he mans the grill, and I take the chair beside Josie at the table, steering clear of Jeff and Brenda. The kids are playing in the pool. Lucas and Serenity are passed out in a child-sized tent a few feet away from us.

Through the smoke wafting up from the grill, my eyes are drawn to the pool house. Curtains cover every window, drawn tight, blocking me from seeing in.

Or maybe they're blocking Cole from seeing out.

What was that in the bathroom? Residual guilt for being rude, maybe. His twisted version of an olive branch after the way we met. But it felt like something more than that.

Why did Cole care to come check on me?

More importantly, why does that even affect me?

Josie nudges me with her elbow. "You okay, Cal?"

I take a bite of my cheeseburger. "Yeah, just a few stains on my dress. No big deal."

"That's not what I meant."

I look into her worried eyes and offer her a smile. "I'm fine. Really."

She lowers her voice and leans closer. "I'm not a fan of Brenda or her husband. Dan only invited them because Jeff overheard some of the guys in the office talking about the party."

"It's okay. Next party, I'll just wear a name tag that says *Hello, My Name is Infertile Myrtle* so nobody asks me if I have any kids."

She doesn't laugh at my lousy joke. "Have you tried talking to Paul about adoption again?"

The ache in my gut throbs. "He refuses to entertain the conversation."

A frown tugs at Josie's lips. "How are things between you two lately?"

My eyes find Paul across the yard. As if he can feel me staring, his gaze meets mine, and he sends me a wink.

I used to be so enamored with him. We were madly in love, in such bliss together. I still love him now, but it's different. Tainted. Our relationship doesn't have the same innocence and purity it used to.

My hope and happiness are being depleted, and I don't know how to stop the hemorrhaging.

I smile at Paul and swing my attention back to Josie. "Things are good. It was tough for a while, but we've decided to stop trying to get pregnant. It was putting a strain on our relationship."

"But you want kids, Callie."

I drop my burger back onto the plate. "Four rounds of in vitro didn't work. Neither did surgery on the fibroids, acupuncture, supplements, or any of the other things I've tried. Now with Paul's sperm motility ... maybe it's just not meant to be. Maybe ..." I chew my lip. "Maybe I'm not meant to have children."

The thought is a painful reality that I must face.

Josie scoffs. "You can't be serious. You're a better mom than I am, and you don't even have kids yet."

"What else do you want me to say? I've tried everything. I have to accept it and move on."

"But you're willing to adopt. That's an option."

"It's not."

"Why not?"

"Just drop it." I look at her, my eyes pleading. "Please. Not today."

She shakes her head but holds her tongue. "I don't get it, Callie."

And she never will.

She couldn't possibly fathom what it's like.

To accept the fact that your body is defective, even though men's and women's bodies are built to reproduce.

To try and try, each time getting your hopes up, only to have everything crash and burn in a pit of disappointment.

To see those two pink lines on the pregnancy test, followed by seeing a blood-filled toilet a month later.

Needles and hormones and pills.

Frustration and fighting and tears.

Again, and again, and again.

No, Josie will never understand what I've endured.

What I've put Paul through.

He's all I've got now.

And that has to be enough.

SIX

COLE

I NEED to chill the fuck out.

I pace the open room and chug another beer.

Paul doesn't seem like a bad guy. I have no reason to buy into Josie's accusation. And even if he *is* beating on Callie, that's none of my business. It's up to Callie to leave his piece-of-shit ass. I don't know the girl. We're not friends. To her, I'm just the scumbag living in the pool house.

Still, something nags me. Something yanking on the wheel every time I try to steer away from Callie Kingston. In the bathroom, she'd recited a ridiculous list of things she's grateful to have.

Things.

Aside from her dog, nothing on that list truly matters in life. Yet it's supposed to calm her. Help remind her of how good she has it, as if material items could ever make it worth whatever she's going through.

And her husband's name wasn't on that list.

What's more, when Paul stepped into the room, Callie's whole demeanor changed. Her body curled inward like a scared turtle retreating into its shell. Panic flashed across her face. She looked like a teenager who got caught smoking in the bathroom at school.

None of that equates to domestic abuse. Those bruises on her arm, though ... I'd finally seen them for myself, and they definitely equate to *something*.

I just can't fathom someone raising a hand to that woman—any woman. Callie radiates kindness and light, with the perfect combination of gentleness and sass. Josie loves her to death, so I know she must be a good person.

I shake my head, pulling at the ends of my hair.

Not my problem.

My front door flies open, and Josie's head whips around until she spots me. "What the hell, Cole?"

"You just burst in here like the Kool-Aid Man. I think I should be the one asking *what the hell*."

She rolls her eyes. "Why are you holed up in here by yourself?"

"Why do you care?"

"You're my brother. Of course I care."

"You don't need me out there. You have plenty to keep you occupied. Always have."

She props her hands on her hips. "What's that supposed to mean?"

"Nothing. Forget it."

A soft knock comes from the door. Callie steps inside, chin down, eyes flitting between us. "I'm sorry to interrupt, but the kids want to know where the sparklers are."

Josie heaves a sigh. "I hid them in my closet so Brandon wouldn't find them. The kid's a little pyro."

"I'll get them," Callie says. "You stay here."

"What's the point?" Josie lifts her arms and lets them fall, her palms smacking her thighs. "I have plenty out there to keep me occupied, right, Cole?"

She storms past Callie who turns to me with a confused expression pinching her features.

I shake my head and toss my empty bottle into the sink.

"She feels guilty, you know," Callie says. "She feels like she wasn't there for you when your parents were sick."

"Wasn't much she could've done while she was popping out babies on the other side of the country."

Callie lifts her chin. "Look, you can resent her all you want, but don't take it out on her kids."

My head jerks back. "Excuse me?"

"Miles wanted to ask you to play volleyball in the pool earlier, but Brandon told him not to. His exact words were '*Uncle Cole doesn't like us.*'"

My gut twists.

"I don't know you, but I'm going to give you some advice. Those kids are your family, Cole, and they're wonderful. Don't take them for granted."

She's gone in the next second, leaving me standing there with the guilt grenade in my hands.

It takes me thirty minutes to muster the balls to show my face outside.

As much as it pains me to be around people like this, I don't want my nephews thinking I don't like them. Callie's right. They're just kids. They don't deserve my anger and bitterness. I have to suck it up. They're the only family I have left.

I took the people in my life for granted once before. Can't let that happen again.

"Hey, Uncle Cole!" Miles runs up to me as soon as I step outside. He holds out an unlit sparkler. "Want one?"

"Sure, kid. Thanks."

His toothy smile beams. "Dad's lighting them over here by the pool. Mom wants us close to the water in case we get lit on fire."

I smirk. "That's because your mom got burned by a sparkler when we were kids."

"She did?" He swings his wide-eyed gaze to his brother. "Brandon! Uncle Cole said Mom got burned by a sparkler when she was little."

Brandon throws his head back and laughs. "Can you tell us the story, Uncle Cole?"

I lower myself into a lawn chair beside him, and Miles plops onto the grass in front of me.

"Your mother thought it was a smart idea to pretend the sparklers were lightsabers."

"Lightsabers?" Brandon asks.

"Yeah. Your mom and I used to love *Star Wars*."

Miles cocks his head. "What's *Star Wars*?"

My jaw goes slack. "I'm sorry. What did you just ask me?"

Dan shakes his head as he tosses me his lighter. "You're lying. There's no way my wife was into *Star Wars*."

I twist around, scanning the yard until I spot my sister talking with Callie and a few other guests. "Josie! You need to come over here right now."

Josie's eyebrows draw together as she makes her way over to us with Callie in tow.

"What's wrong?" she asks. "Did someone get burned?"

I heave a sigh for dramatic effect. "I was just telling your boys about that time you got burned by the sparkler, and then I told them how much you used to love watching *Star Wars*. Do you know what they said?"

She shakes her head, eyes bouncing from Brandon to Miles.

"They asked me what *Star Wars* was." I pinch the bridge of my nose. "Your children ... have never seen *Star Wars*?"

Callie stifles a laugh, clamping her hand over her mouth.

Josie blinks rapidly. "I ... well ... we haven't had time to sit down and watch movies."

I scoff. "Brandon is almost a teenager! You mean to tell me that you haven't had time to watch a single movie in twelve years?"

Dan folds his arms over his chest, feigning offense. "Didn't even know you liked *Star Wars*, babe."

"Uh, neither did I," Callie says, raising her hand.

Josie hisses. "Don't encourage him."

"Well, that's it." I rub my palms together. "We're going to have a *Star Wars* marathon this weekend."

Brandon and Miles shoot up from their seated positions.

"Yeah!"

"This is gonna be awesome!"

"Watch the sparklers!" Josie yells as the boys run in circles, waving their sparklers over their heads. "Your eyebrows won't grow back in time for school in September!"

My gaze skates over to Callie, though I'm not sure why I'm looking for her approval.

Also, I'm not sure why my chest swells the way it does when I find her eyes already on me.

She shoots me a wink. "Nice job, Uncle Cole."

I drag my fingers along the back of my neck. "Yeah, well, the princess gives good advice."

She smooths her hands over the back of her dress as she lowers herself to sit on the grass. "Really wish you'd stop calling me that."

"I won't say it anymore if it really bothers you."

"It does." She pulls her bottom lip between her teeth. "But not because you're wrong."

Ah, shit. "Hey, listen. Forget about what I said. I was angry."

She's quiet as she continues worrying her lip, plagued by whatever thoughts are looming in her mind.

Thoughts I want to hear.

I've asked myself why all day. Why am I drawn to my sister's friend? She's a pretty face, nothing more.

But then I *feel* more. Like the brokenness inside me can somehow detect another lost soul. Someone who can understand me.

Or maybe misery just likes company.

The still water in the pool reflects in Callie's green eyes. Her gilded curtain of hair falls over her shoulders, blond wisps blowing across her delicate features in the warm breeze.

I know I shouldn't be staring. She's married for fuck's sake.

But Callie Kingston, in her stained dress and white sweater to cover her bruised secrets, is beautiful.

Breathtakingly so.

51

"Do you miss New York?" Her soft voice breaks the silence between us.

I pick at the label on my beer bottle. "That's tough to answer."

Her head turns, the full weight of her stare landing on me. *Try,* she silently tells me.

And for some reason, looking into her vulnerable eyes, I want to.

"I've lived in New York my whole life. Always loved it. The hustle and bustle, the busy streets and crowded places everywhere you go. I love the full effect of each season, hot highs and freezing lows, and everything in between."

A smile dances on her lips. "Sounds amazing."

"You've never been?"

She shakes her head. "Been a Cali girl my whole life. I've always wanted to see the snow."

"You should go in January then. Most of the tourists leave after the holidays."

"Paul has no interest in traveling to New York."

I arch an eyebrow, the words burning my tongue in defiance as they fight to escape. "So that means *you* can't go?"

She laughs, dropping her chin, trying to mask the sadness flooding her eyes.

Yeah, that's what I thought.

I search the yard to find Paul playing cornhole with some of the other husbands.

I don't know him. But he makes more money than he knows what to do with. Entitled. And I'd bet he doesn't appreciate any of it. People like him aren't taught how to. They take and they take, and once they have it all, they start taking the things that don't even belong to them.

Greedy.

"So why was my question tough to answer?" Callie asks. "You never finished."

I shift in my seat, polishing off my beer before setting the bottle into the grass. "I miss the New York I used to know. Before ... before everything happened."

She hugs her knees to her chest, almost like she's bracing herself for my answer. "What happened?"

I scrub my hands over my face, as if to physically wipe away the horrific images that assault me every time I ask myself that question.

What happened?

I destroyed everything.

Had everything I'd ever wanted, and I doused it with gasoline, lit a match, and torched it.

Burned my life to the ground.

I didn't mean to, my conscience screams.

Doesn't fucking matter, though, does it?

Doesn't change the outcome.

Resentment and hatred grate my teeth. "You think spouting a few lines about the things you're grateful for can minimize your problems, that the good in your life outweighs the bad. And maybe it does. Maybe your troubles aren't that big. Or maybe you're just fooling yourself. But I don't have anything to recite. No tangible item could possibly make me feel better about what I've lost."

Callie's eyes glisten as she takes in what I've said, but she doesn't look hurt. She doesn't seem offended that I just called her out on her bullshit therapy exercise.

No, it's worse than that.

The things I see etched on her face are a sucker-punch to my gut.

Understanding.

Recognition.

Grief.

Loss.

This woman knows darkness, and she knows it well. More than she lets on.

And fuck if I don't have the overwhelming urge to wrap her in my arms and bear the weight of her pain.

Scoop her up and take her away from this place.

Beat the fuck out of anyone who's tried to hurt her.

"Cal, you ready to watch the fireworks?" Paul struts halfway across the lawn, too lazy to walk the rest of the way to come get his wife.

Callie squeezes her eyes shut, a fleeting moment so she can collect herself. Then she plasters on a smile and hoists herself up.

"Ready!"

Something claws at my insides as I watch her slip her hand inside her husband's. Something possessive and jealous.

Both of which I have no right to feel.

"Everything okay, brother?"

My head snaps up to Josie, who's looking from Callie to me like she can see the thoughts swarming my mind.

I push off my knees to stand. It's time to go.

"I know what you're thinking," she says.

"No. You don't."

"You forget how well I know you, Cole."

"You know the person I used to be." I walk backwards toward the pool house. "And that man is lying at the bottom of a grave back in New York."

SEVEN

CALLIE

"Jeff and Brenda seemed nice yesterday."

I lift a shoulder and let it fall. "Sure."

Paul sets his water bottle on the island. "You didn't like them?"

"I didn't say that."

He smirks. "I know you, Cal. It's written all over your face."

"They weren't *not* nice." I wave my spatula in the air. "They just went on and on about how great it is to have a nanny because they don't want to take care of their own child."

"Ah." Paul nods. "That's why you don't like them."

I twist the knob to shut the burner off and toss the last pancake onto the plate. "Again, I never said I didn't like them."

"They need a nanny. Brenda owns a boutique down in Newport Beach."

I roll my eyes. "Of course she does."

Paul chuckles. "I'm just saying, it's not like she's a stay-at-home mom with a nanny."

"You're right." I walk around the island and take the stool next to him. "It's nice that she gets to do something. Get out of the house."

A heavy sigh leaves his lips as he places his fork onto the marble. "Back to this?"

"I just figured we could discuss it now that we're not ..." I let my sentence trail off.

"Now that we're not having children," he finishes.

I nod. "Can't the discussion be back on the table?"

"You don't need to work, Callie. Jeff doesn't make half the money I'm bringing home. Brenda works because they need another income to sustain the kind of lifestyle that we're all living here."

He laces our fingers together. "What will people think if they see *you* getting a job?"

"I don't care about what people think. It isn't about them." I swivel to face him head-on. "This is about what I want, Paul."

His brows collapse around pensive eyes.

This topic hasn't been broached since we'd started trying to conceive years ago. We put it on the back-burner because I had such a difficult time getting pregnant, and I'd wanted to put all my energy into that. Miscarriage after miscarriage proved that it didn't matter how much energy I put in, though.

You can't make something happen if it's not meant to happen.

"If I'm not meant to be a mother, I at least want to be *something*." I squeeze Paul's hand. "I want to feel like I have a purpose in life."

He leans in and presses his lips to my forehead. "You do have a purpose in life. You're my wife. Isn't that enough for you?"

"I ... that isn't ..."

I struggle to find the words. Maybe there isn't a way to describe how I feel. Words can only take you so far.

Paul is a man. He's never been told that he doesn't have to work. He's been bred *to* work. It's expected of him.

And I'm expected to stay home.

I'm expected to feel fulfilled as a wife and nothing more.

I'm expected to feel satisfied by the success of my husband.

Yet I don't.

And I'm afraid to tell Paul the truth.

Paul shoves his plate away, his chair scraping against the floor as he pushes it back to stand. "Yes, Callie. *Yes* should've been your answer. I should be enough for you. But I forgot: I'm only useful to you if I can get you pregnant."

"Paul, wait. That has nothing to do with this."

He tosses his napkin onto the counter and storms out of the kitchen, leaving me to fall deeper into the abyss of guilt.

∼

"AND WHAT DID you say to him?"

I shift my gaze to the bright-yellow tulips sitting in a vase on the coffee table between us. "I didn't say anything. I didn't know what to say."

Melissa, my therapist, scribbles something onto her notepad. Probably something along the lines of *Callie is pathetic and weak.*

"Did you really not know what to say to Paul? Your mind was completely blank when he said that to you this morning?"

I lift my eyes to meet hers. "No, it wasn't blank."

She leans forward. "What were you thinking?"

"That it's not fair for me to stay home."

"Why?"

"Because I want to work."

"Why do you want to work?"

"Because I want to do something with my life instead of sitting home every day."

"So," she says, leaning back against her leather chair and crossing her legs. "You *did* know what to say to Paul."

I nod.

"You just didn't *want* to say it."

I nod again.

"Why not?"

"Because I didn't want to hurt his feelings."

"And what about *your* feelings, Callie? When do your feelings get validated?"

I hike my shoulders and let them fall.

They don't.

"Let's do an exercise. Pretend I'm Paul. Tell me everything

you'd want to say to him if you knew he wouldn't feel hurt by it. If you knew he'd hear you and accept what you say."

"Okay." I inhale in a long, slow breath while I compose my thoughts.

"I'll start," she says. "Aren't I enough for you, Callie?"

"No, Paul. You are *not* enough. It takes more than another person to make me feel complete, more than a husband to feel fulfilled. I want to have something that is my own. I want to do something that I'm good at. I want to create. I want to feel inspired. I want to be my own person while you are out being your own person, and then I want to come home to you at the end of every day and share in our separate endeavors."

Melissa's eyes narrow. "Keep going. What else?"

Hot tears sting my eyes, my hands shaking. "I want to adopt a baby. We've tried getting pregnant, and it didn't work, and I understand why we can't keep going down that road. I've accepted it. But I don't want to give up. Not when there's another option. We can adopt a beautiful baby, and we can have the family we've been trying to create."

"Good," Melissa says, jotting notes as I talk.

Salty droplets roll down my cheeks, but I don't wipe them away. I let them stay there, serving as proof that I *do* have feelings, and they *do* matter. This is the only place I allow them to surface.

"I want to be able to tell you how I feel without you getting angry, without you turning the attention back on you. I want you to listen to me and actually understand me. I want to feel valued. I want to feel useful. I'm sick of feeling guilty for the things I feel. I'm sick of lying to my friends about our marriage. I'm sick of feeling empty inside. And most of all, I'm sick of pretending everything's okay. It's not okay, Paul. I am not okay!"

I bury my face in my hands as the sobs take over my body.

"Good, Callie." Melissa rises from her chair and places the tissue box in my lap. "This is good."

What Melissa doesn't understand is that my words, my feelings, my tears mean nothing once I leave this room. In here, we can pretend like Paul will hear me. We can practice articulating what I should say. But the problem isn't that I don't have the words to say to Paul.

It's that my words aren't worth saying.

They're not worth the fight that will come after they leave my mouth. The hostility they will incite.

That's why I choose not to say them.

"How have your panic attacks been since our last session?"

I dab my eyes with a tissue and exhale. "I've felt them coming on, but I practice the breathing techniques you taught me. I also made a list of things I'm grateful for, like you told me to do, and that helps."

"I'm glad to hear those exercises have been helping. I have something else that might help." Melissa holds up a pale pink notebook with the word *Journal* in gold foil script letters on the cover. "I give this exercise to all of my clients who have trouble expressing themselves verbally. Each day, I want you to write something in here. Doesn't have to be long, whatever you have time for. But writing your thoughts can help reduce stress and anxiety. It helps to get it all out in a safe space. Like you do here."

I lean forward and take the journal from her, running my fingers over the matte cover. "Thank you."

When my session is over, I fix my smudged make-up in my car before heading home.

It's dark downstairs when I step into the foyer. Paul's probably upstairs in his office, so I make my way to the stairs. I always leave therapy feeling spent, and I look forward to soaking in a hot bath.

"Where are you going?"

My shoulders tense when I spot Paul in the dining room, drinking at the table with the lights off.

"Oh, I thought you were upstairs. I was going to take a bath."

"Come have a drink with me." Paul tilts the crystal decanter, refilling his glass with the amber liquid.

My nose scrunches. "You know I don't drink scotch."

"Sit with me while I drink."

His tone is sharp and demanding. The Paul I know is being

replaced with the person who comes out when liquor is added, which seems to be occurring a lot lately.

I offer him a tentative smile. "Or you can come upstairs with me, and we can both enjoy a relaxing bath. Make love with the jets on like we used to."

My attempt at sounding sexy falls flat. He's too far gone at this point.

Paul stares into his glass, watching the ice swirl around as he flicks his wrist in circles. "Do you even *want* to fuck me?"

My eyebrows hit my hairline. "Is that a serious question?" I set my purse and the journal down, moving slow as I venture toward him, leery of getting too close. "Of course I want to."

He huffs out a humorless laugh. "Why would you want to fuck me if I can't get you pregnant?"

My body stills, realization setting in.

Maverick's ears pin back, and his tail suctions underneath his body as he slinks out of the room.

"Paul, I thought we discussed—"

"I bet you want to fuck *him*, though." His eyes lift, glaring at me from under his furrowed brows. "Bet *he* could get you pregnant."

"Who? Paul, what are you saying?"

He downs the contents in his glass and slams it down on the table, pushing to his feet. "You know who. I saw the way he was looking at you last night."

Cole?

My face twists. "I really don't know what you're talking about. I want you and only you, Paul. Please, let's go upstairs and relax."

He stalks toward me, and fear constricts my breaths as I brace myself for what's to come.

He slides the back of his hand along my cheekbone, though his touch is anything but loving. "Say it again."

"Say what?" My voice comes out like a meek whisper.

"That you want me and only me." He leans in, the smell of alcohol thick on his breath, his words laced with possession. "Tell me you're mine."

My heart breaks for my husband.

After my fibroid surgery, the doctor said there was no reason why I wouldn't get pregnant. When we continued failing, though, the doctor took a look at Paul. *Low sperm motility* was the term he used. Might as well have been a death sentence. Paul was devastated and hasn't been the same since.

I know he feels inadequate because he can't get me pregnant. I want to argue, to tell him that it's not his fault. But it's late, and he's drunk.

So, I slip my hand into the waistband of his shorts and look in his eyes when I say, "I'm yours, Paul. You're the only man I want."

I once meant this with every fiber of my being. Now, I say it because I know it's what he needs to hear.

His eyes close as he groans. "Again."

My lips brush against his, and I squeeze his hardening length. "I'm yours. I belong to you."

He yanks the straps of my dress down my shoulders and fumbles with the clasp on my bra. I reach behind my back and unsnap it for him, letting it drop to the floor.

He kisses me, sloppy and aggressive. He stumbles as he walks me backwards toward the staircase, his movements clumsy. Pushing me against the wall, he shoves my dress down the rest of the way and hikes my leg up around his waist. He's too unstable to take his time, to touch me the way I like. Once he frees himself from his pants, he plunges inside me, fast and hard.

I stifle the groan that shoots into my throat, swallowing the pain.

We're not making love tonight.

This isn't about me.

It's about him.

And I succumb.

Things are easier when I just comply.

EIGHT

COLE

Five Years Ago

"Top off. Now."

Penny tears her shirt over her head and flings it somewhere across the room.

I shuck my pants and kick them behind me.

I grip Penny by the back of her neck and kiss her hard, my tongue plunging into her sweet mouth. She opens wider for me, letting a little moan escape as she drags her fingernails through my hair.

"I've been dying to be inside you all night, Penny."

I hoist her up and walk us to the edge of my mattress. When I drop her down, her hair fans out on the white pillowcase like a dark river I want to drown in. My hands slide down her tight body, working the button on her pants before I yank them off. I drop my mouth to her stomach, kissing and nipping and licking every inch of exposed skin.

"Thank you for coming to dinner tonight," she says, squirming underneath me. "It means so much to me that you were willing to meet my parents."

"I'd do anything for you, Penny." I unsnap the clasp on her bra and toss it over my shoulder. "I want to give you everything and make you happy, because you make me the happiest man alive."

She takes my face in both of her hands and gazes at me with watery eyes.

My hands still, everything coming to a halt. "Baby, what's wrong?"

She shakes her head, and a tear escapes, rolling down the swell of her cheek. "Nothing is wrong. Everything is perfect. You are perfect."

I lean onto my side and pull her close until we're nose to nose. "I love you, Penelope Murdoch. I don't know if this is too soon to say this, but I honestly don't care. I love you, and I'm going to make you my wife one day."

She touches her forehead to mine. "I love you, Cole, and I can't wait to be your wife."

I place a chaste kiss on her lips, brushing her tears away with my thumb. "I don't have the kind of money you're used to. I don't think your parents would approve of you marrying someone like me."

"I don't need money. All I need is you. My parents will see how well you treat me, how happy you make me. That's all that matters. Me and you."

"Just the two of us, Penn. Forever."

"And maybe a little one running around too." Her smile fades, and her eyes suddenly go wide. "Oh, no. What if you don't want kids? We didn't talk about this. We didn't have any of the important talks we're supposed to have!"

I chuckle, rolling onto my back and pulling her on top of me. "Of course I want kids. I want to make a family with you. Watch your beautiful belly grow. Hold our baby in my arms and rock him or her back to sleep in the middle of the night."

"Her. I think our first one will be a her."

My eyebrows lift. "Is that right?"

She giggles as she nods. "I just feel it."

"Okay. A little girl that looks just like her mama. I'm down with that."

She rolls her hips against me. "What do you say we start practicing?"

"I say I love the way you think."

Penny leans in and presses her lips to mine. "I'm going to love you forever, Cole."

"Me too, Penny."

Always.

NINE

COLE

"No."

Josie throws her hands up. "Why not?"

"Because I'm not a babysitter."

"You're right. You're not." She folds her arms over her chest. "You're an uncle."

"No."

A frustrated growl rips from her throat. "You're impossible! I don't understand why you can't watch the kids for two measly hours so your big sister can go to dinner for her anniversary."

"I don't understand how *you* can't understand why that might be hard for me."

"Why don't you help me understand, Cole?"

I shake my head. "Forget it."

"Exactly." Josie huffs out a laugh and runs her fingers through her hair. "How can I understand anything that goes on in that head of yours if you don't talk to me? You never talk to me."

"Nothin' to talk about."

"If you won't talk to me, maybe you should talk to a professional. Callie sees a therapist and—"

"No!" My fists clench at my sides. "End of discussion."

She blows a puff of air through her lips. "The boys have been looking forward to watching *Star Wars* with you all week. All you'd have to do is press play, and they'll sit there. I'll put the twins down before I leave, so you won't have to deal with poopy diapers or bottles or anything."

"It's not about the diapers or the feeding, Josie."

She steps closer to me. "Then what *is* it about?"

I stare into her eyes, ashamed to say it aloud, the words burning my tongue like acid.

It's about being alone with the kids.

Unaccompanied.

Unsupervised.

Trusted.

My chin drops, and my voice quivers. "You shouldn't want me to watch your kids."

Josie's lips part, eyes widening in surprise. "Cole, what happened is not your fault. You—"

"Don't." My razor-sharp tone causes her shoulders to jump. "Don't you dare finish that sentence."

She chews her bottom lip, and I know she wants to press on. My sister isn't one to leave anything well enough alone.

But she heeds my warning.

With a nod, she turns around and walks out of the pool house.

GUILT GNAWS at my conscience for an hour before I give in and make my way to Josie's house.

Don't know what I'm going to say, but I have to make up for refusing to watch her kids. She's letting me stay in her pool house for free, giving me a place to stay and food to eat. I'd be a selfish prick if I didn't try to help her and Dan out when they needed it.

The faint sound of voices floats through the house as I look for the happy family. The kitchen and dining rooms are empty, so I head toward the living room.

"Yes! Now it's your turn!" Brandon's voice gets louder the closer I get. "Come on, Callie!"

Callie.

I despise the way my pulse thunders at the sound of that woman's name.

Eliciting something inside me that I shouldn't feel.

Not for her.

Not for anyone.

Not ever again.

I hang back behind the corner, assessing the scene. Dozens of pillows and blankets line the floor, and the coffee table is shoved against the wall to open the space. Brandon and Miles are perched on top of each armrest, black streaks across their faces like war paint, shirtless and chanting like skinny little savages.

"Callie! Callie! Callie!"

Where's the woman in question, you ask?

She's balancing herself on the back of the couch, legs planted in a wide squat, arms stretched out in front of her, tongue between her teeth like she's rallying all of her concentration for what she's about to do. Her hoodie is tied around her neck like a cape. The now-yellowed bruises on her arm serve as her own war paint—the scars from the real-life battles she's been in.

"All right, boys," she says. "Give me a countdown."

"Three! Two! One!"

Callie launches herself into the air and does a front-flip before bouncing onto the pillows, sticking the landing.

Well, I definitely wasn't expecting that.

The boys cheer, diving off the couch to high-five Callie, who then raises her arms and flexes her non-existent biceps.

Can't remember the last time I smiled—a true, genuine smile—but catching a glimpse of a carefree Callie Kingston being silly with the boys has the corner of my mouth curving up.

That should be my cue to leave. I should acknowledge the danger sign and walk away.

But Miles spots me lurking. "Uncle Cole!"

Callie spins around, green eyes wide.

I step further into the room, though my feet should be carrying me back to the pool house. "What's going on in here?"

"We're wrestling!" Miles spreads his arms out wide. "I'm Mayhem Miles."

Brandon slams his fist into his palm. "I'm Brandon the Bruiser."

I arch an eyebrow at Callie. "And who are you?"

Her cheeks tinge a deep shade of pink. "I'm just playing around with them."

I shake my head. "After a move like that, I'd say you need a fitting name."

"Callie the Crusher!" Miles shouts.

"Callie the Cannon," Brandon offers.

She scrunches her nose as she laughs. "No, no. I don't need a name like that."

No, those aren't right. She's not one for violence. She isn't rough or loud or in your face. Callie possesses a silent strength, unaware of all that she's capable of.

Don't say it.

Don't say it.

Don't say it.

But the words are tumbling out of my mouth before I can catch them. "Callie the Courageous."

Callie's full, pink lips part, and her magnetic orbs lock with mine.

"That's perfect!" Miles holds out his fist, and I tap my knuckles against his.

Callie lifts a brow. "Why are you here?"

I don't miss the accusatory tone in her voice. No doubt Josie told her that I'd refused to babysit.

"Came to talk to Josie."

"Mom left, like, twenty minutes ago." Brandon smacks my arm with the back of his hand. "Hey, can we watch *Star Wars* tonight, Uncle Cole?"

"I should go."

"No!" the boys whine in unison.

"You don't have to leave," Callie says. "I'll make some popcorn. You guys go get the movie started."

"Yes!" Brandon drags Miles by his elbow toward the basement.

As soon as the sound of their feet beat a drumline on the stairs, Callie plants her hands on her hips and glares at me. "You made your sister very upset tonight."

My shoulders droop as I heave a sigh. "That's why I'm here. Wanted to apologize."

"Why wouldn't you help her out? She's helping *you*. It's the least you could do."

"I know."

"Then why? Why's it so hard for you to spend some time with your family?"

I scrub a hand over my jaw and lift my eyes to the ceiling. "It's complicated. It ... it's painful for me."

Those keen eyes of hers soften as she considers me a moment. "I get that." She gestures to the baby monitor clipped to the waistband of her leggings. "It's easier for me when the twins aren't here. But when they're awake, when Serenity looks at me and reaches her arms out for me ..." She shakes her head with a wistful smile. "It kills me."

My head tilts, and I move toward her, unable to stop the magnetic intrigue that consumes me every time I'm around this woman. "Why's that?"

She unties the sweatshirt from her neck and pulls it over her head as she makes her way into the kitchen, retreating into her turtle shell.

I follow, like a dog being lured with a treat.

Callie searches the cabinets until she finds a box of popcorn. I lean my hip against the counter, watching and waiting, while she places the bag in the microwave and sets the timer.

"I can't have kids." Her back is still to me, and her voice is low. "I've gotten pregnant a few times. Almost went a whole trimester once." She glances at me over her shoulder. "But I miscarried every time."

Fuck.

69

Awareness spins around me. "That's why you got so upset by that couple at the Fourth of July party."

She nods, finally turning to face me. "Doctors said I had submucosal fibroids, so I had surgery to try to remove them. It should've worked, but it turns out Paul's sperm isn't strong enough. The odds are against us, so he ... *we* decided to stop trying. Many people don't get it. They have kids, and they go about their lives, not realizing what a blessing their family truly is."

"They take it for granted," I grate out, hatred and disgust coursing through my veins.

"It's difficult to be around people like that. But it's not their fault."

I choke out a bitter laugh. "The hell it isn't."

"They just don't know what it's like, and I'm glad for that. Nobody should have to go through this. I've put such a strain on my marriage and ..." She lets her sentence trail off.

She said *she* put a strain on her marriage. Not the situation, not the infertility or the fibroids. *Her*. As if it's her fault. It's not, though I won't tell her otherwise.

Everyone always tries to absolve you of the guilt you place on yourself, as if their words can wash away the truth.

Callie's eyebrows draw together, and again she asks, "Why is it painful for you to be around Josie's kids?"

Agony throbs in my chest like a caged lion trying to escape. I'm tortured by the memory of my past, yet tortured just the same from keeping it locked inside. Damned if I do, and damned if I don't.

So I don't.

Doesn't matter either way. I doubt even Callie could fathom what I've been through.

And for some reason, I don't think I could stand the way she'd look at me if I told her.

The microwave beeps, pulling her attention off of me. It buys me enough time to escape from the kitchen and get to the basement.

Like the coward I am.

Callie doesn't say a word about it when she comes down and hands the boys their bowls. She plops down on the couch cushion beside me and situates a large bowl between us. Brandon presses *play*, and for the next two hours, I let the world fade away.

It's after nine when the front door thuds closed upstairs. My nephews are still glued to the screen, while my eyes are glued to Callie. She fell asleep halfway through the movie, and I haven't been able to focus on anything else.

Long lashes fan out against her porcelain cheeks. Soft, steady breaths pass through her parted lips. Her tiny body is curled beneath the blanket. Secrets and pain surround her, calling out to me like a beacon—someone who understands.

Desire fists my stomach, and I have no right. I don't even know this woman, yet she's stirring things inside me that I don't deserve to feel.

She needs a savior. A white knight to rescue her.

I'm not that guy.

I'm a destroyer.

I'm the wrecking ball who tears everything to the ground until there's nothing left.

Cole the Killer.

TEN

CALLIE

I NUDGE the car door shut with my hip as I balance the bags in my arms.

My keys slip out of my fingertips, and when I dip to catch them, one of the paper bags breaks open, and everything spills out into the driveway.

I groan and flick my eyes skyward. "Seriously?"

I kneel down and set my bags onto the ground. Collecting the packets of seeds and various garden tools, I stuff them into the other bags.

The rumble and stutter of Cole's truck thunders down the block. He pulls in front of Josie's house and kills the engine, lifting his chin when he spots me through his open window.

I wave. "Hey, Cole."

He swings open his door and steps out of his truck, eyeing me from under the brim of his hat. "Why are you on the ground?"

"Stupid bags always break. I miss plastic."

He strides over and takes the bags from me, stacking them on top of each other. "Paper's better for the environment. Hold them from the bottom, like this."

I snatch my keys off the concrete and offer him a sheepish smile. "Thanks for the tip."

He nods his head toward my house. "Open your door. I'll bring these in for you."

"You can bring them through the backyard, actually."

One corner of his mouth turns up. "Don't want me getting dirt on your perfect floors?"

"I'm building a garden." I arch an eyebrow. "Though, you are pretty dirty. Where do you go when you're out all day?"

"Work."

"And is your job to roll around in mud?"

"Construction."

My gaze skates over his biceps as I imagine him in a yellow hardhat with a tool belt slung low around his hips.

Bad, Callie. Stop ogling your best friend's brother.

"You know how to build a garden?" he asks as I punch in the code to my back gate.

"Not a clue. But I'm going to learn."

"How?"

"YouTube."

He walks across the lawn and sets my bags down on the patio table. "YouTube?"

I plant my hand on my hip. "Yeah, so?"

"And you're going to make a garden bed?"

I shrug, pretending like I know what that is. "Shouldn't be difficult."

"Where's your wood?"

I slide my sunglasses to the top of my head. "Wood?"

"For the garden bed. And the saw to cut the wood. You have one of those?"

I gesture to the shed at the far corner of the yard. "I'm sure there's one in there."

"Does your husband build things?"

"No."

"Then why would there be a saw in the shed?"

"I don't know. That's what a shed is for, storing tools, isn't it?" I lift my hands and let them smack against my thighs. "What's with the Spanish Inquisition?"

He blows a stream of air through his nostrils and shakes his head. "Give me five minutes. I'll be right back."

I scoff. "I didn't ask you to do this for me."

"I'm not," he calls over his shoulder while he jogs to the gate. "I'm going to *teach* you."

Warmth pools in my stomach, and it trickles out to my arms and legs.

He's not going to do it for me—or pay someone else to do it.

He doesn't tell me that I can't do it myself.

He's going to *teach* me how.

Finally, someone who doesn't want to control what I do.

An excited squeal bubbles up into my throat, and I rush inside to change.

Maverick lifts onto his hind legs and puts his paws on my chest, licking my face.

"Hi, my love." I scratch behind his ears and push him down. "I have to change, and then you're coming with me outside."

He barks and springs up the stairs ahead of me.

After I throw on a pair of cut-off denim shorts and a ratty, old tank top, I twist my hair into a high bun and push a red bandana-style headband onto my head.

"Let's go chop some wood, Mav!"

When I slide open the back door, Maverick pushes past my legs and charges toward Cole, who's setting up some kind of table on the grass.

And *dear God* he's wearing a tool belt.

"Maverick! Get down. No jumping."

"Ah, he's excited. Let him jump." Cole cups Maverick's face in both hands and bends down to let him lick his cheek.

Maverick's tail swats the air so hard I can feel the breeze. I grimace as he bounces on his hind legs to get closer to Cole's mouth. "Okay, boy. That's enough. Leave the poor man alone."

Cole glances at me and then does a double-take. His eyes blaze a trail down to my bare legs before cutting back to Maverick. "Cute dog."

"Thanks." I gesture to the table. "So, what's all this?"

"This is my makeshift sawing table. You're going to measure the wood, and prop it up on here when you cut it."

"Where'd you get all that wood from?"

"Had scraps in my truck."

"I can pay you for it."

He holds his palm up. "I'm not taking your money, Callie."

Something about the desperation in his eyes makes me not want to press the issue, so I let it go. "Where do we start?"

"First, figure out where you want the garden."

I cock my head and scan the yard. "How about over there?"

"What are you growing?"

"Vegetables."

He nods and waves me along as he starts walking toward the spot. "Vegetables need a good amount of sunlight. You should start small and then build on as you get more comfortable with it."

I use my hand as a visor over my eyes. "How do you know so much about this?"

His chin drops, and his voice softens. "My mom loved growing vegetables. She was the only one on the block who had the concrete in the backyard removed and replaced with soil."

A smile blooms on my face. "What did she grow?"

"Zucchini, tomatoes, eggplant, cucumbers, and some herbs. She liked to make her own sauce with fresh ingredients."

"I bet it tasted amazing."

"It did. Josie tries to replicate it, but it just isn't the same." His eyes dart up to mine. "Don't tell her I said that."

I wink. "Secret's safe with me."

"What made you want to start a garden?"

I pick at the frays on my shorts. "Just wanted something to keep me busy, I guess."

He scratches the back of his neck. "If this is wrong to ask, just tell me, but don't you get bored sitting home all day?"

Maybe it's because of the honest way he asked, or maybe I'm

just dying to be honest with someone for once. Dying for someone who understands.

I look into Cole's cobalt eyes, and I let the word *yes* fall from my lips. "That's why I want to grow a garden. I love to cook. I've always dreamed of opening my own restaurant." I laugh, shaking my head as if it will shake the thought from my mind. "Somehow, growing a vegetable garden seemed comparable. It's stupid, really."

Cole takes a step toward me, and ever so slowly, he tucks his finger under my chin and lifts it until I'm sucked into his hypnotizing gaze. "It's not stupid at all, Callie. You should go after the things you dream about. The things that make you happy."

My heart pounds, and my knees tremble under me, but not because I'm scared of Cole. It's because I'm scared of believing him. Scared of the notion that it is, in fact, possible to have the things I long for.

To feel happiness again.

"I can't," I whisper.

Cole's eyes tighten. "Why not?"

I want to open up to him, want to fling myself into his arms and beg him to take me far, far away. But that would only continue to mask the problem. *My* problem.

Cole can't save me. I don't need saving. I'm not some damsel in distress locked in her ivory tower. I make my own choices, and I've made my bed here. I have a wonderful life filled with wonderful things. Life's not always perfect, but I have to appreciate what I have.

Things could always be worse.

I pull away from Cole, and he lets the conversation die. He shows me how to measure the area and then the pieces of wood. I'm eager to get my hands on the saw, but he says it's best to remeasure before we cut anything. I don't argue. This is the longest he's gone without a scowl on his face.

I like this side of him. Easygoing. In his element. Calm. Nothing like the wound-up, abrasive version I've come to expect.

With the tool belt on. Let's not forget that part.

It turns out, I get enjoyment out of sawing. It's an exertion of physical energy and manual labor that makes me feel strong and capable. Sweat beads along my skin as I push and pull the saw, back and forth, back and forth, and when I cut through each block, a surge of confidence runs through me.

I *needed* this.

I pound the nails into each corner, and once the box is constructed, we stand back and admire my work.

Cole removes his hat and wipes his forehead with his T-shirt, revealing a spectacular set of abs. Deep grooves separate each cube, and two ridges are carved into each side of his pelvis. Droplets of sweat trickle down his torso, and my eyes follow them on their descent, leading down into the waistband of his tattered jeans.

Heat crawls over my skin, leaving a trail of goosebumps behind.

Cole puts his cap back on, and his face twists in disgust as he glances over my shoulder. "Uh, I think your dog's eating something."

I snap out of the trance I'm in and rush over to Maverick. "Stop that! Gross, Maverick! Come on."

Maverick darts away from the scene of the crime and takes off running around the outskirts of the yard.

I groan. "The vet said he eats his own poop because he's anxious."

"Looks like he's doing it because he likes it."

I snort. "I think maybe you're right."

"What does a dog have to be anxious about? They have the life."

I open my mouth to answer, but then the back door slides open, and Paul steps out onto the patio. Maverick barks and runs toward him like he's been shot out of a cannon.

My stomach flops when I see the perplexed expression on Paul's face, his brown eyes bouncing between me and Cole.

I push up a smile and wave my arms like Vanna White, gesturing to the garden bed. "Hey. Look what I made!"

Paul moves slowly, like a lion ready to pounce on its prey.

Cole steps forward, moving in front of me, angling his body.

Like a shield.

When Paul reaches me, he moves around Cole and snakes his arm behind my back and pulls me against him. His lips dip down to meet mine, but they're hard and unforgiving.

I pull back to look at him. "It's a garden box."

"I see." He glares up at Cole, his fingers digging into my hip.

Cole's scowl is back in place, fists balled at his sides.

"Cole offered to teach me how to build it," I say, attempting to break the awkward ego showdown.

"I bet he did."

The corner of Cole's mouth twitches. "I'll get this cleaned up and be out of your hair."

"Thank you for your help." I pry myself out of Paul's possessive hold. "I really appreciate it."

"Anytime." Cole gives me a tight nod and turns to collect his things.

Paul stands still as a statue, watching Cole until he's out of our yard. Then he turns and walks into the house, leaving me outside as if I'm not even here.

"Come on, Maverick. Let's go in. It's dinnertime."

Maverick trots behind me, and when we step into the kitchen, Paul's already scooping Maverick's food into his metal bowl.

"How was your day?" I approach him with tentative steps.

"Go take a shower. You're filthy. We'll talk over dinner."

My stomach twists into a knot. I rush up the stairs and make my shower quick. Letting my hair air dry, I throw on a pair of lounge shorts and a T-shirt and head back downstairs.

Paul's sitting in the dining room with the lights off again, drinking a glass of scotch. I wonder how many he's had while I was upstairs. The setting sun casts a sliver of light through the window, streaking across his face, giving him a menacing glow.

"Want the light on?"

He shakes his head. "Just hurry up with dinner. I'm starving."

My head jerks back, but I say nothing. I need to diffuse the situation, not make things worse.

I throw together a quick pasta primavera dish and toss in some sautéed shrimp. I heat up Paul's favorite garlic bread in the toaster oven, and when everything's finished, I carry it into the dining room.

"Wasn't really in the mood for shrimp," he says when I place his dish in front of him on the table.

"Oh, I'm sorry. Want me to make something else?"

He gulps down the contents of his glass and slams it on the table, making my shoulders jump. "No. This is fine."

"Are you sure? There's chicken in the fridge. I can make it in twenty minutes."

"I said it's fine. Sit."

Chewing on my lip, I take my seat across from him and start eating.

After a few minutes pass, Paul asks, "Why didn't you tell me that Cole was coming over today?"

I place my fork down and wring my hands together under the table.

Here we go.

"I hadn't planned on it. When I got home, one of the bags broke as I was taking them out of the car, and Cole came over to help. He asked if I had the wood to make the garden bed, but I didn't know what he was talking about, so he offered to show me how to do it. Gave me the wood for free too."

Paul nods as he pours himself another drink. "I don't want him here alone with you."

My eyebrows pinch together. "Why not?"

He watches me over the rim of the glass while he takes a long sip. "Because we don't know him. He's a stranger, and I don't want you alone with him."

"He's Josie's brother. Not exactly a stranger."

Stupid, Callie. Why are you arguing?

Paul's jaw tenses. "Josie hasn't seen him in years, and Dan said the guy's got issues."

"Issues? What kind of issues?"

"I didn't ask. I just need you to listen to me. I don't want him hanging around here anymore. Got it?"

I nod once and lift my fork again. "Got it."

79

Silence falls between us as we continue to eat. It feels as if the storm is passing, the dark clouds beginning to retreat. That's why I'm caught by surprise when Paul's glass whizzes past my head.

The crystal explodes when it hits the wall beside me, shards flying onto the table and floor. Maverick yelps and runs out of the room.

My heart thunders in my chest like a hundred galloping horses. I wish I could hop on one of them and ride it away from here. Away from what's about to happen.

I push back from the table and begin cleaning up the glass, too afraid to look at Paul.

His chair scrapes against the floor. "Stop cleaning, Callie."

My hands shake as I use my napkin to sop up the liquid around me. "It's okay. I just want to get the glass off the floor so Maverick doesn't—"

Paul's hand is on the back of my head, fisting my hair as he yanks me up. "I said stop cleaning!"

I swallow the scream that wants to break free.

Be brave, Callie.

Paul shoves me against the wall, holding me there with his forearm across my chest. His brown eyes harden, shades darker than usual, shadowed by the severe angle of his eyebrows. Gone is the handsome, golden-haired man that I fell in love with. There's a hollowness to him now, a fury replacing his soul.

"Do you want to fuck him, Callie?"

"No!"

His arm presses harder against me. "You're lying."

"I'm not! Paul, please stop. I'm not lying." My body trembles, fear and adrenaline coursing through my veins.

When you're in a dangerous situation, people say you have one of two choices: fight or flight. You react on instinct, without thinking. Your body knows what to do. Either you kick your attacker in the balls, or you run away.

But I can't do either of those things, because my attacker is my husband.

I can't fight back. He'll always be stronger.

And there's nowhere for me to run. No safe haven. This is my home.

I'm stuck.

My hands come up, trailing the skin on Paul's arms, attempting to soothe him with my touch. "You're hurting me," I say, my voice a whisper.

"Well, I'm hurting too." His eyes are glassy, unfocused. "All I ever wanted was to give you a family."

"I know that." My hands cup his face. "It's not your fault. We tried everything we could."

His lips press into a firm line. "And it still wasn't enough. I'm not enough."

"Don't say that."

He digs his arm into me, my chest feeling like it's going to crack under the pressure. "If I were enough, you wouldn't be running around with that asshole behind my back!"

I shake my head, tears streaming down my face. "No, Paul. I'm not running around with anyone. I love you. Only you!"

He steps back, releasing me, seeming to snap out of his stupor. He thrusts his fingers through his hair, yanking on the ends of it, blowing a stream of air through his lips.

Then, without warning, he swings his arm and backhands me across my cheek.

A cry rips from my mouth as my hand comes up to cover the throbbing skin. I squeeze my eyes shut, turning to face the wall, cowering against it, bracing for the next blow.

But it doesn't come.

I hear glass crunching under Paul's shoes as he moves, followed by his footsteps echoing in the hall. I keep my eyes closed until I hear the slam of the front door.

Maverick's collar jingles, his nails clacking against the floor as he tries to enter the room.

"Maverick, no. Stay." I move toward him with my hands up, and pain slices through my bare foot. "Ow, shit."

He whimpers and sits in the doorway, head cocked with his ears back.

81

"I'm okay. Everything's okay. Just have to get this glass off the floor."

Blood smears in a trail behind me as I walk around the table. I tie a linen napkin around my foot, wincing as I tighten the knot. I'll worry about my foot later. Right now, my focus is on sweeping the glass away and clearing the dinner plates.

I go through the motions, working until it looks like nothing ever happened in the dining room.

A hysterical laugh bursts from my throat when I think back to the nickname Cole had given me the other night. "Callie the Courageous. Hardly."

More like Callie the Contemptible.

I grab a bag of peas from the freezer and hobble up the stairs to the bathroom. Propping myself against the sink, I twist my leg to inspect the underside of my foot. After I pluck the glass out and disinfect the area, I bandage it up and carry the peas into my bedroom without so much as a glance in the mirror.

I don't have to look. The throbbing pain tells me that my face is swollen, that the bruise is already marking my skin.

Maverick curls up beside me as I pull the covers over my legs, resting his head on my chest. I press the freezing bag against my cheek and close my eyes.

In the calm stillness of my darkened room, the sadness I've shoved down for the past hour creeps out. My chest tightens as a silent tear rolls down my temple and into my hair.

I put myself in Paul's shoes and try to understand his anger. If I can understand why he reacts the way he does, learn what triggers him, then maybe I can prevent this from happening again. I've gotten good at tiptoeing around his temper.

Paul *isn't* a wife beater. He isn't a bad person. He loves me, but he's frustrated, and he's hurting. We've been under a lot of stress, and rightfully so. Infertility puts a strain on every relationship. Add in the way he's been feeling since the doctor told him that it's his fault we can't conceive, and it's the perfect storm.

But that shouldn't make husbands hit their wives, my conscience screams.

I blow out a breath. "Everything's going to be okay."

And it will. We just have to put this behind us.

It's late when Paul crawls into bed, reeking of liquor.

I keep my eyes closed and pretend to be asleep.

His fingers are gentle as he grazes the tender, puffy skin on my cheekbone. "I'm sorry, baby," he slurs, placing a kiss on my temple. "I'm so sorry. I love you."

Then he rolls over and falls asleep.

Maverick.

California king bed.

Walk-in closet.

Dream kitchen.

Yard with a pool.

Mercedes.

But for the first time, the exercise doesn't make me feel better. It doesn't calm my mind. Instead, I question what Cole said at Josie's Fourth of July party.

Are all of the lavish things I own really worth *this*?

ELEVEN

COLE

What the hell am I doing?

I pause at the curb and look down at the bags in my arms.

I'd stopped at the nursery on my way home from work and picked up a few things for Callie's garden bed.

She hadn't asked me to.

Her husband certainly doesn't want me there.

And I didn't need to be spending my extra money.

So again, I ask myself: *What the hell am I doing?*

Something just doesn't feel right. Something deep in my gut. Felt it the moment I saw the look in Callie's eyes when Paul came home two days ago.

Fear.

On top of that, Josie said she'd invited Callie over yesterday, but she declined, stating she was sick.

Yet she looked fine the other day.

I keep telling myself it's none of my business.

But if something happens to that woman—sweet, innocent Callie—and I could've done something to stop it, it'll add guilt right on top of the heaping pile I've already buried myself under.

Against my better judgment, my legs carry me to Callie's front door, and I ring the bell.

Maverick barks on the other side of the door, but nobody answers.

I set the bags down by my feet and knock after a minute goes by. "Callie, it's Cole."

The curtain covering the window sways, a shadow flashing by.

"Come on, Callie. I know you're in there. Just saw you in the window."

The door cracks open, barely wide enough for me to see Callie. She's wearing a baseball cap that's too big for her head, pulled down low over her eyes.

"I'm sick," she says softly. "You don't want to come any closer."

I bend my knees and lower my head in an attempt to see into her eyes, but she jerks her chin down to her chest.

"What do you want?" Her voice sounds strained.

I gesture at the bags by my feet. "Got you some things for your garden."

Her lips part. "Oh. That's ... that's so kind of you."

My heart thumps against my chest, alarm spiking through my veins. "Callie, are you all right?"

She nods, the brim of her oversized hat jerking up and down. "Just not feeling well."

I bend down and gather the bags. "Well, at least let me bring these around back for you."

"It's fine. You can leave them—"

Maverick wedges himself between the door and Callie's legs and leaps up at me. He knocks the bags out of my arms, tearing one of them, and everything tumbles onto the ground.

"Maverick!" Callie hisses, crouching down to collect what fell.

I nudge his paws off my chest and use this opportunity to snatch the hat from Callie's head. She gasps and attempts to shield her eyes with her hands.

But it's too late.

Every muscle in my body goes stiff, and my stomach bottoms out. I clench my jaw so hard that it feels like my teeth might shatter.

A bright-purple splotch stains her right cheek, on the bone just under her eye.

"What. The. Fuck. Is. That?"

Callie's eyes well as she stammers. "It's nothing. Really. I tripped and fell and—"

"You're seriously going to give me the I-fell-and-hit-a-doorknob excuse?"

Her bottom lip trembles, and she shakes her head. "No. Not a doorknob. It was ... it's ..."

"Go ahead. I'll wait while you think of a believable story." I fold my arms over my chest, restraining myself so that I don't hoist her over my shoulder like a caveman and take her away.

Maybe that's what I should do.

"Cole, it's not what you think."

"And what is it that I'm thinking, hmm?"

Her arms fall at her sides, and she lowers her gaze.

"Say it." I edge closer to her, forcing her green eyes to look up at me. "I want to hear you lie to my face."

"Cole, please," she whimpers.

"Fine. If you won't tell me, I'll just wait until Paul comes home, and then I'll ask *him* what happened to your face."

"No!" Her hands fly up to her mouth.

And there it is.

The truth hanging there in the space between us.

My voice turns sinister. "He hurt you."

"Please. It's not that big of a deal."

My eyebrows hit my hairline. "Not that big of a deal? Are you kidding me?"

Tears stream down her face now. "You don't understand. Please, you can't say anything to Josie."

"You're not fooling her. You know that, right?"

She looks so pitiful, so broken, standing there with her hair a wreck and that bruise on her tear-stained cheek. A fragment of my heart splinters off and drops at her feet. I want to help her. Want to fix it for her. But I don't know how.

"Thank you for all of this," she says, waving her arm at the bags scattered below. "I appreciate it more than you know. But you can't be here. I need you to go."

"Before he gets home." It's not a question. I know what she means.

She hesitates before giving me a slow nod.

I don't know what the fuck to do. Logic tells me Callie is a grown-ass woman who can take care of herself. This isn't my business, and I shouldn't get involved.

But another part of me—the louder part—is screaming at me to do something. Get her out of here.

I settle somewhere in between. "Give me your phone."

Callie's eyebrows pull down. "What?"

"Give me your phone. I want you to have my number in case ... in case you need it."

"That won't be necessary."

"I'm not leaving until you do." I hold my hand out.

She groans and walks back into her house.

While I wait, I crouch down to stroke Maverick's head. "You have to protect her, Mav."

He rests his head on my knee and lets out a heavy sigh.

Callie returns with her phone a moment later, and I punch in my number.

When I give her phone back, I clasp her hand. "You don't have to go through this, Callie. You deserve better."

Then, I turn and force myself across the street.

I hear the boys laughing as I enter through Josie's back gate. They're kicking a soccer ball around the yard while my sister sits in the grass playing with the twins.

"Hey, brother. How was work?"

I stalk over to her, unable to contain my rage another second longer. "You were right."

Her eyebrows dip down as she stands. "Right about what?"

I stab the air with my index finger in the direction of Callie's house. "Her husband hits her."

Josie's hand clamps over her mouth. "How do you know this?"

"Just went over there to drop off a few things for her garden.

She wouldn't answer the door at first, but when she did, she was trying to hide under a hat." I scrub my hands over my face. "She has a bruise on her face, Josie. He hit her in the face."

Her eyes go wide. "How do you know it was him?"

I pace along the side of the pool. "She couldn't even tell me how it happened. She started stuttering, and I called her out on it."

"Oh, my God. I knew it! I knew something was wrong. What are we going to do?"

I arch an eyebrow. "I'll tell you what I'd like to do."

"No, Cole. We have to be smart about this. If Paul finds out Callie told someone, things could get a lot worse for her."

Worse than getting hit in the face?

I stare down at my hands. They're large and calloused. Strong from years of manual labor. Man's hands. How could a man put his hands on a woman? I try to imagine it, but the thought turns my stomach.

Even after everything went down with Penny, not once did I think of raising my hands to her. How can Callie's husband live with himself? How can he think this is okay?

Moreover, why is Callie accepting this and staying with him? Covering for him?

Josie must be thinking similar thoughts, because she keeps shaking her head like she's unable to fathom what's happening.

I throw my hands up. "Yeah, the only plan I'm coming up with is to beat the piss out of him."

"Believe me. I'd love nothing more than to give that piece of shit a taste of the Luciano siblings." Josie lets out an exasperated laugh. "Remember the good old days?"

A smirk pulls at my lips. "I think we were in the principal's office more than we were in our classes."

Josie grins. "Poor Mom. She was beside herself every time she got a phone call from the school."

Mom.

My chest clenches.

Josie's smile fades. "I really miss her."

"Me too."

"Was she ..." She glances down at the twins. "Did she ever say she was angry with me for not coming to visit as much?"

I shake my head. "She wasn't too coherent toward the end, but she'd always ask me to show her the boys' pictures. It made her happy to see her grandkids."

Josie swipes a fallen tear from her cheek. "I wish she and Dad could've met them."

I clear my throat, stuffing the emotion down. "Well, I'm going to jump in the shower. Been a long day."

"I'll talk to Dan when he gets home. He's the level-headed one. Maybe he can come up with a plan to help Callie."

"I'll, uh, come by for dinner tonight." I lift my eyes to hers. "If that's okay."

A smile breaks on Josie's face. "Of course it's okay."

I nod and make my way toward the pool house.

"Hey, Cole?"

"Yeah?"

"I'm really glad you're here with us."

"COME ON, baby girl. Mommy needs to eat."

Serenity whimpers and buries her face in Josie's neck.

Dan holds his arms out, reaching for her. "Come to Daddy. Give Mommy a break."

"No!"

"I've never seen her like this," Josie says. "She doesn't have a fever or anything."

Brandon claps his hands. "Wanna come to big brother?"

"No!"

Serenity squirms in Josie's lap. It looks like she wants to get down, but when Josie attempts to move her to her high chair, Serenity clings to her shirt, not wanting to let go.

"She's allowed to be fussy," Dan says, shoving a piece of bread into his mouth. "Girl's an angel most of the time."

Lucas tosses his sippy cup onto the floor. I bend down to pick it up and place it on his tray. Not two seconds later, he tosses it over again.

He giggles. "Cole pick up!"

I glare at him.

He giggles again.

"This one's gonna give you trouble," I say to Dan as I lean over and swipe the cup off the floor. This time, I set it down on the table, just out of Lucas's reach.

Now it's his turn to glare.

Dan chuckles. "Tell me about it."

Serenity wails, and both Brandon and Miles cover their ears.

"I'm going to try putting her down. Maybe she's tired." Josie pushes back from the table and carries Serenity out of the kitchen.

"Can we be excused?" Miles asks.

Dan glances at their plates and nods. "Clear your dishes first."

The boys scramble to their feet, and after they dump their dishes into the sink, they disappear into the basement.

Dan shakes his head with a smirk. "Welcome to the circus."

"It definitely keeps you guys on your toes."

He sits back against his chair and crosses his arms over his chest. "Josie told me about Callie."

I swallow the food in my mouth and drop my fork onto the table. "You're friends with Paul."

He nods with a heavy sigh. "Can't imagine the guy doing something like that. I've known him for years."

"You never know what goes on behind closed doors."

Trust me. I should know.

"That's true." His eyes tighten. "How bad did she look?"

Bile works its way into my mouth. I haven't been able to get the image of her face, the bruise, the hopeless look in her eyes, out of my head all day.

I lift my hand and gesture to my cheekbone. "He got her right here. Decent-sized bruise."

Dan's face contorts as his head jerks back. "Jesus."

Josie returns with the baby monitor, Serenity's cry blaring

through the speaker. She plops down into her seat and chugs the contents of Dan's beer bottle.

"She's just going to have to cry it out." She points a finger at Lucas. "And don't you get any ideas, tough guy. I can only handle one screamer tonight."

Lucas bangs his fists on his tray. "Lucas tough guy!"

Josie grins. "Not tougher than Mommy, kid." She turns her attention to Dan. "So, what are we going to do about Callie?"

Dan runs his hand over his buzz cut. "I think you have to talk to her first. You're her best friend. Tell her you know about what Paul's been doing. Let her know we're here to help her in any way we can. See what she says."

Josie splays her fingers on the table. "But what if she doesn't leave him? Most women in her situation stay with the monsters who beat them."

"You can't force her to do something she's not ready to do," Dan says. "All you can do is let her know that she has a safe place here if she needs somewhere to go."

Josie chews on her lip, and I know Dan's answer isn't good enough for her.

I know this because it isn't good enough for *me* either.

Dan stands and brings his plate to the sink. "I have a video conference with a client. I'll be in my office if you need me. We can finish talking about this later." He bends down and plants a kiss on the top of Josie's head.

As he walks into the hallway, a loud, gurgling semi-explosion sounds from the tiny human sitting next to me.

Josie and I whip our heads around to look at him.

Lucas giggles. "Poopy."

Josie's head falls onto the table with a groan. "Sure. Wait until Daddy's gone."

I pull up the neck of my shirt to shield my nose. "God, that's foul. What are you feeding this kid?"

She lifts her head to glare at me, and for the first time since I've been here, I realize how tired she looks.

Before my sister moved out to California, she and I were a team.

Our family didn't have much, but we stuck together and helped each other out. She was my best friend for a long time, and I felt the significant loss when she left. She started a new life with her new family, and I'd resented her for it. I assumed she cared about money, expensive homes, and luxury cars more than she cared about the family she left behind.

But looking at her now, at the table full of dirty dishes waiting to be washed, the toddler screaming her head off upstairs, and another one who I'm pretty sure just shit the motherload up the back of his onesie, while the older boys play downstairs, undoubtedly turning the basement into a disaster zone ... it gives me a different perspective on Josie's life here. One I couldn't appreciate without seeing it for myself.

We used to have each other's backs.

I guess we still should.

I toss my napkin onto the table and push out of my seat. "Clean your kid's ass. I'll be right back."

I jog halfway down the basement stairs and peer at the boys over the railing. "Hey. Your mom needs help. Get up here and clear the table. Brandon, you wash the dishes, and Miles will dry. You got me?"

The boys drop their video game controllers and follow me up the steps without a complaint.

Then, I suck in a deep breath and make my way up to Serenity's bedroom.

The poor girl's voice sounds raw from all the screaming she's been doing. Her cry cuts off when I step into her darkened room. She eyes me warily through the slats in her crib as I flip on the small lamp on the nightstand in the corner.

"You're makin' a lot of noise for someone so small," I whisper, taking tentative steps toward her.

Immediately, her arms shoot up for me. My chest cracks open, and I wince at the physical pain.

Fuck.

No, I can do this.

I *need* to do this.

It's for Josie.

I reach into the crib and scoop Serenity up into my arms. She buries her face in the crook of my neck and fists my T-shirt in her little hands. I rub my hand along her back, and she releases a tiny sigh.

Tears sting my eyes, but I will them away.

I can do this.

I carry Serenity to the rocking chair by the window and lower us into it. She snuggles against me as if she can't get close enough. I rock her gently as I continue to rub circles on her back.

Grief strangles me while agony sears my insides. The feel of this little life in my arms, her warmth, her innocence, her pure light … it's too much. I squeeze my eyes shut, desperate to cling to the remaining threads of my sanity, but the tears spring free. A sob chokes out, and I squeeze Serenity tighter.

As if she knows, as if she can understand my sorrow, she lifts her hand and presses her palm to my wet cheek.

I'm not sure who's comforting who anymore, but it feels like we both need this.

And then, without even thinking about it, I start to sing. It's a song I know well, the lyrics haunting me every night along with the ghosts of my past.

I only get halfway through the song before Serenity falls asleep in my arms, but I sing it all the way through.

A while later, the door cracks open, and Josie tiptoes inside, slowly lowering a sleeping Lucas into his crib.

"You got her to sleep," she whispers.

I nod. "She's been out for a while." I ease out of the rocking chair and bring Serenity to her crib.

Josie places her hand on my shoulder. "Thank you so much."

I nod as we gaze down at her sleeping angel.

"How do you do it?"

Josie tilts her head. "Do what?"

"How do you sleep at night?"

Understanding and sadness washes over my sister's face. "It's not easy. I check on them, all of them, at least a dozen times. I wake up in the middle of the night and creep into their rooms, making sure they're okay." She smiles. "Sometimes Dan is already in here. He worries too."

My eyes burn, and I swallow around the boulder that's forever lodged in my throat.

Josie edges closer. "Cole, what you went through ..."

I shake my head violently. "No."

"Please, let me just say this. Once, and you'll never hear another word from me again."

My fists clench at my sides, and I grit my teeth, bracing myself for what she's about to say.

"No one should ever have to go through what you and Penny did. It's not right, and it's not fair, and I'll never understand why things like that have to happen. Never. But it happened." Her eyes bore through mine in the darkness. "Somehow, some way, you have to pick yourself up and move forward. You can't stay stuck in this purgatory of torture and self-loathing. It'll take some time, but you can start a new life. Find someone new, start a family. Try again."

She pauses, gazing at Serenity and then back at me. "I see how much you love her. How much you love my kids. You could make an incredible father someday if you just allow yourself to have that."

"Yeah, Father of the Fucking Year." I move to pass her, to get out of this room, out of this house. I need air.

Josie grips my forearm. "Cole."

I remain staring straight ahead, waiting for her to finish.

"Nothing that happened is your fault. You hear me?" Her fingers tighten, biting into my skin. "Nothing. That happened. Is your fault."

I shake her off and get out of there as fast as I can.

TWELVE

COLE

Four Years Ago

I WIPED my sweaty palms on my slacks.

Yeah, I was wearing dress pants.

Hoped I didn't look as ridiculous as I felt.

The fancy French doors swung open, and Annette, one of the maids, greeted me with a smile.

"Cole, what a pleasant surprise! Come in."

"Thank you, Annette. How are you?"

"I'm well. Is there a dinner I don't know about? Where's Penny?"

"No, no. I came here to speak with Mr. Murdoch." I cleared my throat. "Is he available?"

"He's in his study. Follow me. Let's see if he's off that conference call."

My knees trembled as I walked through the foyer.

A *foyer*.

Who was I kidding? I didn't belong there.

How would I ever be able to provide Penny with the life she deserved? The life she was used to.

Maybe I was making a mistake.

Maybe I should've set Penny free and let her find someone else. Someone in her circle. Someone better suited for her.

But when I thought about what that meant—losing Penny forever—I just couldn't do it.

My heart swelled when I pictured Penny's sweet face, those brown eyes looking up at me with love and adoration.

She loved me.

Maybe love was enough.

"Mr. Murdoch?" Annette rapped her knuckles on the open door. "I have a special guest here to speak with you."

Mr. Murdoch smiled when he saw me. "Cole, come in. Thanks, Annette."

I held my head high and strode into his office.

"Have a seat, son." He gestured to the stiff leather chair that faced his desk. "What can I do for you?"

"Well, uh ... I ... I love your daughter, sir. Very much."

His eyes narrowed as his smile faded. "She's very taken with you too."

I nodded. "I came here because I'd like to ask for your blessing." My throat tightened as I dug into my pocket and pulled out the small black velvet box. "I'd like to ask Penny to marry me, sir."

Mr. Murdoch's eyebrows lifted. "Well, then. Let's see this ring."

I leaned over and slid the box across his desk.

He popped the lid open and rolled his lips together. "It's not as small as I expected it to be."

My stomach dropped. "It's not as big as I wanted it to be either."

He waved his hand and set the box down in front of him. "It's not about the size of the diamond."

Was he kidding?

I couldn't stop the tilt of my head.

Mr. Murdoch grinned. "You seem surprised."

"With all due respect, sir." I swept my arm around his lavish office. "It looks like the size of the diamond matters very much."

He chuckled. "What I mean is, the size of the diamond doesn't matter if the quality isn't there. I'd much rather have a one-carat with a perfect quality over an over-sized, showy diamond that has visible flaws."

He clasped his hands over his stomach as he leaned back in his chair. "That's the thing about marriage: You don't want anyone to see the flaws. The cracks, the imperfections. You have to be willing to do whatever it takes to maintain the quality of the marriage."

I sat up straighter. "I will do whatever it takes to make your daughter happy, sir."

"I know you will, son. I have no doubt. But I can help. I can make things easier for you."

"What do you mean?"

"You're a hard worker. I know the long, grueling hours you put in at those construction sites. You have a good work ethic. I respect that."

"Thank you."

I sensed a catch coming.

"But you don't make good money there, do you?"

Ah, there it was.

"What are you getting at, sir?"

"I'd like to hire you. My company works with contractors and architects. We're breaking new ground all the time. I could pay you the salary you deserve." He leaned his elbows on his desk. "The salary worthy of my daughter's hand."

THIRTEEN

CALLIE

"Damn, Callie."

I roll my eyes and smile. "Stop."

"Don't act all shy now." Josie smacks her palm against my ass. "You're going to be turning heads in this outfit tonight. Better get used to the attention now."

I glance down at my pale-pink tank and white, frayed denim shorts. "It's just a tank top."

"It's not *just* a tank top. It's the perky tits, and the flat stomach, and the thighs without cellulite." Josie gestures to herself. "I used to have all that before four kids sucked the life out of me."

"You still got it, babe." Dan strides into the room and wraps his arms around his wife. "Look just as good as the day I met you."

"Eww, guys." Brandon's nose scrunches as he walks toward the couch. "Get a room."

I ruffle his hair as I sit on the edge of the armrest. "Trust me, you don't want them getting a room. Not unless you want a new baby brother or sister."

Josie points her index finger at me. "Don't you wish that on me, Callie Kingston."

Dan chuckles. "Seriously. We're at capacity."

Brandon looks up at me. "If they have another kid, I'm coming to live with you."

I wrap my arm around his shoulders. "You can stay with me any time, B."

"And Callie has a dog," Dan says. "The boys are trying to convince us that we need a dog."

"I need a dog like I need another hole in the head," Josie mutters.

I laugh and turn to Brandon. "Why don't you come by and walk Maverick? He's got a ton of energy that I'm sure he'd love to get out."

Brandon springs to his feet. "Really?"

I nod. "I can even pay you like a dog walker. Come by every day for the rest of the summer."

Brandon flings his arms around me. "Thank you, Callie! This is gonna be epic!" Then he takes off running into the hallway, no doubt to tell Miles about the exciting news.

"Those boys love you, you know," Josie says.

"And I love them." I stand and smooth out my shirt. "You ready to head out?"

"Go," says Dan, shooing Josie toward the front door. "Get out now while you still can."

Once we're in Josie's car, I relax against the leather seat. "I've been looking forward to this all week."

"Me too. Feels like forever since I've been out of the house without the twins attached to each hip." She reaches over and squeezes my knee. "I'm glad we're doing this."

I'd been anxiously awaiting a visit from Josie after Cole left my house last week. He'd stormed off after seeing the bruise on my cheek, and I was sure he was going to out me to his sister. Lying about the marks on my arm were one thing, but I wouldn't have been able to talk my way out of it if Josie had seen my face.

But Cole kept quiet.

And the bruising faded.

Like it always does.

When we pull up to the restaurant, Josie hands her keys to the valet. We opt for a high-top table near the bar and order drinks and appetizers.

"How's your garden coming along?"

"It's great, thanks to your brother." A small smile tugs at my lips. "He helped me get it started. Gave me some pointers and brought over a bunch of supplies."

"He's very handy." She's quiet for a moment, pondering as she stares down into her wine glass. "He has a big heart. Always loved helping people. Everyone on our block in our old neighborhood adored him."

"Really?"

"I know it's hard to picture now, but he used to be so friendly and full of life. That's why it kills me to see him wasting away in that pool house all the time."

My mind drifts to those tormented eyes of his. "What happened to him? Was his divorce really that bad?"

"It's more than that," she says with a sigh. "But yeah. The divorce was rough."

I want to pry, curious about what more there is to Cole's story. But if Josie wanted to tell me, she already would have. It's not her story to tell, and I get that.

"Divorce has to be scary," I say. "I can't imagine where I'd go or what I'd do if Paul and I split up."

Josie straightens in her chair. "You wouldn't have to worry about that. You'd come stay with me and Dan. We'd help you get on your feet."

"I know you'd be there for me. I just meant long-term. I don't have a job. I don't have my own money." I pop a mac-and-cheese bite into my mouth. "I give Cole a lot of credit for coming out here and starting over. I don't know if I could do something like that."

Josie's hand covers mine. "You can do anything, Callie Kingston. You hear me?"

I laugh. "Yes, best friend. I hear you."

"I'm serious." She slides her wine glass to the side of the table. "You could stay with us for as long as you needed to. We have plenty of room. You have a college degree, so you'd have no trouble finding a decent job to start out with. Plus, you'd get alimony from Paul in the divorce settlement."

My eyebrows press together. "Geez, Josie. I wasn't being serious about divorcing Paul."

Her eyes narrow as she crosses her arms over her chest. "Maybe you should be."

Realization slaps me in the face.

Shit shit shit shit.

"Cole told you."

She grimaces as she leans forward. "Callie, why wouldn't *you* tell me? Why are you hiding this?"

I roll my eyes, angry with myself for not seeing this ambush coming. "That's what this girls' night is really about."

"No. I mean, yes, but ... I'm scared for you, Cal. I just want to talk about what's going on."

"Nothing's going on. Everything's fine."

"Are you kidding?" She lowers her voice to a whisper. "Your husband is putting his hands on you. How is that *fine?*"

My stomach twists into a knot. I need to do some major damage control, and I need to do it fast.

"Look, Cole jumped to conclusions when he saw me the other day. I told him not to say anything to you because I didn't want you to worry over nothing. Paul was helping me in the garden, and I got too close, and he accidentally elbowed me in the face." I wave my hand. "The bruise was barely visible. It wasn't a big deal."

Josie grits her teeth. "Why are you lying to me?"

"You know Paul. You've known him for years. You know he wouldn't hurt me. Not on purpose."

Disbelief contorts her features. "He's obviously not the man I thought he was."

"Josie, it's not—"

"How long has this been going on?"

"It hasn't—"

"How long have you been keeping this from me?"

"I'm telling—"

"Why are you protecting him?"

"Enough!" My palm slams on the table, garnering the looks from several people nearby.

Josie sits back against her chair, a smug smirk on her face. "Good. So, you *do* have some fight left in you."

"I don't expect you to understand," I mutter.

"So help me, Cal. Help me understand."

I massage my forehead with my fingertips. "You know how I've been for these past couple of years. I became obsessed with getting pregnant, and it was all I could focus on, all I could see. I put Paul under so much stress, and now he thinks that he's only good to me if he can get me pregnant. I did that. I put this huge strain on our marriage, and now ... I just need to fix it so we can go back to normal."

Josie's eyebrows shoot up. "Are you saying you *deserve* this? That you deserve to be abused?"

"You have a perfect marriage and a perfect family. You don't know what it's like to feel like everything around you is crumbling."

"You're right. I don't understand. I don't understand how my best friend can lie to my face about the fact that her husband is mistreating her."

I shake my head. "You don't have to understand. What I need is for you to be my friend."

"I *am* being your friend. This is what friends do. They talk about shit, and they help each other. They don't sit idly by while their friend is in trouble." She reaches for my hand again. "Please, Callie. Let me help you."

"You can help me by dropping this. Forget about it. And please, don't say anything to Dan. The last thing I need is Paul catching wind of this."

The incredulous look on Josie's face kills me, like she doesn't recognize me. I want to be honest with her—God, do I want to—but things between me and Paul are finally getting better. I don't need this ruining everything. Not now.

"I don't know if I can do that," Josie says, her voice low. "I don't know if I can sit and watch you go through this, not saying a word, pretending like everything is fine."

My heart sinks.

I fight back tears as I dig into my wallet and toss a fifty-dollar bill onto the table. "Then I guess the only way you can help me is by taking me home."

~

I HAD a terrible night's sleep, so I'm still in bed when the doorbell rings the next morning.

Maverick, who was snuggled under the covers with me, shoots off the bed and barks the entire way down the stairs.

When the bell rings again, followed by knocking, I flip the comforter off my legs and peek out my bedroom window.

Brandon is standing outside, hands in his pockets.

"Shit." I tie my robe tightly around my waist as I dash down the stairs. "Coming!"

I swing open the door, and Brandon smiles wide. "Hi, Callie! I'm here for dog walking!"

On cue, Maverick leaps up to lick Brandon's face.

Totally forgot about that. I'm surprised Josie even let him over here after our fight.

But I'd never turn her kids away.

I run a hand through my disheveled hair. "Come on in, B."

He steps inside and closes the door behind him. "Geez. You look as bad as Mom does."

I raise my eyebrows. "Oh, yeah? What's wrong with her?"

"Dad says she drank too much last night." His eyes dart around before landing on mine. "But I heard them talking."

My stomach constricts. "What about?"

"They were whispering, so I didn't hear everything." He hikes a shoulder. "Mom said you guys got into a fight at dinner."

I heave a sigh and wave him into the kitchen. "Want some orange juice?"

"Sure."

I pour Brandon a tall glass and one for myself. "You shouldn't be eavesdropping on your parents, you know."

His shoulders slump. "I know."

I ruffle his hair. "But I'm glad you're here. Whatever goes on between me and your mom doesn't affect you. You're always welcome here."

He nods and takes a gulp of his juice.

"All right. Here's what you need to know about walking Maverick. He loves to sniff everything. Sometimes you have to give him a little tug because he'll stay in one area sniffing every blade of grass if you'd let him."

Brandon giggles.

"He loves meeting other dogs, but you have to be careful because other dogs aren't always friendly."

Maverick sits at Brandon's feet, blinking up at me as if he's part of our conversation.

"He also likes to run. Once you get used to walking him, you can bring your skateboard or your bike, and he can run with you."

Brandon's eyes widen. "That would be awesome!"

I glance down at my pajamas. "I'm going to run upstairs and get dressed. I'd like to come with you on your first walk to make sure everything goes okay. After that, you'll be on your own."

He pumps his fist in the air. "Thanks for letting me do this, Callie."

I squeeze his shoulders. "Of course."

After washing up in the bathroom, my hair gets twisted into a bun. I throw on a pair of running shorts and a tank, and then we're out the door.

I show Brandon how to wrap the leash around his hand. "When Maverick starts to pull you, keep his leash short so he can't get too far ahead."

"Got it." Brandon's eyes narrow, and his lips are pressed into a firm line. He's taking this job so seriously it's adorable.

We walk down the block and across the street, stopping every few feet to let Maverick sniff mailboxes and bushes.

"Do you think you and Mom will make up?" Brandon asks.

"We will," I say, even though I'm not so sure myself. "All friends get into fights every now and then."

"I didn't understand what they were talking about." He pauses, looking down at Maverick. "Uncle Cole seemed really angry."

"Cole was there too?"

He nods. "They've been doing a lot of whispering lately. I don't get it."

I smile and drape my arm over his shoulder. "My parents used to whisper a lot when I was a kid. My mom would always catch me sneaking around so I could hear what they were saying."

"Did she yell?"

I shake my head. "She'd say, 'There will be plenty of time for grown-up secrets when you're older.'"

"Guess she was right."

If only Mom could see me now.

I often wonder what advice she'd give me.

"I'm worried about Uncle Cole."

My feet stop, and I tilt my head. "Why's that?"

Brandon bends down and scratches behind Maverick's ears. "I think he's sad."

I lower myself until I'm sitting on the sidewalk beside them. "Well, he went through a divorce. Those are tough to go through."

"When Mom and Dad said he'd be coming to live with us for a while, they said that he'd lost his family. I didn't really understand what that meant." His curious brown eyes lock with mine. "How do you lose your family? Does that mean they died?"

Oh, God. My chest burns at the thought. Did Cole have children?

"I'm not sure what happened to him," I say. "I know he and your mom lost their parents pretty close together. Maybe that's what she's referring to."

I hope that's all it is.

He's quiet for a moment. "He doesn't like to be around us much."

I tip Brandon's chin. "It's not because of you. I need you to understand that. But sometimes, when you're going through a difficult thing, you don't want to be around other people."

Brandon nods. "Are you sad because you can't have kids, Callie?"

"I am."

"I'm really sorry." He wraps his arms around my neck and pulls me into a hug. "You would make a good mom."

Tears flood my vision as I tighten my grip around this sweet boy. "It's okay, B. I have you and Miles and the twins. You guys are like family."

And the thought of losing them to my fight with Josie only twists the knife in my heart deeper.

FOURTEEN

COLE

"Callie!"

She swings her car door shut and turns her head in my direction.

I jog across the street, pulling off my hard hat. "Hey. I'm glad I caught you."

She glances up at her house before looking back at me, and I can't stand how nervous she looks.

"What's up, Cole?"

"I wanted to come by your house earlier this week, but I didn't know if you'd answer the door."

"I don't think that would've been a good idea."

I heave a sigh and kick a pebble with the toe of my boot. "Look, Josie has been upset all week, and I feel like it's my fault. I didn't mean to cause a fight between you two."

Callie shakes her head. "It's not your fault. She's your sister. I don't blame you for saying something to her."

Of course she doesn't blame me. Callie Kingston never blames anyone but herself. It's infuriating. I wish I could rip those stupid sunglasses off her face and *see* her.

"Why didn't you tell her the truth, Callie? Why are you pushing your best friend away?"

"I can't do this right now." She attempts to walk around her bumper, but I step in front of her.

"She wants to help you. You shouldn't go through this alone."

Her lips form a hard line, nostrils flaring, frustration rolling off of her. "You're one to talk. You've been treating your sister like crap since you got here, and you're hiding away in that damn pool house."

"Yeah, and then someone pointed out how shitty and ungrateful I was, remember?"

"Is that what this is?" She huffs out a humorless laugh. "You're here to tell me what a bad friend I am?"

"No." I edge closer. "I'm telling you that Josie just wants to help you."

"Well, she can't."

"Because you won't let her."

"Can she help *you*, Cole? Can she help you with whatever you're going through right now?"

"That's different."

She plants her hands on her hips. "Is it? Because I don't think it is. I think it's a hell of a lot easier to dole out advice than it is to take it. Maybe you should listen to yourself."

I dip my head down, grinding my teeth together. "What I've gone through is done. There's no undoing it. My sister can't help me. No one can. But there's still hope for you. You don't have to live stuck in this pathetic excuse of a life. You can get out … before it's too late."

She lifts her chin. "I love my life. I don't want out."

"I think you do."

"You don't know anything about me to even make that statement."

I snatch her sunglasses off her face, cursing myself for making her flinch. "Go ahead. Tell me again how much you love your life."

"I do."

But her eyes betray her. They well, and I can see her pain beneath the depths of the lies she tells herself just to survive.

I shake my head. "I'm not talking about a walk-in closet or marble countertops or a luxury fucking car. I'm talking about *your life*, Callie. Those things you recite when you feel anxious? They're just for show, meaningless shit that you collect to justify your existence."

Her bottom lip trembles, and she turns her head to look away from my knowing stare.

"You might tell everyone that you're happy, that you love your life." I carefully turn her chin until she returns her gaze to mine. "But I know you're lying ... to them and to yourself."

"How do you know that?" she whispers.

"Because I was you once. I let myself live a lie because I thought it was easier to stay comfortable where I was, easier to put on a show. But it ate away at me, day after day, and it will do the same to you."

Her eyebrows pull together, her eyes searching mine for more information that I'm not willing to give.

I've already said too much.

"Why do you care about what happens to me?" she asks. "About what I do?"

I've been asking myself the same question all week.

I drop my hand from Callie's face and run it through my hair. "I think the question you need to ask yourself is: Why don't *you* care about what happens to you?"

Her mouth falls open, but she quickly clamps it shut when the door to her house swings open, drawing our attention.

Paul steps outside. "Get in the house, Callie."

She looks from him to me, worrying her lip between her teeth. "Goodbye, Cole."

I lower my voice and lean in. "Josie will still be here for you when your husband hits you again. And he *will* hit you again. You're deluding yourself if you think he'll stop."

"Callie," Paul calls. "Now."

She turns and scurries up the driveway while Paul stalks down the steps toward me.

Callie whips around. "Paul, what are you doing?"

He keeps his eyes fixed on me. "Going to have a chat with Cole. Go inside."

I smirk, crossing my arms over my chest.

Please. Give me a reason to hit you.

He stops when he's almost toe-to-toe with me. "You need to stay away from my wife."

"Didn't realize she wasn't allowed to talk to her neighbors."

"She can talk to whoever she wants." His eyes narrow. "Just not to you."

"And why is that? You feel threatened by me, Paul?"

He chokes out a laugh. "Hardly."

"Then what's the problem?"

"You're a lowlife, and I don't want Callie around a piece of shit like you."

My teeth gnash together. "Yet she's with you."

Anger flares in his eyes, and he takes a step closer.

"Paul, enough." Callie appears at his side, wrapping her slender fingers around his wrist. "Let's go inside."

We remain in a stare down. I use my height to my advantage, glaring down my nose at him, begging him to make the first move so I can lay him out here and now.

"Paul, please." Callie tugs on his arm again.

Finally, Paul relents, backing away. "Stay. Away. From my wife."

I flash him a sadistic grin before I turn and stride off his property, my grin curling into a snarl.

For the life of me, I'll never understand how kind-and-gentle Callie ended up with a prick like him.

I only hope she comes to her senses before it's too late.

∼

"LET'S BREAK FOR LUNCH. I'm starving."

I toss my hard hat onto the ground and replace it with my worn baseball cap.

Billy's face contorts in disgust. "Ah, come on. Take that shit off."

I pull the brim down with a smirk. "Not gonna happen."

"You're in Cali now. You can't be wearing that New York Yankees shit."

"I'm only here temporarily."

"You keep saying that."

Billy is about the only guy here I can stand. Most of the workers are young, arrogant muscle-heads who think they know everything about everything. I tried sticking to myself on this job, but Billy wouldn't have it. Followed me around the first week like a stray dog, going on and on about some stripper he'd fallen in love with last year. Made it impossible to ignore him. He talks a lot, but at least he keeps my mind occupied.

We head to our spot for lunch at Gertie's Diner.

I actually like this part of California, though I'll never admit it to anyone. Lake Arrowhead. It's a touristy town, and it reminds me of the crowded streets of New York. I feel comfortable here. It's about an hour and a half from Josie's house in Orange County. The drive sucks when I'm tired, but it's a job, and I need the money.

Anything is better than working for Penny's father.

Gertie, the owner, greets us when we arrive and take our seats on the retro red bar stools at the counter. "Hello, boys. I'll put in your usual. Filling up your ice waters now."

"Thanks, Gertie." Billy dabs his forehead with a napkin. "It's hot as hell today."

I wave my hand. "Nothing compared to the humidity in New York."

"Ah, yes. And the mouth-watering smell of garbage."

I chuckle. "Knock it all you want. There's a reason New York is referred to as the greatest city in the world."

"He's not wrong." Gertie places two tall glasses of water in front of us.

"See?"

Billy shakes his head. "You're both nuts. I'm hitting the head. Be right back."

Gertie pats my forearm. "Don't you mind him. Some of us need to get away so we can forget about the things that happened back where we're from. Though, I suppose it helps us remember all the things we appreciate too."

I gulp down my water and nod. Gertie might be an elderly woman, but she's got her wits about her. She's sharp—too sharp. Sometimes, she looks at me as if she can see my heartache playing like a movie across my face.

She leans in. "How are you doing today, sugar?"

"Fine. How are you, Gertie?"

She wags her long, wrinkled finger at me. "One of these days, you're going to tell me the truth. None of this *fine* bullshit."

"Not likely."

"Well, you'd better tell someone. Can't bottle it up and let it eat away at you. You're too handsome to wither away and waste the rest of your life."

I raise an eyebrow. "So, it'd be okay if I were ugly?"

She grins, showing off her sparkling-white dentures. "No, but don't you go making jokes. It breaks my damn heart watching you walk in here every day looking like a lost soul."

"I'm fine, Gertie. Don't worry about me."

She shakes her head and clicks her tongue before she returns to the kitchen.

When Billy gets back from the bathroom, he yammers on about nothing. I try to listen, but my thoughts keep pulling me toward Callie and the encounter with her husband last night.

What will it take for her to realize that she needs to get away from him? What if she doesn't *want* to get away from him? What if he hurts her—*really* hurts her? What if I can help her? What could I even do? She keeps pushing Josie away. Why would she want my help?

Mom always used to say, "When someone pushes you away, you need to find the strength to hold on tighter." Maybe Callie just needs someone to fight for her, to show her how she should be fighting for herself.

Why do I want that someone to be me?

"Earth to Cole." Billy waves his hand in front of my face. "Come back to reality."

Gertrude deposits our plates onto the counter. "Well, I'll be damned. I've seen that look before."

I lift my gyro and take a mammoth-sized bite so as to not answer any questions she throws my way.

"What look?" Billy's head whips between the two of us.

"Ask your friend." Gertrude winks at me. "Maybe you're not so lost after all, kid."

"What's she talking about?" Billy asks.

"Don't know."

He sighs before digging into his BLT sandwich. "You're in outer space today, man. More so than usual. What's going on with you?"

I take my time chewing and swallow. "The neighbor across the street from my sister is getting hit by her husband. The guy's a real piece of shit."

"Damn." Billy whistles. "I bet she doesn't want to leave him. Women always want to stay with the men who abuse them."

My head jerks back. "Really? Where did you get that information from?"

"My cousin's friend gets beat on by her boyfriend. He proposed to her last month. Guess what she said."

I shake my head. "I can't understand it. Why would anyone stay with someone who's physically hurting them? It doesn't make sense to me."

"What doesn't make sense?" Gertrude drags her stool over so she can sit and chat with us.

"Cole's neighbor is in an abusive marriage."

Gertie gives me a solemn look. "My first husband used to hit me."

I almost choke on my gyro.

Billy sputters too. "You? But you're such a badass, Gertie. How could you let a man put his hands on you?"

"Now, there's your first problem. Passing judgment when you don't know the first thing about it."

I lean forward, placing my elbows onto the counter. "Help me understand, Gertie. I want to understand."

She runs her red fingernails through her silvery teased hair. "It was a long time ago, but I don't suspect much has changed for women today. You're fed a fairytale when you're younger, and so you try everything in your power to make that fairytale come true. You don't see the signs along the way, the red flags. Or maybe you do, and you just don't realize how bad things will be until you get there. When someone hits you, someone you love, someone that claims to love you, you take responsibility for it. You blame yourself. You don't want to see the person you've grown to care about as a monster. You want to believe in the fairytale, that everything's going to work out in the end."

She huffs out a breath. "But strong or weak, it doesn't matter. Anybody can be a victim of abuse. Getting hit doesn't mean you aren't strong. It means you haven't learned your worth yet."

I stare down at my fries, contemplating for a moment.

How could a woman like Callie be so unaware of her worth?

As if she can read my mind, Gertrude tips my chin up until my eyes meet hers. "And it's not up to you to show a woman her worth. You hear me? That's a journey she needs to make alone."

I've said it from the beginning. Callie's life is none of my business. I have my own shit to focus on, and I'm no expert on relationships. Look how my own marriage turned out. My help would only make things worse for Callie.

Maybe instead of holding on tighter, I need to let go.

FIFTEEN

CALLIE

August 2ND

I had another panic attack today. The exercises Melissa gave me are no longer helping. Not since the fight with Josie. Still haven't spoken to her. It's been two weeks. This is the longest we've gone without talking. I miss her. I want to reach out to her, but I don't know what to say. She made it clear that she doesn't want to be my friend as long as I'm with Paul. Maybe once things between me and Paul get better, I'll give her a call. I wish I knew when that'll be.

Paul has been drinking every night. I take a bath and go to bed early just to avoid any confrontation while he's in that state. It seems to be working to keep his temper at bay. I can't figure out what else I can do to get us past this. It's exhausting trying to be perfect, and my stomach is in constant knots.

Maybe there's nothing I can do.

Maybe things will never get better.

What does that mean for us?

What will it mean for me?

"You've been writing in that thing a lot lately."

I jump at the sound of Paul's voice. He strides across the room, and Maverick's tail thumps against my leg.

"Melissa told me to write in it every day."

"What a good student." He leans one knee onto the white comforter and presses his lips to mine.

I laugh and shove his shoulder. "Don't patronize me."

He grins and yanks his tie over his head. It's been a while since he's come home from work in a good mood, since he hasn't gone straight to the bottle of scotch. I miss *this* Paul, the person he used to be when we first got married. Happy. Sweet. Full of life.

Is it possible for that man to come back?

I have to try.

My eyes follow his fingers as he undoes each button on his shirt, and I reach out to take over for him. Kneeling on the mattress, I push his shirt off his shoulders and pull the material down his arms until it falls to the floor. I brush my lips over his bare chest, placing kisses along his skin as I make my way to his cubed abdomen. I work the buckle on his belt and drop his pants, palming the growing bulge in his boxers.

Paul's lips are on mine in an instant. His kiss is slow and sensual, and he takes his time peeling off my clothes. Then he lifts me in his arms and carries me into the shower.

It feels like it's been so long since Paul has made love to me like this. Like this isn't a means to an end. Like he isn't just taking what he wants. We're showing each other how much we care for one another and making each other feel good. Loved. That's what sex used to be about. His gentleness spurs me on and opens me up to the possibility of getting over this rocky time.

Things can get better.

He can get better.

With our bodies pressed together under the hot spray of the water, I'm filled with hope.

Hope can be dangerous, but it's all I have left to hold on to.

After Paul exits the shower, I take my time washing my hair, basking in the sated after-sex glow. Then I towel off, letting my hair air-dry, and walk back into the bedroom.

All that hope dissipates when my gaze lands on Paul, standing over my night table with my journal in his hand.

Open.

A mixture of confusion and anger contorts his face. "*This* is what you've been writing in here?"

"Paul, that's private." My voice is a meek whisper, fear constricting my airways.

"Our marriage is *private*. Yet you're writing about me, about us. What the hell, Callie?"

I wrap my robe around my naked body, knotting the strap as if it will protect me. I venture closer to Paul, my body trembling with every step.

"It's supposed to be an exercise to help me when I feel anxious."

He flips to the page I wrote today and stabs it with his finger. "Why won't Josie speak to you, and what do I have to do with it?"

I scrub my hands over my face, unsure whether I should tell him the truth.

Maybe it's better to get it all out.

Maybe that's the only way we can move forward.

Maybe the secrets and the lies have been burying me, little by little, and the only way for me to dig myself out of this pit is by confronting this head-on.

Confronting *him*.

"Josie found out. She found out that you ..."

Come on, Callie.

"You ..."

Paul's eyebrows dip down. "That I *what?*"

Be courageous.

Courageous Callie.

I swallow around the lump in my throat and look into Paul's eyes. "She found out that you've been hitting me."

Paul tosses the journal onto the mattress and stalks toward me. My muscles lock, cringing in anticipation.

"She found out? Or you told her?"

I shake my head. "I didn't tell her!"

"Then how did she find out, Callie?"

"Because ... Cole ... he came by the house and saw the bruise on my cheek."

His face reddens as a crazed look takes over his eyes. "Cole."

I hold my breath, waiting in the terrifying silence that hangs between us.

Paul inches closer, backing me toward the wall.

"I didn't mean for her to find out, I swear. But it's over now. It's behind us. You don't have to hit me anymore. We can move past this together."

Paul's fist cocks back, and I squeeze my eyes shut, but it hurtles into the wall instead, inches from my head.

Maverick barks wildly beside us.

Paul's knuckles are bloody as he pulls his hand out of the hole he put in the Sheetrock. "You think I want to hit you, Callie? You think I enjoy this? You think I like being this way?"

Tears stream down my cheeks as I shake my head. "No! I know you don't. That's why I forgive you, why I still love you. I know we can make this work, but you have to stop hurting me." I whimper. "You can't keep hurting me, Paul."

"It's too late for that now!" he yells. His fingers wrap around my neck, gripping so hard that I can't breathe. "Everyone knows the truth! How are we supposed to move on and pretend like none of this ever happened?"

I claw at his hand, his wrist, his arm, smacking him as I sputter, unable to suck in a breath. My eyes plead with him to let me go, to let me breathe.

Why is he doing this?

Why is he hurting me?

Why am I letting him?

His grip around my neck tightens, and he lifts me until my toes dangle above the floor. Then he tosses me onto the bed.

Run!

Coughing and clutching my neck, I gulp down deep breaths as I scramble to my feet and run into the hallway.

Maverick bolts downstairs ahead of me.

"Where are you going?" Paul's voice thunders.

I stop at the top of the stairs and turn around to face him, mustering as much nerve as I possibly can. My throat is raw, my voice hoarse. It hurts to speak.

But I know I must.

My voice is all I have.

"I'm leaving, Paul. You're hurting me, and you're not thinking straight. We can talk after you've calmed down."

I don't wait for him to respond. I spin around and race down the stairs. I swipe my purse off the entryway table and twist the lock on the front door, my fingers fumbling as they quiver.

Paul reaches me as soon as I swing open the door, grasping my wrist and yanking me backwards. "You are not leaving this house!"

The wild desperation in his eyes terrifies me. I pull back, attempting to shake myself free from his grip. "Yes, I am. Please, Paul. Let me go!"

His open palm smacks against my cheek, and then he grips my jaw so hard it feels as if it'll crack under the pressure. "You are mine; do you understand me? You are not leaving this house!"

Adrenaline surges through my veins. "I won't go back in that house with you like this."

He grits his teeth and winds up to hit me again, but I jam my knee between his legs with all my might.

"Son of a bitch!" Paul hunches forward and releases my arm.

The grass crunches under my feet as I flee across the lawn.

Go!

Go!

Go!

I don't check the street before crossing, and the blare of a horn jolts my body as I freeze like a deer in the headlights. Brakes screech as the rusted bumper of a broken-down truck stops mere inches away from me.

The driver's door flings open. "Callie! Are you okay?"

I blink rapidly, my heart pulsing in my throat as Cole rushes toward me.

"I almost hit you. What are you doing?" His eyes rove over me. "Why are you in your bathrobe?"

My lips open to speak, but a gasp comes out instead. Paul's fist crashes into the side of Cole's face, blindsiding him.

My hands fly up to my mouth. "Paul, no!"

Cole staggers backward, and Paul lands another punch. He's about to strike again, but Cole lunges toward him, ramming his shoulder into his midsection and flipping him onto his back in the middle of the road.

Cole straddles Paul and hammers his fists into his face, over and over. Left, right, left, right. Blood explodes with every punch he lands, and all I can do is shriek.

"What the hell is going on out here?" Josie rushes into the street.

"Paul ... Cole ..." I can't get the words out to explain what's going on, or why it's happening.

Dan jumps in and attempts to pull Cole off of Paul, whose arms now lie limp at his sides on the ground.

"Enough!" Dan catches Cole by the crook of his elbow and stops his next punch. "Enough, brother."

Cole's chest heaves as he stands. Blood trickles down his cheek from the cut just under his eye. His knuckles are raw, and blood covers his white T-shirt.

But it's nothing compared to Paul.

I kneel beside my husband, hovering over him, cradling his mangled face in my hands. "Come on, Paul. We have to get you inside."

He moans, barely able to open his eyes.

I glance up at Dan. "Do you think he needs a hospital?"

"You should let him rot in the street." Cole gets back into his idling truck and peels out in the opposite direction.

Dan bends down and throws Paul's arm around his neck. "I'll get him into the house. Josie, take Callie inside."

I shake my head. "I want to help."

Dan's eyes meet mine. "You're the one who needs help, Callie. Go. I've got him."

Josie wraps her arm around my shoulders. "Come on."

I watch as Dan helps Paul to his feet and walks him back toward the house.

My house.

And now, it's no longer a home.

~

A SOFT KNOCK on the door draws my attention away from the window.

"Come in."

Josie sticks her head inside the guest bedroom. "Mind if I join you?"

"Of course not." I turn my head to gaze back out the window overlooking her backyard. "It's your house."

Josie sighs and lowers herself onto the corner of the mattress, the down comforter puffing up around her. "It's yours for as long as you need it to be."

"I don't deserve your hospitality."

"Hey." Josie places her hand on my shoulder. "Look at me, Cal."

I shift on the bed and set my watery eyes on my best friend. "I'm so sorry, Josie. I'm sorry I lied to you. I'm sorry I didn't call you after our fight. I just ... I'm so lost and scared. I don't know what I'm doing."

Josie wraps her arms around me and pulls me into an embrace. "You have nothing to be sorry about. Just because we had a fight doesn't mean we aren't friends."

Quiet sobs rack my body, wave after wave of emotion consuming me, and Josie holds me while it all floods out.

"I don't know how I got here. Things weren't supposed to go this way."

"I know," Josie whispers. "Life doesn't always go along with the plans we make for ourselves."

"I don't know that I'd blame life." I sniffle and edge back to look into Josie's eyes. "I made these choices. I was in the driver's seat. I did this."

Josie's head tilts. "I have to ask ... how long has this been going on?"

I look down at my hands in my lap. "In college, he'd get mad and punch a hole through the wall or throw his phone across the room." I shrug. "I chalked it up to him being a typical guy with a temper. Guess I should've seen this coming."

Josie squeezes my hand. "There's a big difference between hitting a wall and hitting a person."

I nod. "We started fighting a lot after we realized that we couldn't have a child. Sometime around the third miscarriage. There was so much tension between us, and I was depressed." I shrug. "He'd grab my arm or shove me, and that escalated into hitting. It comes out when he drinks, but tonight was the first time he put his hands on me while he was sober. I just kept hoping that he'd turn back into the person he used to be when I fell in love with him. Like somehow, I'd be able to control it. Maybe if I tried harder, if I didn't make him angry, if I did what he said ..." I offer a pathetic shrug.

"This is Paul's issue." She grips my shoulders and dips her head, leaning in. "There was *nothing* you could've done to stop it. You didn't cause this."

I run my fingers through my hair. "Are you sure you're okay with me staying here?"

"Of course. Don't be ridiculous."

"I don't want to involve your kids in this or cause any issues for you guys."

She shakes her head vehemently. "You are family, Callie. You will stay here for as long as you need to. There's no timeframe."

Tears spring into my eyes again as panic tightens in my chest. "What am I going to do, Josie? Where do I go from here?"

"You don't have to figure it all out tonight. Or tomorrow, for that matter. We'll take it day by day. Together."

I know I'm lucky to have a friend like Josie. I know many people go through this alone. Still, it feels like I *am* alone. The idea of navigating a divorce, finding a new place to live, figuring out how I'll earn an income ... it's all making my head spin.

Maverick.

California king bed.

Walk-in closet.

Dream kitchen.
Yard with a pool.
Mercedes.
But the things that once calmed me no longer belong to me.
I just lost everything.

SIXTEEN

COLE

"Cole! Oh my God! Cole!"

I flung off the covers and bolted out of bed as fast as my disoriented body would move. "Penny, what's wrong?"

Penny's agonizing cry amplified as I skidded to a stop in the nursery doorway. She was curled up in a ball on the floor beside the crib.

Dread pooled in my stomach, filling me up with every step I took. "Penny." My voice was a hoarse whisper. "What's wrong?"

My body jerks awake, and my eyes flutter open, darting around the darkened pool house.

Swallowing hard, I stretch my T-shirt up to dab the mixture of sweat and tears from my face. My head drops as I lean my elbows onto my knees, sucking in a few deep breaths until my heart rate slows.

Will these nightmares ever end?

I head to the fridge and chug a bottle of water before popping off the top of a beer. My knuckles are still throbbing from beating the piss out of Paul earlier. I open and close my fist a few times, stretching my fingers. Hand might be broken. That'll be a pain in the ass at work tomorrow.

Fucking worth it, though.

My stomach contracts, followed by a low rumble. I skipped dinner at Josie's, wanting to give Callie some space. I've been wondering how she's doing. Not sure if I should check up on her or if she'd even want to see me.

The way she looked when she ran out in front of my truck, her eyes wide with terror ... I can't get that look out of my head. No one should have to go through something like this. No one should live in fear of their spouse.

Definitely not Callie.

I swipe an ice pack from the freezer and wrap it around my hand as I head out into the backyard. Hopefully, Josie has leftovers. But when I make my way across the lawn, blond hair catches my eye.

Callie is sitting at the edge of the pool in an oversized T-shirt with her bare legs dangling into the water. Her hair falls in messy, matted waves around her shoulders. She's so damn beautiful, even with tears brimming from her puffy and red-rimmed eyes.

But it's the purple marks around her delicate, pale neck that have my insides twisting.

The bastard choked her?

She lifts those penetrating green eyes of hers as I approach. "What are you doing up?"

I arch a brow. "I could ask you the same question."

She drops her gaze to my hand. "Are you okay?"

This woman.

I huff out a laugh. "You're seriously asking *me* if I'm okay?"

She hikes a shoulder and shifts her attention to the still water. "It's easier to focus on someone else."

I lift my bruised hand. "Even easier to take it out on them."

The corner of her mouth twitches, but she bites her bottom lip to stop the smile from fully blooming.

Makes me want to try for another.

"You hungry?"

She shakes her head. "I don't really feel anything right now."

"It's like that in the beginning."

She considers me a moment. "Did you want your divorce?"

I heave a sigh and scrub my hand over my jaw. "Yes and no."

She gives me a small smile. "Do you ever actually answer a question?"

"Depends on the question."

She laughs softly, and warmth pools in my chest. "Well, why don't you have a seat, and I'll keep asking questions until you give me a straight answer?"

"Mind if I heat up some food first? Was on my way to raid Josie's fridge."

Her chin drops to her chest. "Oh, I'm sorry. Of course. Go ahead. I didn't mean to bother you."

I kneel down and tuck my finger under her chin, tilting her head until she's looking back at me. "Nothing you do could ever be a bother to me. You hear me?"

Her eyes bounce back and forth between mine, and then she nods.

I drag myself away from her and make us each a plate in Josie's kitchen before going back outside. Then, I place the dishes between us and lower myself onto the ground.

"If there's one thing I learned while being married, it's that you never believe a woman when she says she isn't hungry."

Callie smiles. "Sounds like you learned that the hard way."

I shove a forkful of potatoes into my mouth. "Yup. Lost most of my fries that night."

"Ouch." She pushes the peas around her plate. "How long were you married?"

"A little over four years."

"Why'd you get divorced?"

I take my time chewing, contemplating the best way to state my answer. "She cheated on me."

A gasp leaves her lips. "Oh, Cole. That's awful."

I nod, shoveling more food into my mouth. "Definitely came as a surprise."

"How did you find out?"

"Came home from work, and there they were."

Her hand clamps over her mouth. Then, her eyes narrow, and she lowers her hand. "What a bitch!"

The steak I'm in the midst of swallowing almost gets lodged in my throat, and I sputter as I clutch my chest. My eyes squeeze shut as I throw my head back, and a deep bellow rips out of me.

Callie covers her face with her hands. "I'm so sorry. I shouldn't have said that. I don't even know her."

That makes me laugh even harder, and I slap my palm against my thigh, unable to speak or catch my breath. I can't remember the last time I laughed, let alone a laugh this hard, but I can't help myself. Kindhearted, sweet, reserved Callie just called my ex-wife a bitch.

Finally, I wipe the corners of my eyes. "Oh, man. That was amazing."

"And super inappropriate. I should keep my opinions to myself."

"No, Callie. You most definitely should not keep your opinions to yourself." I turn my head to face her, sobering as the smile fades from my face. "Is that what you've been told?"

She shrugs and looks away. "I guess my opinions never really mattered."

"Just because they didn't matter to one person doesn't mean they don't matter to anyone else."

Silence falls between us.

I push my plate aside. "When I caught my ex cheating on me, her father wanted to keep it a secret. Cover it up. He didn't want anyone in his circle to find out because of how it would make his family look." I laugh and look up at the sky. "I told him I'd keep the divorce quiet and that I didn't want to start a war. I just wanted to be done. Done with the job I hated. Done with our life together. But he told me that he didn't want us to get divorced. That it was in the best interest of his company to keep everything under wraps and looking copacetic."

Callie's eyebrows draw together. "He expected you to stay married to the woman who was having an affair behind your back?"

I nod. "He's a rich and powerful man. All he cares about is how he's perceived in the public eye."

Recognition flashes in her eyes. "That's why you blew up at me the first day we met."

I blow out a stream of air through my lips. "Yeah, I'm sorry about that. You didn't deserve that. Not at all."

"It's okay. Now I understand why."

"Doesn't give me the right to explode on an innocent person."

She lifts her fork and takes a bite of her steak. "So, what did you say when he told you that?"

"At first, I agreed. I think I was still in shock. A lot had happened leading up to that point, and I guess I wanted to pretend that none of it was real."

"But you couldn't go on pretending forever," she says quietly.

"No, and neither can you."

She watches the ripples as she kicks her legs back and forth in the water. "I really thought I could fix everything that was broken in my life. My body, my marriage. It's normal to want to turn a blind eye to what's going on. Bury your head in the sand. Ignorance is bliss, they say."

I smirk. "Yeah, until it isn't. It's a smokescreen that leaves you feeling empty inside."

"That's exactly how I feel right now. Empty. It's a hard pill to swallow when you realize that you're not meant to have all the things life has to offer."

I lift my eyebrows. "Maybe you were just with the wrong person, and the universe didn't want you to raise a child in that kind of environment."

Callie tilts her head. "I've never thought about it like that before. You know, doctors have said that it's possible to have a baby with fibroids. I just haven't had that kind of luck."

I reach over and squeeze her hand. "Maybe your luck will start to change now that you've taken a step in the right direction for yourself."

She covers my hand with hers. "Maybe it will for you too."

Looking into those big, hopeful eyes of hers, I don't have the heart to tell Callie that things won't turn around for me.

There isn't a light at the end of my tunnel.

There's only darkness and despair.

It's what I deserve.

I slip my hand out from under hers and stack our plates. "You should get some rest."

"Wait." Her fingers wrap around my wrist. "Please don't leave yet. Can you just sit out here with me for a little longer? We don't have to talk."

I should go.

Shouldn't even be indulging in this time with her right now.

Yet my mouth can't form the word no. Not when she's looking at me the way she is.

Like she needs me.

Like my presence helps her in some way.

If I'm being honest, her presence helps me, too.

And that's a big fucking problem.

I place our dishes back down on the ground and settle into my spot beside Callie. I'll sit out here with her just a little while longer.

A little quiet time together can't hurt.

Can it?

SEVENTEEN

COLE

Three Years Ago

"Can we look yet?"

Penny laughed. "The box says to wait three minutes."

I paced the perimeter of the bathroom. "Well, this is taking forever."

"Come here." Penny lifted her hand, and I clasped it in mine, lowering myself to sit beside her on the tile floor. "What do you want the outcome of this pregnancy test to be?"

"I ..." I blew out a stream of air through my lips and looked into Penny's big, beautiful eyes. "I know we didn't plan for this to happen so soon, but I want it, Penny. I want the test to be positive."

She smiled as she took my face into her hands. "I do too."

I nuzzled my nose against hers. "Would be a pretty great wedding gift."

She giggled. "I can't wait to marry you tomorrow, Cole Luciano."

"And I can't wait to make you my wife." I pulled Penny onto my lap, and as soon as I pressed my lips to hers, the timer on her phone dinged.

I threw her off me and bolted for the pee stick.

Penny's laughter faded into the background as I gazed down at the two pink lines.

One line meant negative.

Two lines meant ...

"Positive. It's positive. Penny, you're pregnant!"

She wrapped her arms around my neck, smiling the biggest smile I'd ever seen on her, and looked up at me with watery eyes. "We're having a baby."

Tears blurred my vision. "A baby."

"A little boy who looks just like you," she whispered. "With captivating blue eyes and a heart of gold."

"Or a beautiful little girl who looks like her mama, with warm brown eyes and the most genuine soul."

"Maybe we'll get lucky and have one of each." She pulled back to look at me. "Don't twins run in your family?"

"They do, but let's not get ahead of ourselves." I lifted her up and carried her into our bedroom. "We'll start with one and work our way up to two."

Penny laughed as she bounced back onto the bed. I crawled on top of her, and she wrapped her legs around my waist.

"Have I ever told you how much I love your laugh?"

She bit her bottom lip and nodded.

"And these lips," I said as I kissed them.

I trailed kisses down her chest and stopped at her stomach. I pushed up her T-shirt and showered her stomach with affection. "I'm going to take care of you," I whispered. "I'm going to do everything I can to be the best father and husband."

Penny took my jaw in her hands and pulled me up until I was looking in her eyes. "I love you so much."

"I love you more than you'll ever know."

"We're going to be a beautiful family, Cole."

A family.

"Always."

EIGHTEEN

CALLIE

IT'S ALWAYS DISORIENTING WAKING up in someone else's bed.

Even before you open your eyes, you can tell that you're not at home. The sheets feel different against your skin. Your neck is out of whack from the pillow you aren't used to sleeping on. The whir of the air conditioner seems louder. But waking up in Josie's guest bedroom is an entirely different experience altogether. The noise level here with four kids, two of which are crying toddlers, is off the charts.

Though I'm only across the street from my house, it feels like I'm waking up in another life.

I suppose I am.

Dan's words from last night echo in my mind. *You're the one who needs help, Callie.*

It's true. I need help.

How could I expect to help Paul when I'm such a mess inside?

Questions continue to assault me as I pull the white comforter up and hug it close. What am I going to do now? Where do I go from here?

I miss Maverick's morning wet-nose kisses. Tears well at the thought of him looking for me when he wakes up. Part of me misses Paul too. I know I shouldn't miss someone who hurts me, but I can't help it. I still care about him. I've loved him for over a decade.

I wonder if I always will.

I'm not ready to face the day. To face the truth. To face Josie and her beautiful family. Reality is too real. Too raw. Too frightening.

Funny how living in a house with a man who hits me doesn't seem so scary when I'm faced with the possibility of starting over.

Without him.

Alone.

I huff out a humorless laugh as my tears drop onto the pillow.

I must be really messed up.

I wallow in bed until a knock draws my attention to the door.

Josie sticks her head into the room. "You up?"

I push myself up to sit against the headboard. "Not sure I actually slept."

She closes the door behind her. "We can be kind of loud. I was hoping we didn't wake you."

I shake my head. "You didn't. And you don't have to tiptoe around me. I'm in *your* house. You guys need to go about business as usual."

The mattress dips down as Josie lowers herself onto the edge. "You're crying."

I nod, quickly swiping the evidence away. "Thinking about Maverick. Wondering how Paul's doing. Not really sure what to do with myself today."

"Right now, all you need to worry about is what you're having for breakfast. We'll keep an eye out for when Paul leaves for work, and then you can go see Mav. We'll pack some clothes and essentials while we're there too. Dan also has the number of his lawyer friend for you."

I press the heels of my hands to my eyes. "I don't know if I'm ready for that yet."

"Well, at least you'll have it when you are." She pauses. "Callie, everything is going to be okay. I know it seems scary right now, but you're going to get through this. I'm here for you, and I'm going to help you. I won't let Paul hurt you again."

I know she won't, but the real question is, why did *I?*

"Come down and have something to eat when you're ready. We can come up with a plan. I know that's what's bouncing around in that head of yours."

I offer her a small smile. "Sure."

I wash up in the bathroom, using a spare toothbrush, and try to use my hair to cover the bruising along my neck. The last thing I want is for Brandon or Miles to notice it. They're innocent kids and shouldn't be subjected to the violence in my life.

Out of all the bruises Paul's given me, this set of purple finger marks is the most upsetting. It physically pains me to look at myself in the mirror like this. The man I love, the man I married, tried to choke the life out of me.

Why?

Before I spiral any further, I force myself out of the bathroom and down the stairs.

"Callie!" Brandon and Miles charge toward me, knocking over their chairs at the kitchen table.

"Whoa." I brace myself for impact as they crash into my midsection. "What's all this about?"

"You and Mom aren't fighting anymore," Brandon says. "And you're going to live with us!"

I laugh, squeezing them as tight as I can. "For a little while."

Miles looks up at me, his glasses crooked from our embrace. "It'll be like a really long slumber party. We can have wrestling matches and watch movies!"

"Okay, boys." Josie waves them over from the table. "Let Callie sit and eat. You two need to finish your plates, as well."

I take a seat next to Lucas's highchair and ruffle his hair. "Good morning, handsome boy."

He holds out a mushed piece of waffle, and I pretend to go after it, but he quickly shoves it into his mouth. Serenity giggles, and I shoot her a wink.

"Here. Eat up."

My eyes widen when I see the full plate Josie's pushing my way. "Are you expecting company?"

"Just shut up and eat. Breakfast makes everything better."

I shake my head. "You didn't have to do all this for me."

"You know I cook when I'm anxious."

"Mom's worried about you," Brandon says.

Miles hits his arm. "You're not supposed to talk about it, Mom said!"

Josie buries her face in her hands. "Smooth, boys. Real smooth."

I smile. "It's okay. This is your house. We can talk about whatever you want here."

Brandon's big brown eyes meet mine from across the table. "Did Paul really hurt you, Callie?"

I nod. "He did."

"I'm glad Uncle Cole beat his face in."

"Brandon!" Josie points her index finger at him. "That is *not* something you can say, and what have I told you about eavesdropping?"

His head drops. "Sorry."

I slide my hand over the table and wrap my fingers around Brandon's forearm. "Look at me, B."

He lifts his tear-filled gaze.

"I understand why you feel that way. Your mom just doesn't want you to think that hitting someone is a solution to your problems. What Uncle Cole did was wrong, just the same as what Paul did was wrong. Okay?"

A tear slides down his face as he nods. "I'm just so mad at Paul."

"We all are," Miles chimes in.

"I think Paul needs help. Sometimes, people have problems that can't be solved on their own. It's hard to understand why they do the things they do, and they don't mean to be the way they are."

"So, hopefully, Paul gets the help he needs." Josie claps her hands. "End of story. Now clear your plates and go be kids."

Brandon hugs me once more before running off with Miles.

Josie heaves a sigh. "They hear everything. There are no secrets in this house, I swear."

"It's okay. They have questions, and I'd rather them have correct information than to wonder and come to their own conclusions."

"You're right, though. Paul does need help. Do you think he'll talk to a therapist?"

I shrug. "I'm not sure. We have a lot to talk about, but I'm just not ready to face him yet. I haven't even turned my phone on."

"A little break is perfectly fine. You'll decide when you're ready. You're safe here in the meantime."

I rub small circles on my temples. "I wonder how he's feeling today. His face was so ... bloody."

"Dan made sure he was okay before he left last night. He's going to be bruised for a while." She brushes an imaginary crumb off her lap as she mutters, "Serves him right."

I smirk. "Heard that."

She shrugs.

"I can't imagine he'll go to work today with his face looking like that. We might not be able to get into the house."

She grabs her phone. "I'll talk to Dan. We'll figure it out and get you back in there."

I push my plate away, my stomach too twisted up in knots to eat. "I have therapy today. Do you mind if I use your shower and borrow some clothes?"

Josie's hand clamps over mine. "You don't have to ask. Go. Take whatever you need. This house is yours."

Mine.

What do I have left that's mine?

"I wish you would've told me sooner, but I'm glad you were able to get yourself out of there."

"I'm sorry, Melissa. I should've told you."

My therapist shakes her head and offers me a soft smile. "I didn't say that to force an apology out of you, Callie. I just hate that you went through this alone for so long. I could've helped you. That's what I'm here for."

"I know. I just ..." I shrug. "I don't know why I didn't say anything. I think I was scared of what it would mean to say it aloud."

"It's okay not to know. You're not expected to have all the answers. This is still so new. You need time to go through your range of emotions at your own pace."

"I think I'd feel better if I had a plan. I can't just sit around and do nothing."

"That's the anxiety talking. Sometimes, especially in the begin-ning, you *need* to sit around and do nothing. Be one with your thoughts. Listen to what your heart is telling you. Why don't you start by making a list? Organize your thoughts."

I nod slowly. "I could write it in my journal."

"Absolutely. Write everything and anything you're thinking and feeling. It helps to sort through the noise in your head."

Melissa stands and pulls a flyer out of a drawer in her desk. "You should also consider going to one of these support group meetings. You don't have to talk if you don't want to, but it helps to listen to other people who understand what you're going through."

I take the flyer from her and stare down at it.

Women's Support Group.

Tears flood my vision for the hundredth time today. "Thank you," is all I can muster.

"The first step is the hardest, and you've done it. This is huge, Callie. Take this time to reflect on who you are and who you want to become. Think about what path you want to take moving forward. It's up to you. You have the power to change your story."

"Paul's always had the power."

"Because you let him have it."

I huff out a humorless laugh. "Pathetic, huh?"

"You were in survival mode. Relinquishing the power to him was what kept you safe all these years. But now, you broke that pattern. You left, and you took the power with you."

"I don't feel powerful at all."

"Just because you don't feel it doesn't mean it isn't there. It's a gradual process."

Gradual.

Slow.

All the things I don't want right now. I wish I could press a giant fast-forward button on my life and get to the part where I'm past all this.

"The most difficult part of this whole thing," Melissa continues, "is coming to terms with the fact that you allowed someone to hurt you. You'll question yourself, if you haven't begun doing that already, which is natural. But I want you to remember what we talked about when you first started your sessions with me. Your father had narcissistic tendencies, which turned you into a people-pleaser. Being the child of a narcissist, you were blamed for things that you didn't do, things that you had no control over. This, in turn, created a need to *fix* within you. Hear me when I say *you cannot fix anyone but yourself.* You can change, and grow, and become a stronger person who doesn't feel the need to fix everyone around them. Right now, you need to focus on fixing yourself."

Though I leave Melissa's session feeling mentally and physically drained, I also leave feeling more focused than when I started.

Maybe I can do this after all.

I just need to fix myself.

If only I knew where to start.

Josie's waiting for me in the parking lot as promised. My clothes, my car keys, and everything I own are in my house, and Paul hasn't left all day. I hate relying on Josie to drive me around, but there's no room for pride right now. She's my best friend, and I need her.

"Dan is with Paul right now," she says when I buckle myself into the passenger seat. "You and I will go in there together to get your stuff. You can talk to him if you feel ready to, but I'll be by your side. I won't leave you alone with him."

I nod as the knots in my stomach pull tighter.

Will Paul be angry? Will he beg for me to come back home? Will he feed me more empty promises?

More importantly, will I crumble under the guilt of his heartache?

Stay strong, Callie.

You've come this far.

Be brave.

Callie the Courageous.

Cole's wrestling nickname for me has become an anchor of strength. I know it's silly. It probably meant nothing more than clever alliteration to him. But it meant something to *me*. The way he looked into my eyes when he said it that night made me feel seen. His gaze pierces through my armor of lies—always has, since the day we met—and he hears the words I leave unspoken.

How? How can someone I barely know make me feel so understood?

I still don't know Cole's whole story, the burden he carries around like a heavy cross on his back. But I want to. And maybe therein lies my problem. I want to bear the weight of everyone's problems except my own.

As we roll to a stop in front of my house, I decide it's time to focus on my problems, once and for all. Face my demons.

Face *him*.

Josie lets me lead and follows me up the walkway. I'm unsure if I should knock or walk in. I hesitate, and then Dan swings open the door to spare me.

"Hi, Callie. He's in the living room."

"Thanks, Dan."

At the sound of my voice, Maverick comes galloping into the foyer. His legs slide out from under him as he struggles for traction on the tile. I bend down to meet him, and he leaps into my arms, frantic as he licks my face.

I bury my face in his fur. "I know, bud. I've missed you too. It's okay. I know."

"He's been beside himself since you left."

My head snaps up at the sound of Paul's voice, and I gasp when I catch sight of his face. Both eyes are swollen, the left completely shut, and deep-purple bruises line his cheeks and jaw.

"Jesus," Josie whispers behind me.

I push to my feet and take a few tentative steps.

Paul rushes toward me, arms outstretched, and a sob escapes

him. I remain where I stand and let him wrap his arms around me, engulfing me in his embrace.

"We've both been a mess here without you. I'm so sorry, Callie. I'm sorry. Please believe me."

He crushes me against his body, tighter with each passing second. I pat his back gently to console him, absorbing his raw emotion pouring out and making it my own. Tears threaten to spill over my lids, but I blink up to the ceiling to keep them at bay.

He finally releases me and edges back, only a little. "You seem happier to see Maverick than you do me."

"Can you blame her?" Josie interjects before I can say a word. "Maverick didn't strangle her the other night. *You* did."

"Josie, please." I reach out and squeeze her hand. "I've got this."

She shakes her head at him, her top lip curled into a snarl. "We let you around our children. We let you into our home. And *this* is what you're really like? This is what you've been doing to Callie all this time?"

Paul runs his fingers through his disheveled hair, pulling at the ends of it. "I'm sorry, Josie. I'm sorry about everything."

"Yeah, well, so am I. I'm sorry Callie ever fucking met you."

Dan wraps his arm around her waist. "Come on. That's enough. Cal, we'll be in the kitchen if you need us."

Josie whips her head over her shoulder. "So don't try anything, asshole. You think my brother beat you badly? I'll rip your dick off so fast you won't even know what hit you!"

I cringe, covering my face with my hands as Dan ushers her into the next room.

Paul blows out a breath through his lips. "Do you want to sit so we can talk?"

I nod and follow him toward the couch. "I don't know where to begin," I admit, taking a seat on the cushion beside him.

"Then let me." He takes my hands into his and stares down at them. "I'm so sorry, Callie. I know you've heard it before, and you probably don't believe me, but I truly am sorry for hurting you."

"I know you are."

His eyebrows shoot up. "You do?"

"I know you regret putting your hands on me. I know this isn't something you take pleasure in. But apologizing doesn't do anything to fix the problem, Paul. An apology becomes a lie if you keep doing the thing you're sorry for."

He nods. "I get it. Just tell me what I can do to fix this. I want to fix it, Callie. I don't want to lose you."

"I don't know how to fix the kind of problem you have. I think you need to go to therapy, or anger management."

"Done. I'll do it. I'll go tomorrow."

I chew my bottom lip.

"Is that enough?" he asks. "If I get help, will that make you come back home?"

"I ... I don't know."

His head jerks back. "What are you saying?"

"I don't know." I pinch the bridge of my nose between my thumb and my index finger. "I don't have a solution. I don't have an answer for you. All I do know is that you need help, and so do I."

His hand clamps over my knee. "We can go together. We can work through this. I know we can."

"I think we need to go separately before we can go together."

"Fine. I'll go alone. Whatever you want me to do, it's done."

That doesn't sit right with me. "Paul, do you realize what you just said?"

His head tilts. "What?"

"You said you'll do whatever *I* want you to do. But this isn't about what I want. This is about what you need. What you should want for yourself. I don't want you to go to therapy because you think that's what will get me to forgive you. I want you to go to therapy because *you* want to."

"You know what I mean, Callie. Of course I want to go and get help."

"Why now? Why not last month, or the month before that, or last year? Why do you suddenly have the urge to go to therapy?"

"Because you left. Because I realize now that I'm going to lose you if I don't stop and change."

My heart sinks. "And if I had never left? Then you'd be perfectly fine hurting me and going around and around this sick merry-go-round we're on?"

Paul shakes his head emphatically. "You're twisting my words. I never said that."

Irritation surges in my stomach. It rises up through my chest and into my throat. The words I've kept on a low simmer inside me for so long are now searing my tongue, and they bubble out of me like hot acid.

I pull my hair over one shoulder, exposing my neck. "Look what you did to me, Paul. Look at this! Again and again, you've gotten so out of control that you put your hands on me. Any time I've spoken up, any time I've tried to tell you how I feel, any time I've told you what I want, you snuff me out like a candle, as if I don't matter. As if my words don't mean anything to you. You've made me feel worthless and insignificant! You get to do and say whatever you want, but I have to sit in silence. I have to obey. I have to follow your rules. Why is that? Why don't you want to hear what I have to say? Are you so insecure that you can't stand the thought of me doing something for myself?"

"No, Callie. That's not true."

"Isn't it?" Rage and resentment fuel the fire that's ignited within me. "You want me to be yours, Paul. To *belong* to you. But I'm not a possession. I'm a person. I wanted to be part of an *us*, a partnership where I could still be me. Somehow, I ended up losing myself along the way."

Paul's index finger jabs the air between us. "You lost yourself once you became obsessed with having kids. That's all you cared about! You forgot about me, about our marriage. You only wanted to have sex when your stupid fertility app told you to. Do you forget how depressed you were? Do you not remember lying in bed, day after day, because you refused to come to terms with the fact that having a baby isn't going to happen? And who took care of you during that time? Who picked you up off the bathroom floor and held you while you cried? Who went to endless doctor's appointments and treatments? Who took care of you after you insisted that surgery was going to cure you? Me, Callie. It was me! So don't act like I've been this horrible monster, because we both know that isn't true."

Guilt spills over the flame, cooling me down for a moment. "You're right. You did take care of me. And I take responsibility for the part that I played in ruining our marriage. I know what I put you through, and I blame myself every single day. I wouldn't have been able to get through that time without you by my side."

Paul's expression softens as he cups my face. "It kills me that I wasn't able to give you the family you've always dreamed of."

A tear slides down my cheek. "I know it does. It kills me I wasn't able to give you children."

"But we have each other." He pulls me closer and presses his lips to my forehead. "We still have each other."

"I don't know what we have anymore, Paul. I don't even feel like I have myself at this point. I don't know who I am, or what I'm doing with my life. I want to work. I want to go out and experience life." I pause before pushing out the rest of my words. "And I want to adopt a baby."

"We can do all of that. You can work, and we can fill out an adoption application tomorrow."

I pull back, and Paul's hands drop into his lap. "Just like that? All of a sudden you're singing a different tune?"

He heaves a sigh. "I know I didn't want those things before, but I want to be with you more than anything else. You're all that matters to me. So, whatever you want, I want you to have it. Don't you see? I'm willing to make this work."

More tears stream down my cheeks, frustration nearly choking me. "Why couldn't you have wanted to make it work before? Why couldn't you have been this open, this compassionate, this under-standing? I've tried to have this conversation with you on multiple occasions, but you shut me down every time! You made me feel like I was wrong for wanting to explore other options. Why, Paul? Why?"

He pulls me against him, and I bury my face in his chest, weeping.

How can it be that the man comforting me is the same man who raised his hands to hurt me?

How am I finding solace in the same arms that broke me down?

Why do I miss the person I fled from?

I feel sick. I don't know what to do. It's like someone threw my head and my heart into a blender, and everything got all jumbled.

I know what I want for myself, but I don't know whether I can achieve that if I stay with Paul. Is he capable of change, really and truly? Have abusive men become calm, loving husbands?

Paul has beaten me down mentally and physically for so long that I can't even trust my own thoughts. Are they mine? Are they his? Or are fear and guilt warping my reality?

I lean away from him, wiping my eyes with the backs of my hands. "I need some time to think, Paul."

His eyebrows dip down. "Think about what?"

"About what I'm going to do."

"You need to think about whether or not you want to be with me?" He scoffs, shaking his head. "How can you say you love me but not know if you want to be with me?"

I rise from the couch and look down at him. "The same way you can tell me you love me and hit me."

NINETEEN

COLE

I HAVEN'T SEEN Callie since we sat by the pool last week.

Yet the saying *out of sight, out of mind* hasn't proven to be true.

I half-expected her to return to Paul, to crawl back into the comfort of her familiar patterns, but she hasn't.

Josie filled me in on what happened when Callie packed some of her belongings from her home. All the things she said to Paul, how she didn't give in and let him weasel his way back into her life with empty promises and flat-out lies.

Courageous Callie.

My heart soars with pride. I'm not even going to attempt to analyze why.

So, when a flash of blond goes past the large window at Gertie's, my head snaps around, and my heart skips a beat. My feet carry me outside before my brain even realizes what I'm doing.

"Callie!"

She spins around, and a smile blooms on her face when she spots me. "Hey, Cole. What are you doing here?"

I nod my head in the direction of the diner. "Grabbing lunch. What about you? This is far from home."

She points toward a building behind me. "Just came from a job interview."

My eyebrows shoot up. "Really? How did it go?"

She shrugs. "Everyone keeps telling me I don't have experience for the jobs I'm applying for. Don't know how to gain experience if nobody hires me."

"Ah. That's the worst part of job hunting. I'm sorry."

She waves her hand. "It's fine."

I know her eyes underneath those sunglasses would tell me otherwise.

"Are you busy now?" I ask. "Feel like joining me for lunch?"

She adjusts the strap of her purse on her shoulder. "You wouldn't mind?"

"Not at all. Come on."

Billy's brown eyes almost pop out of his head when Callie takes the red stool beside me.

"Callie, this is Billy. We work together at the construction site."

She leans over and clasps her hand in his outstretched one. "It's nice to meet you, Billy."

"Likewise."

His eyes rove over her as she shakes off her blazer, revealing a silky royal-blue tank. Can't blame him for staring, because her creamy skin captures my attention as well. It's the most skin I've seen her expose.

I suppose this is how she normally dresses when she doesn't have any bruises to hide.

"What's good here?" She pushes her sunglasses up onto her head while she flips through the menu.

"Everything, sugar." Gertie smiles wide as she presses her hands onto the counter. "Then again, I'm biased. I own the joint."

"Then I'll let you surprise me." Callie flips her menu closed. "I'm not picky."

Gertie looks between the two of us before her gaze settles back on Callie. "I'm Gertrude, though everyone here calls me Gertie."

"It's a pleasure to meet you, Gertie. I'm Callie. I'm a friend of Cole's."

"Friend?" Billy blurts out. "Cole's got friends?"

I flip him off.

Callie laughs. "I'm the only one, I think."

"Can't imagine why." Billy claps me on the back. "He's so charming and friendly. Always has a smile on his face."

"All right, all right." I point at Callie. "You're not invited to lunch anymore."

She grins and nudges me with her shoulder. It makes me happy to see her like this. Different. Lighter.

"You're all dressed up," Gertie says. "Do you work around here?"

Callie shakes her head. "Just came from a job interview. I've been striking out all week."

"Where did you apply? I know everyone on this street. I can put in a good word for you."

"Oh, that's sweet of you. I had an interview at Tommy's Coal Fired Pizza."

"As a waitress?" Billy asks.

"As a part-time chef."

Gertie's eyebrows lift. "You cook?"

"Well, my grandfather owned a small restaurant when I was a teenager. I used to help him cook and create different recipes. I loved it. I wanted to take over the business after he passed, but my father insisted I go to college and get a degree instead."

"You're hired."

All three of our heads snap to Gertie.

"I'm sorry?" Callie asks.

"You need a job, and I'm looking for some help in the kitchen. You'll be the perfect fit."

Callie's eyebrows dip down. "Are you serious? You're really willing to hire me on the spot like this?"

Gertie narrows her eyes at me. "Do you vouch for your friend? Will she be a reliable worker?"

I look into Callie's eyes, wide and round as saucers. "You won't find anyone better."

Gertie claps. "Then it's settled. You can start tomorrow." She takes Callie's menu and saunters into the kitchen.

Callie's mouth is left open. "I can't believe that just happened."

"Everything happens for a reason." Billy winks. "It's a good thing Cole spotted you walking by."

Callie's hand touches my forearm. "Thank you so much. I owe you one."

I shake my head. "You don't owe me anything. I'm happy to help."

She slumps forward onto the counter, resting her head in her hand. "I'm so happy I don't have to go on any more interviews. I've only been on four, but that was torture."

"Gertie will take you under her wing," Billy says. "She's great. You'll love working for her."

Billy continues to talk through most of lunch, as usual. Callie laughs at all his lame jokes, and her smile has the corners of my mouth tipping up too. It's a nice reprieve from the mundane workday.

After we say goodbye to Callie and pay the bill, Gertie stops me before I reach the door.

"That was her, wasn't it? The woman you told me about?"

I nod. "She left her husband. Moved in with my sister for a while. It's been tough on her. I really appreciate you giving her a job."

Gertie pats my shoulder. "Don't you worry about it. I'll take good care of her."

"I know you will, Gertie."

"She's beautiful, too."

I hike a nonchalant shoulder. "Sure."

"I see the way you look at her." She clicks her tongue. "And though it might be a little too soon for her, she looks at you the same way. She just doesn't know it yet. So, you be patient. Don't rush it. Give her space."

I hold my hands up on either side of my head. "There's nothing to rush. Trust me."

"Boy, how can I trust you when you don't even trust your own damn self?"

I shake my head. "See you tomorrow, Gertie."

"Uh-huh. That's what I thought."

Crazy old lady.

WORK ENDS EARLIER than it usually does.

I don't mind working long hours, but today is especially hot, so I'm thankful to be done. I'd give anything to have a truck with working AC right about now.

I'm disgustingly sweaty when I pull up to Josie's house. Sounds of the kids playing in the backyard echo as I walk up the path to the gate, but I don't see Josie or Dan's SUVs in the driveway.

Laughter and splashing amplifies when I enter the yard and lock the gate behind me. I spot the top of Brandon's head as he swims across the deep end, legs kicking water everywhere behind him.

These kids shouldn't be in the pool while no one's home to supervise. Something could happen to them. Anger spikes my heart rate. With my eyebrows dipped down and my scowl in place, I open my mouth to scold him.

But I freeze mid-step when my eyes land on Callie. She and Miles are sitting on the steps in the shallow end, watching the twins slap at the surface of the water.

Golden waves hang loose around Callie's shoulders, wet at the ends that stick to her skin. A pale-blue bikini top ties around her neck, accentuating her full chest. My eyes trail down her toned stomach to the matching blue bottoms that tie on either side of her hips. Her shapely legs have a sun-kissed sheen to them, and I drink them in until they disappear under the water. She looks like a goddamn fantasy.

My throat goes dry, and desire fists deep in the pit of my stomach.

"Uncle Cole's home!" Brandon shouts.

Callie's head shoots up, and Miles waves excitedly.

"Unkey Cole! Unkey Cole!" Lucas chants.

I unclench my jaw and blow out an exhale. "Hi, guys."

"Come in with us," says Miles.

Brandon holds up a beach ball. "We can play volleyball."

I shake my head. "It's been a long day, and I need to shower."

"Please, Uncle Cole. Come in for a little while and play with us." Miles interlocks his fingers and pleads with me.

Callie swims over to the edge of the pool where I'm standing, craning her neck and squinting up at me. "Do you have your phone on you?"

"Yeah, why?"

"Do you mind if I shoot a text to Josie? I left my phone inside."

"Sure." I crouch down and hand her my cell.

As she takes my phone, Callie's other hand shoots out and grabs my wrist. She yanks on my arm, and I lose my balance. I fall forward, face-first into the cool water.

When my head pops up, the boys are laughing and cheering. I sputter and spit, pushing my hair out of my eyes.

And Callie Kingston is wearing a shit-eating grin on her face like the little she-devil she is.

I arch a brow. "You needed to text Josie, huh?"

She tosses my phone onto the grass and shrugs. "Didn't want to ruin your phone in the water. You're welcome."

I advance toward her, one step at a time. "How thoughtful of you."

She backs away as I edge closer. "I'm a pretty thoughtful person."

"Is that right?"

"Yep."

She's got those stupid sunglasses on her face, and I want to snap them in half. Want to see her eyes go wide when I lunge at her.

She squeals as I dive forward and hoist her up.

"Cole, don't you dare throw me. Cole ..."

I jump and release her into the air. She flails and smacks the water, going under beside Brandon near the deep end.

The boys now cheer for me, and Callie points at them when she reemerges. "You're supposed to be on my side!"

"Sorry, Callie," Brandon says. "But that was hilarious."

She catches her sunglasses before they float away and sets them on the ground outside the pool. She glares at me, but I know there's no malice there. The smile on her face gives her away.

"Throw me!" Miles shouts. "Me next!"

Callie and I spend the rest of the afternoon taking turns tossing the boys and playing volleyball while the twins circle us in their floats.

When Serenity starts to get fussy, Callie takes her out of her float and hugs her to her chest. "They're probably getting hungry. I'll go get dinner started so Josie doesn't have to worry about it when she gets back."

"Where is she?"

"She's shopping for Miles' birthday party. She was going to take the twins and leave the boys here alone, but I told her I'd watch them."

"Why don't I barbecue for us?"

Callie's eyebrows shoot up. "You'd do that?"

I shrug. "It'll be quick and easy. You go get the twins situated, and I'll see what meat Dan has in the fridge."

She nods. "Come on, boys. Let's dry off."

At the door of the pool house, I peel off my wet jeans and wring out my T-shirt, laying them on the grass to dry. I step inside, and when I turn around to close the door, my eyes lock with Callie's from across the yard. She whips her head around as soon as I catch her staring and busies herself with drying off the twins.

Why does that excite me?

Why does being around that woman make me feel like I'm a kid again? As if I don't have a care in the world. As if my wretched past never happened. As if we actually stand a chance. A chance at what, I have no fucking clue. But Callie makes me feel something I shouldn't.

Hope.

It's fucking absurd.

There's no hope for me.

I'm ruined. Broken.

I don't have any business imagining what it'd be like to hold that woman in my arms and kiss her pain away.

I don't deserve to forget what I did.

And being with Callie makes me want to forget.

Hatred and grief coil my muscles, and just like that, I'm bitter and wound-up tight again.

I change out of my wet boxer-briefs and throw on basketball shorts and a T-shirt. When I exit the pool house, Josie is back, showing Callie and the boys what she bought from the store.

Josie smiles. "Heard you got wet, little brother."

I smirk. "Not by choice."

"Well, the boys sound like they had a blast. Callie, too. She told me that you got her a job at the diner."

I slip my hands into my pockets. "I did."

Josie's expression softens, and she throws her arms around my neck. "Thank you for helping her. She really needed this."

I pat her on the back. "I know she did."

Josie steps back and gazes at Callie, who's listening to Miles talk about his birthday party with a genuine smile on her face.

"I think she's going to be okay, Cole," Josie whispers.

"She will be."

Her eyes flick up to mine. "And you?"

"I'm fine."

"You have a huge heart. I know it's broken, but it's not gone. I see the way you are with the kids, the way you treat Callie. You're a good man, Cole. You deserve to be happy again. And you can be, if you just let yourself."

I shake my head and start walking toward her sliding glass door. "I'm going to make dinner."

"This doesn't have to be a life-sentence, you know," she calls after me. "People have gone through this, and they've moved on and started over."

She's baiting me, and I know it. Yet I can't stop myself from firing back at her.

I whip around and stab my finger in the air. "You don't know what you're fucking talking about, so why don't you stop telling me what to do as if you have a clue what I'm going through?"

Callie and the kids stop talking, looking up at me with wide eyes and open mouths.

But Josie crosses her arms over her chest, clearly not ready to back down. "I don't have to know what you're going through to know that you're throwing the rest of your life away. You spend all your time alone, drinking yourself into oblivion in that damn pool house." She takes a few steps toward me. "You're punishing yourself for a crime you didn't commit. It wasn't your fault, Cole. How many times do I need to tell you for it to sink in?"

"You saying it doesn't make it so!" My nostrils flare as my anger boils over. "You weren't there! You didn't see the way she looked." I choke on my words as the image sears my brain. "I have to live with what I did for the rest of my life. I see it every time I close my eyes. It's fucking torture. And you will never understand. Not with your perfect life. You don't get to talk to me about this."

"Then talk to someone who can help you." Josie gestures to Callie. "Callie's been through the wringer, but you don't see her sulking around and snapping at the people who care about her. She's going to therapy."

Callie stands, lifting her hands in front of her. "Please don't bring me into this. Everyone's different."

"Yeah," Josie says with a bitter laugh. "Some people want to get help, and others are just too fucking stubborn."

"Fuck you, Josie." I turn around and storm back to the pool house.

"Cole, wait." Callie's feet crunch on the grass behind me as she runs after me.

But I don't wait.

There's nothing she can say that will make this better.

That will make *me* better.

I slam the door shut just as Callie reaches it.

I need to keep her out.

Away from me.

TWENTY

CALLIE

"There's something you should know about me before I sign these papers."

Gertie lifts one penciled-in brow and looks at me from over the rim of her glasses. "That's never a sentence an employer wants to hear from her newly hired employee."

I laugh. "Well, I haven't escaped from the mental ward or anything like that. But I have anxiety. Sometimes, I'll have a panic attack out of nowhere, and I can't stop it."

Her head tilts. "What is it you need from me when that happens?"

I shrug, averting my eyes to my white apron. "No one's ever asked me that before."

"Oh, dear." Gertie's hand comes up to cup my face, and it trembles slightly. "I'd be honored to help you. Just tell me what I can do when you feel it coming on, okay?"

I nod, swallowing the emotion in my throat. "Thank you."

"Well, I suppose I should share a secret with you now." Gertie heaves a sigh, planting her hands on her hips. "I know you might be a bit surprised to hear this, but I'm getting old, Callie."

I bite my bottom lip to stifle a laugh. "You don't look a day over thirty."

She pats her silver bouffant and smiles. "Flattery gets you everywhere."

"So, what does your age have to do with anything?"

"My hands don't work like they used to." She holds them out in front of her, demonstrating how shaky they are. "I'm looking to take less of a hands-on role here. That's why I'm so glad you came along. It's like fate brought us together."

My eyebrows lift. "That must be a very hard decision for you to make."

She nods. "It's killing me to think about not being in front of that stove every day, but it's also killing me physically."

"Well, good for you for taking care of yourself."

"I have to, dear. Lesson number one: Take care of yourself. Nobody else will do it better than you can."

I hum as I let her wise words sink in. "That's a lesson I'm working on."

"Glad to hear it, sugar. It's never too late to learn how to love yourself. Now, sign those papers, and let's get cooking!"

The morning flies by. When lunchtime rolls around, I smell like fried oil, and the balls of my feet throb. But I wouldn't trade this for anything in the world.

I love it here.

After the lunch rush dies down, Gertie saunters over to me and bumps my hip with hers. "Your friends are here. Why don't you take your lunch break and eat with them?"

"My friends?"

"Billy and Cole."

My stomach clenches at the sound of Cole's name. "Oh, are you sure that's okay?"

She smacks me with a hand towel. "Of course, child. You need to eat. Can't have you passing out on the first day. I'll whip you up what the boys are having."

I grin and remove my apron and hairnet. "Thanks, Gertie."

I don't know why I'm nervous to see Cole. If anything, he's the one who should be nervous to see me after the way he acted yesterday. But I feel bad for him. Josie didn't need to jump on him like that, especially not in front of me and the kids.

"You weren't there! You didn't see the way she looked."

I was up half the night wondering what he was talking about. It makes me sick to think about what he went through.

Billy's face lights up when he spots me exiting the kitchen. "Hello, Miss Callie. How's the first day going?"

Cole's eyes meet mine, and I offer him a smile. "It's going great. I love it already."

"Knew you would." Billy chugs half of his iced water. "Lucky us, we get to see you every day now."

My cheeks flush as I walk around the counter and take the seat on the stool beside Cole. "Do you mind if I sit with you guys? I'm on break."

"Of course we don't mind." Billy smacks Cole's arm with the back of his hand. "Isn't that right?"

He nods once. "I'm glad to hear your day is going well."

I lean in so Billy can't hear me. "Cole, I'm really sorry about yesterday. Josie was out of line, and—"

"Don't. It's fine."

I chew the inside of my cheek. "Your sister cares about you. She has a huge heart, and she hates to see anybody suffering." I shrug. "She just wants to help."

"Well, she should help the people who want her help."

I nod. Then I nudge him with my shoulder and attempt to be playful. "At least you've got the pool house to escape to. I'm stuck with her in the house."

I expect Cole to chuckle or at least flash me a smirk. Instead, his eyebrows collapse as he puts those stunning steel eyes on me. "Do you want to take the pool house? I could switch with you if you'd prefer it."

My mouth falls open, and I can't seem to form a response.

Is he seriously willing to give up his isolation in the pool house for *me*?

"God, no. Cole, I was just kidding. I would never ask you to switch with me."

He hikes a shoulder. "I know you wouldn't. That's why I'm offering. You went from that big mansion to a room inside my sister's mansion. It's gotta be an adjustment."

I shake my head. "No. Absolutely not. That pool house is yours. I'm fine in the guest room."

"All right," Billy says, leaning over. "Anybody want to tell me what we're whispering about?"

"No," Cole says before I can answer.

Billy wags his finger. "Secrets, secrets are no fun."

"You finish that sentence, and I'm going to punch you."

Billy chuckles. "How do you deal with this guy?"

I grin. "He's not so tough underneath his scary exterior. I'd even dare to say that he's sweet."

Cole shakes his head and pulls the brim of his hat lower, but I swear I see a smile trying to peek through.

"Pffft. Sweet? I can't even picture it."

"Did Cole ever tell you how we met?"

Billy shakes his head. "He mentioned that you live across the street from his sister."

I'm about to tell Billy the story, but Cole suddenly springs to his feet.

I swivel on my stool to see what's going on, and my stomach drops when I see Paul standing inside the diner.

"Paul, what are you doing here?"

He walks toward me, slowly, with his hands out in front of him like he's approaching a scared animal. "I'm not here to cause trouble."

Then his eyes land on Cole, and his entire demeanor changes. "What's he doing here?" he growls.

Cole steps forward. "I should be asking you the same question."

I stand between the two of them, looking up at Cole. "Please, don't cause any problems for me on my first day."

His eyes widen. "He's the one causing problems. He shouldn't be here."

"Let me talk to him. Please, just stay calm."

Cole's jaw flexes as his eyes shoot daggers at Paul.

I look at my husband and jerk my head in the direction of the kitchen. "Come with me."

I lead him down the hall, and Gertie's eyes narrow when she sees Paul follow me in and close the door.

"Gertie, this is my husband, Paul. He came to talk. Do you mind if we talk back here while you're cooking?"

"Sure, doll."

Paul's eyes bounce between me and Gertie, and he shifts his weight from one leg to the other. "Can't we go somewhere a little more private?"

I fold my arms over my chest. "You're at my place of work, and I don't have a lot of time. What's wrong? Why are you here?"

His shoulders slump. "You won't answer any of my calls or texts. I just wanted to see you."

My eyebrows hit my hairline. "That's why you're here?"

He takes a step forward, reaching out for me. "I miss you. I want you to come back home."

His eyes are glassy and bloodshot. He looks ...

"Are you drunk?"

He scrubs a hand over his jaw. "It's been so hard without you, Callie."

"I told you I needed some time, Paul. It's only been a week."

"How long do you need to figure out if you want to be with me anymore? We're married, for God's sake. We should be *together*."

"We should be. But you made it clear that you can't control your temper around me."

Paul's eyes slice to Gertie, whose back is facing us while she flips a couple of hamburgers on the grill.

Always worried about what everyone else thinks.

"Have you found a therapist?"

He shakes his head. "Not yet. But it's at the top of my list of things to do."

At that, Gertie glances over her shoulder, and I have to bite my lower lip to keep from smirking at her pissed-off expression.

"Look, Paul. I asked you for time to think, and you haven't even taken a step toward getting help. We're nowhere near ready to be together again."

His eyebrows press together. "But you have plenty of time to get a job and hang out with Cole."

I scrub a hand over my face. "I've told you how important it is for me to get a job. Cole was kind enough to get me this job, so he's allowed to be here."

"Yeah, I'll bet he's kind."

"What are you insinuating?"

He rolls his eyes. "Nothing."

My patience snaps. "I'm sorry you're upset, but I've been upset for a very long time. I will contact you when I'm ready to talk. In the meantime, you should get started on that to-do list of yours."

Paul's fists curl at his sides, his cheeks tinged with red.

Gertie spins around. "You heard the woman. Go. Get your shit together." She swats her spatula through the air several times until Paul turns around and storms out of the kitchen.

A relieved breath whooshes out of me, and my knees feel weak. "I can't believe I just spoke to him that way. I don't know where that came from."

Gertie pulls me into an embrace, squeezing me until I can't breathe. "I'm so proud of you, sugar."

I shake my head and touch my palm to my cheek. "I don't know what I'm going to do, Gertie."

She slides her hands up and down my arms. "You don't have to figure it all out now. This is still new. Let him stew in his sadness. It'll be good for him. It humbles a man when he doesn't get everything he wants."

"It's like I can't think straight when he's around. When he's gone, I can hear my own thoughts and feel my own emotions. But when I'm with him, all I can think about is how he's feeling. I don't know how to be myself with him because I'm afraid it'll upset him."

Gertie points her finger in my face. "Now, you listen to me, and you listen good. I'm not going to tell you what to do, but I am going to tell you this. The right person won't ask you to sacrifice who you are for his love. Losing yourself in a relationship is never an option. You're the most important thing you've got. You can love someone with your whole heart and still stay true to yourself. If he doesn't like that, then he's not the one for you. Do you understand?"

I swipe away my tears as they force themselves to the surface. "What do you do if you've already lost yourself?"

"You find your way back." Gertie turns me by my shoulders, facing me toward Cole, who's leaning against the doorframe with his hands in his pockets.

Something about the way he's looking at me with concern etched onto his features makes my chest ache.

"Just came to see if you're okay."

I nod with a sniffle. "I'm good."

"Good."

We stand there, staring at each other, until Gertie clears her throat. "Who's ready for lunch?"

THE REST of the week goes by as quickly as my first day at the diner.

Gertie even let me add some of my own dishes to the specials list. Customers raved about them, and she said I can pick one to add to the actual menu. It means the world to me that she's allowing me to take such a prominent role in her business.

At the end of the day on Friday, I head over to the Women's Support Group that Melissa told me about.

As I sit outside, staring out the window at the run-down high school building, I feel nervous, unsure of what to expect. I haven't decided if I'll feel comfortable enough to share anything with a room full of strangers, but I walk inside with an open mind.

Melissa welcomes me when I arrive inside the gymnasium, and I'm relieved that she's here. She introduces me to several women who are sitting in metal folding chairs strategically placed to form a circle.

I take the seat beside a young brunette woman named Carrie. She has beautiful hazel eyes behind her wire-rimmed glasses.

She sticks her hand out and smiles. "Nice to meet you, Callie."

"You too."

"First time at group?"

I laugh. "Is it that obvious?"

"I remember wearing that same look you have on. It's not so scary once everyone starts sharing."

"Have you been coming here for a while?"

"Two years. It really helped me to find a group of people who understand."

I nod. "That's great."

Melissa surveys the room as she takes a seat across from me. "All right, ladies. Let's get started. How is everyone doing today?"

Several of the women shout out their answers.

Carrie raises her hand. "I'd like to start."

Melissa smiles. "I was hoping you would."

Carrie turns her head to look at me. "Today marks five years since the day I tried to take my own life."

My lips part in surprise, but I recover quickly. I'm not sure what the proper protocol is.

"Why don't you tell Callie your story?" Melissa says.

Carrie inhales and folds her hands on her lap. "I had a verbally abusive boyfriend. He'd put me down because I didn't want to go out and party with him. Looking back on it, we were very different, and I don't know how we ended up together, but opposites attract, I suppose.

"Some nights, he'd take my car and say he was hanging out with friends. They were girls, but he'd swear they were just friends."

Several laughs echo throughout the room, but it's as if everyone knows they're not directed at Carrie. They're laughs that say *heard that one before*.

"Turned out that my ex was an addict, and he was pimping out the girls he'd leave me to see in order to buy drugs." Carrie shakes her head. "When we'd fight, his biggest dig at me was how I couldn't have children, as if it was my fault. He ended up getting someone else pregnant while he was screwing around behind my back. That was the straw that broke the camel's back. It wasn't fair.

Why did she get to have a baby with him, and I didn't? At the time, it felt like dying was my only option."

I reach over and place my hand on top of hers. "I'm glad you're still here."

She smiles. "Me too. I'm stronger now than I've ever been."

Applause fills the room.

Melissa turns her attention to me. "Callie, would you like to say anything?"

I blow out a shaky breath. "Sure."

"You don't have to, of course. You're welcome to listen if you prefer."

"No. I'll share."

"You're brave," Carrie says. "Took me a few weeks before I shared in group."

I huff out a laugh. "I don't feel brave. That's actually something I'm working on. My husband ... he ... my husband hits me."

The words whoosh out of me, and with it comes a flood of emotions. "We had such a perfect relationship in the beginning. Or maybe I just thought it was perfect, and I just didn't see the danger signs flying past me." I shrug. "He changed over the years. He became angrier, more aggressive. I blamed myself because of my struggle with infertility. It put a lot of stress on our relationship, and I can understand why his fuse was so short. I guess I had to put the blame somewhere, because I couldn't figure out why any of this was happening to me."

I look at all the pairs of eyes watching me and lift my chin. "I left him a few weeks ago."

Applause breaks out around me.

"He says he's going to change, that he wants to work on himself. To be honest, I don't know if that's possible."

"Anything is possible if he makes an effort," Melissa says. "But you need to see proof of that before you move forward."

A woman with stunning coppery-red hair raises her hand. "I can relate to what you said about infertility struggles straining your marriage. My name is Chelsea, by the way."

I offer her a smile. "Hi, Chelsea."

"My husband and I tried conceiving for almost two years before we were successful," she says. "I know it might not sound like a long time, I know many others have struggled for longer, and I know how lucky we are that we were finally able to have a child, but that doesn't mean it wasn't still devastating to go through.

"There are pregnant people literally everywhere. I couldn't understand why my body was failing at the one thing it's genetically supposed to do. That ovulation schedule was the worst. Sex became a chore, and I was putting so much pressure on the act. What used to be a sex life like what you'd read in steamy books was reduced to finishing the fastest way we could whenever the ovulation test read positive."

I nod like a bobblehead doll. "Yes, it's awful."

"Were you ever able to conceive?" she asks.

"No."

"Oh." She looks down at her lap. "I'm sorry."

"Don't be sorry, Chelsea. You are so lucky to have been successful. I know how much that must mean to you, and I'm so happy for you."

"She can stay," Carrie says, jerking her thumb at me. "I like this one."

We all laugh.

Melissa gestures to a woman with auburn hair sitting a few seats away from me. "Janae, you've gone through something like this as well."

Janae nods. "My husband and I have four beautiful children. On the outside, you'd never know how badly we suffered. You'd never know that I've miscarried three times. You'd never know that I've experienced a molar pregnancy that led to a D&C. You'd never know that the placenta of my second child grew into my scar tissue from the C-section of my first child. You'd never know that I've almost died during delivery.

"With four kids, people say, *'Look how fertile you guys are,'* and doctors ask, *'Why do you keep trying to get pregnant if you've had so many complications?'* I understand their assumptions, but the judgment hurts. What nobody knows is that I grew up in a violent home, so it was always a dream of mine to one day have a family of my own. I'm lucky to have four healthy children, and I'm lucky to be alive. But it hasn't been easy getting here. And that struggle wore on me and my husband."

It's eye-opening to see that someone with so many children has suffered, too.

We take turns chatting, relating to one another, until a woman sitting beside Melissa slowly raises her hand. A hush falls over the group, and I can tell that this isn't someone who normally speaks up.

She clears her throat. "Hi, everyone. My name is Jennifer. I know I haven't shared my story in all the months I've been coming here. But I want you to know that I've tried. Every night I'm here, I try to speak up, but I don't have the strength to."

Her hazel eyes meet mine. "But if our new friend, Callie, can find the strength to leave her abusive husband, then I think I can try to say a few words to you ladies."

Melissa places her hand on Jennifer's shoulder. "That's very brave of you."

The room stays silent while Jennifer contemplates what she's about to say. "When I was thirty, my sister was dying from ovarian cancer. I was lost and vulnerable. As the story always goes, I met a beautiful man who made me feel special during a time when I needed it most. I didn't expect to get pregnant. It came as a surprise, but I welcomed it. It should've been happy news.

"Unfortunately, the man turned out to be an immature boy, and he didn't want a baby. On top of that, my parents said that I'd disrespected our family by having sex out of wedlock. I felt alone and scared during the most important time of my life. But I was determined to love that baby at all costs. I didn't need anyone's permission or validation. All I needed was my baby."

Jennifer's chin drops, and a tear rolls down her cheek. "I named her Hannah. She was beautiful."

Was.

My gut churns, and I wrap my arms around my midsection, hugging myself as I anticipate the rest of her story.

"Not only did I have to deal with the heartbreak of losing my baby, but I had to deal with other people's responses. You'd think they'd be sympathetic, right?" She chokes out a laugh and swipes the tears from under her eyes. "If I had a dollar for every woman who said to me, *'Oh, honey. This is for the best since you weren't married,'*— as if I needed a man to validate my motherhood—I'd be a very wealthy woman."

She shakes her head. "I cried every time I had to explain the reason for my returns at all the baby stores, or whenever a friend's child would make me a card to cheer me up. I even lost some friends because they didn't know what to say, so they ignored me for fear they'd say the wrong thing.

"Losing your child is unlike anything else. People offer advice, and they tell you cliché quotes. But I can tell you from experience, time is not going to heal this wound. I've just learned to breathe around the hole in my heart. The guilt never goes away, as if I had a hand in Hannah's death. I know I didn't, logically, but still. I was blessed with a daughter three years later, and I still wonder, *why couldn't Hannah have lived too? What could I have done differently?*"

Jennifer pushes up her sleeve to reveal a beautiful tattoo of two flowers on her forearm. "I got this Sweet Pea for my daughter and this Forget-Me-Not for my Hannah in heaven. It serves as a reminder that life is precious."

Melissa leans over and pulls Jennifer into an embrace. Carrie passes the tissue box around the circle since there isn't a dry eye in the place now.

And my mind drifts to Cole.

I don't know his story. I don't know what he's been through. But if it's anything like Jennifer just described, then I don't know how he's burying it inside like he is.

At the end of group, as I'm getting ready to leave, a young woman with dark curly hair approaches me. "Hi, Callie. I'm Jasmine."

"Hi, Jasmine. It's so nice to meet you."

She fidgets with the strap of her purse on her shoulder. "I just wanted to say thank you for sharing your story with us. I haven't felt ready to share mine yet."

I give her shoulder a squeeze. "It's okay. You don't have to talk about it if you're not ready."

Her brown eyes fill with tears. "I've been trying to have a baby for five years, so I can relate to what you're going through. It's a hard pill to swallow when you realize that your dreams won't come true like everyone else's."

I want to offer her hope, to say something that will lift her spirits. But I know from experience that it won't help. Jasmine may never have the child she wants.

And neither will I.

"I'm sorry," she says, wiping her eyes. "I didn't mean to unload that on you."

"No, no. It's okay. I'm glad you did. It helps, talking to someone who understands what you're going through."

Chelsea joins us with her phone in hand. "We should all exchange numbers. I'm an army wife, so I'm new to the area. I could use some friends here."

"Absolutely," I say.

Although I leave carrying the heavy weight of the women's stories, I feel lighter after unloading mine.

And a small, broken piece of me snaps back together.

TWENTY-ONE

COLE

"Go, go, go!"

Miles sprints across the yard and dives behind the side of the pool house.

"Nice footwork, Mayhem." I clap him on the back.

"Thanks, Night Hawk."

Callie stifles a laugh.

I lift my eyebrows, feigning offense. "Are you laughing at my code name?"

She covers her mouth with her hand as her shoulders shake. "No. Not at all."

"You're one to talk, Wonder Woman. Real original."

Her eyes go wide. "What's wrong with Wonder Woman? She's awesome."

"Guys, focus!" Miles points his index and middle fingers at his own eyes and then faces them toward the yard. "They're coming."

I crouch down and peek my head out from behind the corner of the pool house. Brandon and several of his friends are hiding behind a nearby tree.

Miles' friend, Jason, whispers, "What should we do?"

"Get your squirt guns ready."

Callie and the boys pump their guns and take aim at the tree.

"I'm going to run," I say, "and when I do, I want you guys to rain down on those boys with everything you've got."

Miles narrows his eyes. "Copy that, Night Hawk."

Callie cracks up again.

"Screw you, Wonder Woman." But my lips are tipped up into a smile.

I give the boys a silent countdown with my fingers, and then I take off running in plain sight.

Brandon and his friends charge after me, spraying me in the back with their water guns.

"Yeah! We got you, Uncle Cole!"

But Callie, Miles, and Jason are right behind them.

"Now!" I shout.

Brandon and his friends get blasted with water.

Miles does a victory dance. "We win! We win!"

Brandon ruffles his brother's hair. "I want a rematch."

"Why don't we up the ante," Callie says. "Kids versus grown-ups."

Brandon and Miles look at each other and grin. "You're on!"

Callie squeals as I grab her hand, and we run for the nearest tree.

"I have a plan." Callie scans the yard and spots the boys huddled behind a bush. "We're going to rush them."

I lift an eyebrow. "You want to let them win?"

"Trust me." She winks. "Follow my lead, Night Hawk."

I do my best to follow her without gawking. She's in a yellow two-piece, leaving little to my imagination. She has the perfect hourglass figure, curves in all the right places.

"You ready?"

I clear my throat and nod.

Good thing I'm wearing sunglasses.

Callie drops her water gun onto the grass and runs out from behind the tree. I follow suit, wondering what she's going to do next.

The boys fly around the pool house, squirting the both of us, and they stop to high five each other.

But Callie doesn't stop running.

She hoists Miles into her arms and makes a beeline for the pool.

Brandon's mouth drops open when he realizes that I'm running at him full-speed. He spins around and attempts to run away, but I catch him and toss him over my shoulder.

Callie jumps into the pool with Miles in her arms, and I do the same with Brandon. Their friends jump in after us, everyone laughing and cheering.

"Good plan, Wonder Woman."

Callie slaps her palm against mine and brushes her wet hair off her forehead. "Now I look like a drowned rat. Should've thought that idea through."

You look beautiful. "You're having more fun than those trophy wives out there."

Callie grins. "Yeah, I am."

Josie saunters over to us, using her hand as a visor over her eyes. "You two going to come join the adults for a while or what?"

I grimace. "I'm good."

She plants her hands on her hips. "Just let me introduce you to some of my friends. They're asking about you, and I don't want them to think you're being rude."

I hike a shoulder. "Don't really care what they think of me."

"I do."

Callie makes her way to the steps. "Come on, Cole. If I have to be subjected to trophy-wife torture, then so do you."

I grit my teeth. "Fine. But I'm not sitting next to Brenda and her geriatric husband."

"Cole," Josie hisses. "They'll hear you."

"I'll say it louder so they do." I cup my hands around my mouth and pretend like I'm going to shout their names.

Josie elbows me in the stomach. "Don't you dare."

I wrap my arm around the back of her neck and dig my knuckles into the crown of her head. "Don't start something you can't finish, big sis."

She shrieks. "You're getting me all wet, you jerk!"

I let her go with a shove. "Ah, it's just water."

Callie laughs. "You two must've been such a handful growing up."

"You have no idea." I shake my hair out and towel off. "She used to terrorize me."

Josie scoffs. "Yeah, until you had your growth spurt."

"Payback's a bitch."

Josie sticks her tongue out at me. "Come on. Let's go sit by the table."

I'm subjected to introductions and meaningless conversations for the next hour. The only thing that keeps me invested is Callie. She's quiet until she has something to say, something of value, and when she does, I listen with rapt attention.

My mother always used to say that people should talk less and listen more. I think she would've really liked Callie.

I really like Callie.

My stomach, jaw, and hands clench at the same time, as if my body can restrain this feeling to keep it from seeping out. I'm a prisoner in my own mind, daydreaming of the things I could have if my life had gone differently. If I'd made better choices.

Maybe Callie is here to serve as my punishment. The thing I want that I can never have.

At that thought, I push back from the table and head back to the pool house. I gave Josie what she wanted. Now I just want to be alone.

After several minutes, there's a knock on my door.

Callie's standing on the other side of it.

She's wearing a sheer black cover-up "What are you doing in here?"

I war with what to say.

I can't stop staring at you.

I want to hold you and bear the weight of your pain.

You make me feel things I shouldn't.

I need to stay away from you in that bathing suit so I don't pounce on you like a jungle cat.

No, the truth won't go over so well.

"Just needed to get away. I don't exactly fit in out there."

She glances over her shoulder at the couples and their children. "I get that."

"Want to come in? We can hide out together."

"Sure."

"I don't have much to offer you in here. I've got water, beer, and some cereal."

She laughs as she steps inside. "I'm good, thanks."

I watch her as she makes a slow circle around the room. Her eyes bounce around from the bookcase to the flat screen mounted onto the wall, landing on the stack of cardboard boxes in the corner.

"Your things are still in boxes."

I shrug and take a swig of beer. "No point in unpacking. I don't plan on staying."

She frowns as if that news upsets her. "Where will you go when you leave?"

"Not sure."

"Do you think you'll stay in California or go back to New York?"

"I miss New York, but I think I miss the way New York used to be. There's nothing left for me to go back to."

She hums. "I don't know what I'm going to do either."

"Do you ... do you think you'll get back with Paul? Try to make things work?"

She turns around to face me, and I'm hit with the full weight of her green-eyed stare. "I met with a lawyer this morning."

I can't hide my surprise. "You did?"

"He's one of Dan's friends. He says he trusts him."

I lean onto the back of the leather couch. "And how did that go?"

"It was overwhelming. I don't want to drag this out or take Paul for all he's worth. I just want to be happy. I want to be free." She shrugs and looks out the window. "All this money, and it doesn't mean a damn thing."

"Money isn't worth your happiness, but you should take whatever it is that Paul owes to you according to the law."

She laughs a humorless laugh. "That's not what your sister thinks."

"Yeah, well, my sister thinks a lot of things for someone who's never been in our shoes."

Callie nods. "You and Gertie are the only ones I know who understand. It helps."

"I'm glad."

"I wish I could know what you've gone through," she says quietly.

"Trust me, you don't."

"I keep wondering if it's better or worse than what I've been coming up with in my head."

"Why am I even a thought in your mind?"

She walks toward me and sits at the edge of the couch beside me. "It's kind of like when someone has a secret, but they refuse to tell you what it is. So, you're left speculating what the secret could be and wishing the person would just tell you so you didn't have to wonder anymore."

I smirk. "You're just curious then?"

"I think it's more than curiosity. I ... I've grown to care about you, Cole. You've shown me who you are over these past couple of months. I don't see the same person you see when you look in the mirror."

My heart wrenches with yearning. "Hearing the truth will change the way you see me."

"Your mistakes don't define you. It's a chapter in your life, a part of the whole. All I can judge you on is what you've shown me." Callie reaches out and caresses my jaw with the lightest, feathery touch. "And you've shown me nothing but a caring man with a huge heart."

I want to believe her.

I want to lean into her touch.

Allow her to make the pain subside, even for just a moment.

Awareness spins around me, a mixture of lust and need. My fingers itch to get lost in her hair, my mouth craving the unknown taste of hers.

"Tell me," she whispers. "Let me help you carry the weight of your burden like you've been helping me with mine."

"It would crush you."

"But it's crushing you to bear it alone."

I swallow, my throat dry and my voice hoarse. "I can take it. I deserve to."

She shakes her head and lifts her other hand to my cheek, gripping my face in both hands so that all I can focus on is her.

As if I could see anything else while she's in the room.

"No, Cole. You don't deserve to live in hell any more than I do. I used to think I deserved it, but I'm learning that I don't. What happened to us isn't our fault, but what we choose to do with it after is up to us. I saw you laughing with your nephews earlier. Your smile took my breath away. You were happy once. You can find that again. You can feel it again."

My body betrays me, acting on instinct without a second thought. My thumb slides over her bottom lip, and her eyes flutter closed.

I lean in close, so close that our noses touch. "What if I told you that I feel happy with you? Then what, hmm?"

"Cole, I—"

A knock on my door cuts off her words, causing us to jump apart from one another.

What the fuck am I doing?

Another knock. "Uncle Cole, are you in there? We're going to light the candles and sing to Miles."

"It's Brandon," Callie says as if I didn't just hear his voice through the door. Her eyes are wide, burning a hole through me, searching for an explanation for what just happened.

What *almost* happened.

I give her a tight nod. "Let's go."

I don't look at her as I walk by—or for the rest of the night.

TWENTY-TWO

CALLIE

I TOSSED and turned in bed last night for hours.

I shouldn't have tried to go to sleep so early, but I didn't know what else to do with myself.

Cole almost kissed me.

And I almost let him.

I don't know what the hell I was thinking.

What I'm *still* thinking.

The way his hungry eyes looked into mine. The way my lip sizzled when his thumb skated across it. The way my head and my heart were completely in sync for what felt like the first time in a long, long time.

I wanted it to happen.

I'm an awful person.

Cole's vulnerable right now. He experienced something horrific, and he was opening up to me in the pool house yesterday. I took advantage of his trust, all while Paul is alone in *our* home, distraught and waiting for me to make a decision about our marriage.

I'm still married.

It's only been three weeks since I left Paul. I can't be kissing someone else! Or thinking about it.

I bury my face in the pillow and let out an exasperated growl.

Get your life together, Callie.

I reach into the nightstand and pull out my journal.

Get a job. *Check.*

Consultation with a lawyer. *Check.*

Continue therapy. *Check.* ·

Go to group. *Check.*

What's next? It seems like I'm at a stalemate until I decide what to do about my marriage. The lawyer, Will, made it seem very cut and dry. Easy. I suppose divorce *is* easy on paper where there are no emotions involved.

But that paper holds my life. My future.

I don't care about tangible items or Paul's pension. Maverick is the only thing in that whole house that I'd fight for, and according to Will, I'd win that battle. Maverick was a gift Paul gave me for Christmas a few years ago, and gifts can't be taken back by the gift giver.

I'm worried about Paul. How would he handle this if I said I wanted a divorce? Would he be spiteful? Would he hate me? Would he try to hurt me?

Or is he capable of change? Has he gone to therapy in the last few weeks? Is he making an effort to be better for himself, for us, for me?

How would it feel to go back to living together after all this? Is our marriage salvageable? I used to think I could do something to fix us. Now, I'm not so sure. This is bigger than me.

My head throbs. I hate thinking about the answers to these questions, but I need to figure this out.

The sooner I do, the sooner I can find peace.

~

"You look like hell."

I huff out a laugh. "Gee, thanks, Gertie."

"What happened to you?"

I dig the heels of my hands into my eyes. "Couldn't sleep last night. Had a lot on my mind."

She leans her hip against the counter. "Well, let's hear it so I can help."

I shake my head. "I don't want to bother you with my stuff."

"Your stuff is my stuff, sugar. You're helping me run my business. Let me help you with yours. So, come on. Out with it."

I heave a sigh. "I don't know what to do about Paul. I need to make a decision so I don't leave the two of us in limbo, but I don't know what the right answer is."

"The right answer is what you *want* to do. Plain and simple."

"What if I don't know what I want?"

"I have news for you, sugar." Gertie steps closer to me and grips my shoulders. "You already know what you want. You're just afraid to admit that you want it."

"I'm not so sure about that."

"You just need to listen better. Listen to what that little voice inside is telling you."

The corners of my mouth pull downward as I try to hear something, anything.

"Don't frown so much," Gertie says with a wink. "Food tastes better when you cook it with love, not sadness."

I chuckle and get started on this morning's orders. It's so busy I barely have any time to think. I lose myself in cooking. It's therapeutic. It reminds me of better days, when my mom and my grandfather were alive. Before Paul. Before this whole mess started. Cooking brings me happiness.

Would I have to give this up if I went back to Paul?

The thought alone makes my stomach hurt.

As I'm getting ready to leave at the end of the day, Gertie stops me at the door.

"I want to ask you something before you go, sugar."

"Of course."

"Have you had any panic attacks lately? In the last week or two?"

My eyebrows dip down as I think about it. "No. I had one the night I left Paul, but I don't think I've had one since."

Gertie hums. "Interesting."

"Why do you ask?"

She shrugs as she flips the light switch. "I just think that's very telling. That's all. Have a good night, dear."

～

"ARE you sure you don't feel up to coming out? It'll be our treat."

I shake my head. "I'm sure, but thank you so much for the offer."

Josie waves her hand at me. "You're no fun!"

"If she's tired, she's tired. She was working on her feet all day." Dan shoots me a wink as he comes to my rescue.

"Sure, take her side." Josie rolls her eyes and clomps toward the front door in her wedges. "There's food in the fridge when you get hungry, Cal."

"Thanks. Have fun!"

I blow out a breath of relief as I lock the door behind them. Josie and Dan are taking the kids out to dinner, which means I have the entire house to myself tonight.

I take the stairs two at a time and make a beeline for the guest bathroom. I've been dying to soak in a bath since I started staying here, and tonight's the perfect night for it.

While the tub fills, I strip out of my clothes and settle on a meditation playlist on YouTube. Then I light a few candles, shut off the lights, and climb into the warm water.

Closing my eyes, I drift away to the soft sound of the music. I force any and all thoughts out of my mind, allowing myself to forget about everything that's happening in my world right now. I let go and breathe.

After the bath, I'm feeling more relaxed than ever as I wrap myself in my robe and head down to the kitchen to make something to eat.

The doorbell rings.

I check through the peephole, and all of my relaxation goes right out the window.

My shoulders jump as he knocks on the door. "Callie, are you there? It's Paul. I just want to talk."

I'm uneasy about the idea of being alone with Paul. Then again, maybe he's here to tell me he's been going to therapy. Maybe he's trying to change, and we can have a healthy conversation.

Tightening the belt on my robe, I swing open the door.

"Hey, did I catch you at a bad time?" he asks.

His hair is combed, and his white collared shirt is crisp. The bruising on his face has completely faded. He looks better. Lighter.

He looks like my handsome husband.

Can it really be?

I step back and let him in. "No, I just took a bath. I'm heating up some food. Are you hungry?"

He shakes his head. "No, but thank you. I saw Dan and Josie leaving with the kids when I got home from work. Figured I'd see if you were here. I really want to talk."

"I want to talk, too." I gesture to the plush, cream-colored couches in the living room. "Let's sit."

We lower ourselves onto separate cushions on the same couch. Paul reaches over and caresses my cheek with the back of his hand. "I miss you, Cal. You have no idea how much."

"I miss you, too."

And it's not a lie. I miss the man I once fell in love with. I miss our good times. Our companionship.

"You look good," I say. "Have you been going to therapy?"

His gaze drops to his lap. "Not yet. But I've made a list of a few places."

My heart sinks. "Oh."

"It's been crazy at the office. I've been working long hours and on the weekends. I'm on a really important case right now."

I'm *an important case.*

"So then why are you here?"

His eyebrows dip down. "Because I miss you. I wanted to see

where your head is at. I don't think being apart from each other is the best thing for us."

I inch back. "I understand how you feel, but I don't agree. Being apart is what's best for me right now."

"This isn't just about you, Callie. What about me?"

I scoff. "Are you seriously asking that? After everything that happened, you're worried about *yourself*?"

His hands shoot up in front of him. "No, no. That's not what I'm saying. Don't twist my words."

"I'm not twisting anything." I rise from the couch and start pacing. "You keep telling me how much you miss me and how much you want me to come home. Yet, you haven't done the one thing I've asked you to do. You're not making me a priority."

"Come on." Paul stands and grips my forearms. "We're both supposed to make each other a priority. I don't see how what you're doing is putting me first either."

I yank my arms out of his grasp. "We put each other first when we work on ourselves. You need help, Paul."

He steps forward and cradles my face in his hands. "I need *you*, Callie. You. I don't want to lose you. I can't."

The guilt overwhelms me. He's in my space, and my head is swirling. I can't breathe, my chest tight, my throat closing. I place my palms on his chest and push him back gently, but he doesn't budge.

He grips my face tighter.

"Please, Callie. Please, come home with me. Be with me again. I'll be better, I swear."

His lips crash into mine. His kiss is anything but tender. I try to pull back, but he wraps his arms around me and squeezes me, holding me there against him.

Against my will.

I turn my head so I can suck in a breath. "Paul, please. You're hurting me."

"I just love you so much. I can show you. You need to see. You need to feel it again. If you feel my love, you'll come home. I can make you love me again."

My heart thrashes against my chest. "No! Not like this. Please, not like this."

I can't wriggle free. He's too strong. Instead, I let my legs go limp and drop all of my weight in his arms. He stumbles forward and falls on top of me on the floor.

I claw at the area rug beneath me, attempting to slither out of his reach. But he's fast, and he pins me on my back, straddling my hips.

Again, he kisses me hard. Tears stream down my face. I can't get enough oxygen into my lungs, and I begin to panic.

I squirm under him, kicking my legs and smacking his arms, doing anything I can to get away.

He restrains my wrists over my head in one of his big hands while the other reaches between us. The sound of the zipper on his pants echoes in the room.

I scream.

"Shh. It's okay, baby," he whispers in my ear. "It's going to be okay."

"Please don't do this, Paul. Please! I'll never be with you if you do this."

But he doesn't hear my plea.

I don't think anything I say could reach him now.

Panicked and running out of time, I ram my forehead into his, stunning the both of us. His grip around my wrists loosens, and I use the opportunity to stretch my arm up to the glass vase sitting on top of the coffee table.

I smash it into the side of Paul's head, knocking him unconscious. Glass shards are everywhere, and blood trickles from Paul's temple.

But I don't move.

I can't.

I wrap my arms around my midsection and curl up into a shaking ball on the floor.

TWENTY-THREE

COLE

THERE ARE some images you'll never be able to erase from your memory.

Callie lying in the middle of Josie's living room in the fetal position, covered in broken glass, is one of them.

I hear someone crying when I walk into Josie's kitchen. I step through the hallway, and when I get to the living room, my stomach bottoms out.

Paul's passed out face-down on the area rug beside Callie, and she's weeping. I rush over to her and kneel down, scooping her into my arms.

"Callie, what happened? Are you okay?"

Her entire body is trembling, tears running down her cheeks. "Be careful," she whispers. "There's glass."

A strangled sound leaves my throat. "What the fuck happened in here?"

She squeezes her eyes shut and buries her face in my chest. Uncontrollable sobs wrack her body.

Jesus Christ.

"I need you to tell me if you're hurt." I glance down to her arms and legs. "Did he ... did he hurt you?"

She shakes her head. "He tried … he tried to force himself on me."

Paul stirs, groaning, as he touches his fingers to the cut on his head.

Rage flares in the pit of my stomach, and it courses through me like lava. I carry Callie to the stairs and ease her onto her feet. "Go upstairs and lock yourself in your room. Don't come out until I come and get you. Do you understand me?"

Her eyes move to Paul, but I bring her attention back to me. "Look at me, Callie. Do you understand?"

She nods and then runs up the stairs.

Paul is trying to stand when I stalk over to him. I grip him by the back of his neck and drag him toward the door.

"What are you doing?" he grumbles.

"What I should've done from the start."

As I turn the knob, the door pushes back on me. Dan, Josie, and the kids are home.

"Cole, what's going on?" Josie asks.

"Keep the kids out of the living room. There's glass everywhere."

I push past them as Paul struggles to get out of my grip.

Dan follows me down the walkway. "Where are you going?"

I stare straight into his eyes. "I'm going to fucking kill him."

Josie hands Serenity off to Brandon. "Take the twins to your room, boys."

They scurry inside and close the door.

Josie turns back to me. "Don't do anything stupid. I'll call the cops, and they'll deal with him."

I shove Paul onto the ground. "Call the cops. He's going to need an ambulance."

Paul moves to run, but I'm quick to slam him back down with my foot. I mount him and wrap both arounds his neck, crushing his windpipe. "How does it feel to have the life choked out of you, Paul? Huh? How do you like feeling helpless on the ground?"

"Cole, stop!" Josie yanks on my shoulder.

But I don't relent.

"You've made your point," Dan says. "Come on. Don't do something you're going to regret."

Oh, I won't regret this.

It feels good to release some of this tension I've been carrying around. To give Paul a taste of his own medicine. He's sputtering, his face turning red and then purple. I want him to match the bruises he's left on Callie.

Then Josie's voice penetrates my senses. "Think of Mia. She's looking down on you right now. Don't do this. She's watching."

Like I've been shocked with an electric current, I release Paul's throat and stagger backward.

Mia. My Mia.

Dan bends down next to Paul, who's clutching his throat and gasping for air. "Get off my property, and don't come back. You're not welcome here."

Paul grunts as he pushes to his feet. "I didn't mean to hurt her. I just want her back."

Josie shoves past me and swings her hand, slapping her palm across his cheek. "You will never get her back. Ever. Now go!"

Paul's head slumps forward, and he drags himself across the street.

"What the hell happened in there?" Dan asks, turning to face me.

"I went to the kitchen to grab something to eat, and I heard Callie crying in the living room. When I walked in to see what was wrong, they were both on the floor." I glare at Paul's back as he makes his way to his house. "I think he tried to rape her."

Without another word, Josie spins around and bolts into the house in search of her friend.

Dan sighs, running his fingers through his hair. "I'll call my buddy, John. He's a cop. Callie can make a statement and get a restraining order against Paul. That should help her with the divorce."

"Won't put him where he belongs."

"No, but at least it's something."

I shake my head. "Should've let me handle it."

"Do you really think you're capable of something like that?"

"It's what I do."

Dan shouts after me as I turn and walk toward the backyard. "That's not true, Cole."

"Tell that to Mia."

~

I'M surprised to see Callie at the diner the next day.

She's eating lunch at our usual spot at the counter. There are two plates waiting for me and Billy on either side of her.

"There's my girl," Billy says, taking the stool to the left of her.

She smiles, though it doesn't reach her tired eyes. I wonder if she got any sleep last night.

I know I didn't.

"How are you?" I ask.

She lifts a shoulder and lets it fall. "Could've been worse."

"Doesn't mean it wasn't a big deal. You should've taken the day off."

She shakes her head. "I need to keep busy."

"Here we go with the whispering again." Billy rolls his eyes.

I toss a french fry at his head, and he flips me off, garnering a chuckle from Callie.

Gertie makes her way down the counter, refilling coffee mugs as she points a finger at me. "You best not be throwing food in my diner. Just because you're good looking doesn't mean I won't knock you upside your head with my shoe."

"That I'd love to see," Callie says.

My jaw drops open. "Hey, whose side are you on?"

Callie laughs as she nudges me with her shoulder.

Billy takes over the conversation, and Gertie uses the distraction to lean in and whisper to me. "I'm glad you're here. This is the first time I've seen her smile all day."

I nod, speaking around the wad of food in my mouth. "She had a rough night."

"What happened?"

"Her ex came by the house and attacked her. He tried to force himself on her."

Gertie's wrinkly hands ball into little fists. "I could kill him."

"Yeah," I say with a laugh. "I tried to."

Her eyebrows shoot up even higher than they're already drawn on. "You were there?"

"Few minutes too late. I found her on the floor."

She clicks her tongue as she shakes her head. "Poor thing doesn't deserve any of this."

"No, she doesn't."

Gertie looks over the rim of her glasses at me. "She thinks very highly of you, you know."

"She shouldn't."

"Ah, horseshit."

"Uh-oh," Billy says. "Gertie's cursing. What'd you do now, Cole?"

I hold my hands up on either side of my head. "I didn't do anything."

"This is why I'm her favorite. Ain't that right, Gertie?"

"Whatever helps you sleep at night, sugar." She pats Billy's hand as she heads back to the kitchen.

When we're finished with lunch, Callie stops me before I follow Billy out the door. "I just wanted to say thanks for helping me last night."

"You don't have to thank me."

She smiles. "Just accept my gratitude, will you?"

"Fine."

"You're so difficult."

I smirk at that.

"I think I need to look for another place to live," she says as if she's thinking aloud.

My eyebrows lift. "You think that's a good idea?"

She smooths her hand over her hair and blows out a breath through her lips. "I don't want Paul to know where I am, and I hate feeling like I'm putting the kids in danger."

"I've actually been looking for apartments myself. Around here. I like the area, and the prices aren't too bad. I could help you look if you want."

Her face lights up. "Really? You're not going back to New York?"

"I ... I'm not sure. Just looking at my options."

"Well, I'd love your help."

"How about tomorrow after work?"

She chews her bottom lip. "I'm actually meeting with the lawyer. Going to move forward with the divorce."

Relief floods through me. On instinct, my hand reaches out to touch her shoulder.

And she doesn't flinch.

"I'm glad to hear that, Callie. I think you're making the right decision."

She nods. "I know I am. It's just scary."

"Can't be scarier than what you've already been through."

She mulls that over for a minute and then offers me a small smile. "That's a good way of thinking about it."

I wink. "That's the only way you should be thinking about it."

I'm about to push open the door and leave, but then Callie throws her arms around my midsection. I'm filthy from work, but I don't bother to tell her that. Instead, I snake one arm around to her back and one around to cradle the back of her head, holding her against my chest.

We both exhale, and I don't know who needs this more. The angel caught up in chaos, or the demon searching for peace.

Her cheeks are flushed when she pulls away. "Sorry about that. I don't know what came over me."

I tip her chin up so her eyes meet mine. "Remember what I told you about apologizing."

She laughs as she turns to walk back toward the kitchen. "I'll work on that."

"Hey, Callie."

She spins around, a hopeful gleam in her eyes. "Yeah?"

"I'm proud of you."

And then she dazzles me with the most brilliant smile I've ever seen. It steals my next breath right from my chest.

When I meet Billy outside—who no doubt just saw everything—he shakes his head and huffs out a laugh.

"What?" I ask, not really wanting to know what he's about to say.

"Dude, you are so screwed."

TWENTY-FOUR

CALLIE

SEPTEMBER COMES and goes in the blink of an eye.

Lots of changes are in motion. Brandon and Miles are back in school. Josie enrolled the twins in daycare for three days a week. Warm summer nights have turned a bit chillier, though the days are just as hot.

Life moves on around me, but for once, I don't feel stuck. I don't feel like I'm trapped on the inside, watching everyone live and grow on the outside.

This time, I'm living and growing, too.

Paul has been served with a restraining order and divorce papers. I haven't heard him since the night at Josie's last month. Part of me is surprised he hasn't reached out to me. The other part is relieved. I try not to think about it too much. It makes me feel sad for the good pieces of our relationship that I've lost. The happy times we shared. The good news is he's cooperating with my lawyer. Will said that normally it can take up to six months for a divorce to be finalized, but if Paul continues to comply, he can expedite the process so it'll be over before that.

That's all I want, to close that chapter of my life.

Despite what Josie and Cole think, I believe in my heart that

Paul is not a monster. He's not a bad person. He's *human*. He has a problem, and I hope he seeks help for it. The hardest part of moving on hasn't been forgiving Paul. I forgive him for his flaws.

But it's been difficult learning how to forgive myself.

My days are spent at the diner. I love creating new dishes for customers to try, and I love talking with Gertie even more. She has become like family to me. In the evenings, I keep busy by going to therapy or group and spending time with Josie and the kids. Cole and I have been looking for apartments, but nothing has felt like the right place for either of us. Still, I enjoy our time together.

Cole and I have grown closer. I never would've guessed that the rude, scowling man in Josie's backyard—*who looked like the landscaper*—would become such an important person in my life. Though he denies it, he has a heart of gold. I've seen it. I've been on the receiving end of his kind and gentle nature.

If only he'd face what he's running from.

I know he's tortured by something. Something more than his ex-wife cheating on him. Something he blames himself for. I want to take his pain away, to help him heal.

But I know better than anyone that healing needs to start from within.

One night in October, as I'm closing up the diner, I decide to reach out to a few of the women from group to see if they want to have a few drinks with me and Josie by the fire pit in her yard. I could really go for a girls' night in.

Jasmine, Carrie, Janae, Jennifer, and Chelsea show up at nine with bottles of wine and fruit and cheese to snack on.

"Bitch, you forgot to mention you're living in a castle," Carrie says, nudging me with her elbow as she walks through the door.

"No wonder you haven't found an apartment. I'd be dragging my feet too." Janae's eyes roam around the foyer and travel up the spiral staircase.

"I just haven't found anything that feels right yet."

Chelsea drapes her arm around my shoulders as I lead them to the backyard. "How are you holding up?"

"I'm good. Some days are tougher than others, but I feel better now than I did when I was living with Paul. It's like an insane amount of weight was lifted off me. It's crazy to think that I was okay living in fear like that for so long."

"It's not crazy," Jennifer says. "You were comfortable in your situation. It was familiar to you."

Carrie nods. "Change is scary as fuck."

Josie greets us when we step outside. "Who said fuck? I like you already."

The girls laugh, and I introduce them as we take our seats around the fire pit.

Josie hands me a glass of Moscato, and I close my eyes as I take a sip. "I can't remember the last time I had a glass of wine."

"I can't either," Josie says with a pout. "We used to sit out here every night."

"Paul got violent when he drank." I hike a shoulder. "I figured if I didn't drink, then he wouldn't feel the need to either."

"Didn't work, did it?" Carrie asks.

I shake my head.

Carrie leans over and squeezes my knee. "That's all behind you now."

My eyes find Jennifer's forearm. "I keep thinking about your tattoo and how you said it reminds you that life is precious."

She smiles. "I look at it every single day."

Janae's eyebrows lift. "Are you thinking of getting one?"

"Oh, please can we go together?" Josie asks. "We can get matching best friend tattoos!"

I laugh. "I've been thinking about it. For so long, I had to hide the marks Paul left on my body. If I got a tattoo, it'd be my choice. A mark I was proud of."

"Cheers to that!" Janae scoots forward to the edge of her chair with her drink lifted, and we clink our glasses together.

"Jasmine, you're quiet tonight. You okay?" Chelsea asks.

At that, Jasmine bursts into tears. She covers her face with her hands, shoulders shaking.

I rush toward her, kneeling in front of her chair. "What's wrong? What happened?"

"One of my friends found out she's pregnant today."

Sounds of sympathy come from the group, and my heart wrenches. I pull her into my arms, and one by one, the girls join us.

After a few minutes of crying, Jasmine dabs at the corners of her eyes. "Thanks for the group hug. I'm sorry; I didn't mean to put a damper on the night."

"You did not put a damper on anything," Jennifer says. "That's what this group is all about. We talk and we help each other."

"I feel like such a bad friend," Jasmine says, sniffling. "It's not like I'm not happy for her. I am."

"You can feel happy for your friend and still feel sad for yourself," I say.

Josie reaches for my hand. "Is this what you felt like when I found out I was pregnant with the twins?"

I chew on my bottom lip and give her a reluctant nod.

"I'm sorry, Callie."

"It's okay. It's not your fault."

We cry, and we laugh, and we drink, and I can't remember feeling this happy in a long time.

Sometime after midnight, the pool house door opens, and Cole emerges. A hush falls over the group, and I take note of the way everyone's eyes follow him across the yard.

Everyone's except for Josie's, of course. "Hey, brother! Are we being too loud out here?"

Cole smirks and shakes his head. "You're the only loud mouth out here."

She scoffs and flips him off.

"Sorry, ladies. Don't mean to interrupt," he says, his eyes meeting mine. "Just grabbing some food from the kitchen."

"You're not interrupting. I'd tell you to join us, but"—I gesture around the circle of women—"I doubt this is your scene."

"Thanks, but no thanks." He winks and heads inside.

Chelsea nudges me with her elbow. "So *that's* why you haven't found an apartment yet."

My eyebrows dip down. "What are you talking about?"

She rolls her eyes. "Please don't act like you're not aware of that man's hotness."

Josie plugs her ears with her index fingers. "La, la, la, la."

My cheeks heat. *Oh, I'm totally aware.*

Carrie tilts her head. "Is he single?"

"Divorced."

"Just like you," she says.

I hold up my index finger. "I'm still waiting for the paperwork to go through."

"Pfft." Janae waves her hand. "That's a technicality."

"Can we *please* change the subject?" Josie groans.

The girls stay for a bit longer. Then we say goodnight, and I help Josie clean up.

"Hey, Cal, can I ask you something?"

I place the last wine glass in the dishwasher and turn to face her. "Sure. What's up?"

"Do you really find Cole attractive?"

My stomach clenches. "Uh, are you going to hate me if I say yes?"

"Stop. I'd never hate you for that."

I lift an eyebrow. "Why do you ask?"

"Well, I know you two have been spending a lot of time together, and I guess I'm just curious if there's something going on between you."

My eyes widen. "No! Nothing has happened. Did he tell you something happened? Because it didn't."

A smile spreads across her face. "Do you *want* something to happen?"

Looking into my best friend's eyes, I can't bring myself to lie. My shoulders slump as I exhale. "I don't know. I like spending time with him. But I'm not even officially divorced yet. I shouldn't be thinking about anybody else right now. I've been with Paul for so long that it almost feels wrong."

"It's not wrong, Callie. It's not like you've been in this wonderful marriage. You've been hurting for years. And I know Cole's hurting too. I think the two of you would be a great match for each other."

I run my fingers through my hair. "We don't even know if he's interested in me."

She rolls her eyes. "Do you forget who you're talking to? I'm his sister. Trust me when I say that he's into you. I see it written all over his face."

I worry my lip while I ponder that possibility.

"Look, it's food for thought. I just wanted to let you know that it's okay if you're feeling something for him. I love you both, and I want the best for you." She cups my shoulders. "I think it's time you let yourself be happy."

Josie heads upstairs to bed, but I head back out to the patio. I polish off the last of the wine while my head swims with thoughts.

I can't deny the chemistry between me and Cole. Warmth spreads throughout my body when I think back to our almost-kiss on Miles' birthday. He's been nothing but sweet and helpful, and we've developed a friendship over the past few months.

But am I ready to cross that line?

Will I ever feel ready?

How will I know when enough time has passed?

And who creates these rules and regulations about when it's okay to move on?

My gaze drifts to the pool house. The shades are drawn, but a sliver of dim light peeks through.

Is he awake, like me?

I stand. I don't know what I'm doing, yet I can't seem to stop my feet from moving across the lawn. My head is screaming with warning bells, but something inside me is compelling me forward. When I reach the pool house, I lift my fist and lightly tap my knuckles on the door. My heart thumps in my chest while I wait.

The door cracks open, and Cole peers through the space. His hair is a disheveled mess, but I only notice that for a split second due to the fact that he's shirtless. His bare torso stares me in the face, drawing my eyes like a magnet. Thin, plaid pajama pants sit dangerously low on his hips, putting his sculpted abs and V-shape on full display.

My legs turn to Jell-O.

"Callie, are you okay?" He opens the door wider and steps aside, worry creasing his dark brows.

"Oh, yes. I'm fine. I'm sorry, were you asleep? I just assumed you were up because, well, you said you're always up. But I know it's late. I didn't mean to wake you."

A smirk pulls his lips to the side. "I was up. Come in."

I walk inside and glance around. It's dark aside from the small lamp on his nightstand. There's a book laying face-down on the mattress.

"What are you reading?"

"*The Shining.*"

My face twists. "Out here, all alone?"

He chuckles. "I'm not afraid. Reality is often scarier than anything in King's novels."

"That's true."

He watches me as I walk around the perimeter of the space. I stop at a picture frame sitting on the bookshelf and lift it to take a closer look.

A young Cole and Josie are grinning on the beach in their bathing suits with their arms around each other. Cole's eyes sparkle in the sunlight, and it makes my chest ache to see him smile like he doesn't have a care in the world.

His breath is at my ear, and his voice is low as he looks on over my shoulder. "I was eighteen when we took this picture. It seems like a lifetime ago."

"You guys used to be close."

"We were."

I set the photo down and turn around to face him. "You seem like you're getting back to that."

He nods. "You've helped with that."

"You've helped me as well."

He tucks a strand of hair behind my ear but then quickly lets his hand fall back to his side as if it stepped out of line without his permission. "Why are you here?"

I shrug and avert my eyes. "I don't know."

He inches closer and tips my chin up until my gaze returns to his. "Why, Callie?"

How does he do it? How does he always see right through me? He always has. Those cobalt eyes slice through me, finding my darkest parts and exposing them, shining the spotlight on everything I try to hide.

Whatever lie I'd planned to tell dissipates.

"*Why?*" His voice sounds strained, like he's desperate for the truth.

I let my hands do the talking while I search for the right words to say to him. Trembling, I reach out and slide my palms over his broad chest. He shivers as my fingertips trail down over the contoured ridges of his abdomen.

It's reckless and foolish, but I'm too tired to care.

"I want to *feel* again. I want to feel something other than despair and pain. I don't want to think, or plan, or hold back." My eyes lock with his. "I came here to see *you*."

Cole takes my face into his hands and rests his forehead against mine. He squeezes his eyes shut, wincing as if my words have caused him pain.

"Callie," he whispers.

His palms are calloused, but his touch is gentle, barely brushing my skin.

I want more.

"You hold me like I'm this fragile thing. You don't have to be scared to touch me. I won't break."

His eyebrows press together. "But you *are* fragile, Callie."

My lips tug downward. "You think I'm weak because I let someone hit me."

"No." His fingers push into my hair, and he cradles the back of my head, gripping me tighter. "You're not fragile because you're weak. You're fragile because *life* is fragile. It can end in an instant. Every moment we have is fleeting."

Life is precious.

My heart pounds as my gaze falls to his lips. "Then we shouldn't take another second of it for granted."

With a groan, his mouth is on mine.

We collide, and I let go.

Full and smooth, his lips are the softest thing on his hard exterior. Everything about him is a contradiction. He's tender and rough at the same time. Both the calm and the storm, the dark and the light.

And maybe that's how we should be. Maybe that's what makes us human. Maybe there isn't right and wrong, or black and white. Nothing is cut and dry. We have no right to pass judgment on anyone—not even ourselves. We're all convoluted paradoxes ruled by our emotions, searching for what makes us feel alive.

With Cole, I've found that. *He* makes me feel alive.

Our tongues entangle, and a spark ignites into a flame, a rip-roaring fire that consumes us both. I melt into him, pressing up onto my toes so that I can get *more*—more of him, more of this feeling.

Kissing Cole is everything I never knew I needed.

In an instant, he lifts me and pins me to the wall. My legs wrap around his waist, my arms around his neck, hands lost in his hair. It's like I need every part of me touching every part of him, like I can't get close enough.

His fingers dig into my waist, and I smile against his mouth at the thought of his grip bruising my skin—a *good* kind of bruise for a change. One that represents something so different than the bruises in my past.

"I can't get you out of my head, Callie. Can't stop thinking about you, wanting you."

He presses himself against me as he pillages my mouth, and I moan, rolling my hips, craving the friction between us. Fisting my hair, he yanks my head to the side and devours my neck, sucking and biting my sensitive skin.

"Me too," I say on an exhale. "I want you, want this. You feel so right. We can be each other's hope."

At that final word, Cole's body stills. He pulls back to look at me, agony contorting his features. It's as if he has snapped out of a spell and is now realizing what he's just done.

He sets me down on my feet, panting, gasping for breath, and staggers backward.

Away from me.

"Cole, what's wrong?"

But I already know. I said the one word he doesn't want to hear. The one word he doesn't believe in.

Hope.

"I'm sorry," he says weakly, as if he doesn't believe it himself. "I shouldn't have let that happen."

My head jerks back. "Why not?"

He gestures between the two of us. "This can't be."

"We don't even know what *this* is, and you've already come to the conclusion that it isn't possible?"

"Yes."

I huff out a disbelieving laugh. Embarrassment tinges my cheeks, but I use my anger to mask it. "Why not? Please enlighten me on how you've figured it all out in a matter of seconds."

He stalks forward, stabbing his chest with his index finger. "I'm not good for you, Callie. Not long-term. I can't be the man you need, the man you deserve. I have nothing to offer you. You shouldn't feel hopeful with me. I can't give you more than this physical connection. I don't want to lead you on."

I grasp his face in my hands and force him to look at me, as if my eyes can reflect what I see in him. "You have so much to offer. You are kind and caring, and I know you're suffering, but so am I. We can help each other through it."

He jerks his head out of my reach and paces, pulling at the ends of his hair. "We shouldn't do this."

"We just did! And it was incredible. It felt *right*, Cole. I know you felt it, yet now you want to take it all back because you're scared. You know what? I'm scared too. I've gone through hell, but I clawed my way out, and now all I want is to be happy."

"Exactly." His face hardens, and the gates he uses to protect himself come down around him. "I can't make you happy."

"You're right." My shoulders drop in defeat. "You can't make me happy. I'm the only one who can do that. And for the first time in years, I just did something that made me happy. Kissing you made me happier than I've felt in a long time. So, thanks for ruining that."

I spin on my heels and head for the door, willing the tears of humiliation to hold off until I get to my bedroom.

"That's what I do, Callie," he calls after me. "I ruin everything I touch."

I grip onto the door handle for strength. "The only thing you're ruining is your own life."

TWENTY-FIVE

COLE

Two Years Ago

My body jolted awake.

Hungry already?

With a groan, I rolled out of bed and shuffled to the nursery next door.

Mia's shrill wail got louder when I stepped inside her room. "Okay, Mia girl. All right. Daddy's here."

I lifted her tiny body out of the crib and held her against my chest. Her screaming stopped as soon as she was in my arms, and I smiled. "Let's go make you a bottle."

Penny and I had barely slept since we brought Mia home. The first night was easy, but each night got more challenging. Yesterday, Penny poured salt into her coffee, and today I almost drove to the store in nothing but my boxers. Sleep deprivation was driving us mad.

But it was all worth it.

Penny gave birth to Mia Rose just after 3AM last Tuesday.

Watching my incredible wife in action like that was life-changing. It felt like my body was going to explode with love, respect, and adoration. Then I looked at Mia, and my entire world changed.

It was unbelievable how someone so tiny could matter so much.

She was the perfect baby ... until nighttime came. Then she was like a gremlin who got fed after midnight.

I chuckled as I looked down at the angel in my arms. "Bottle's ready, gremlin baby."

I carried Mia back to her room and lowered us into the old, wooden rocking chair—a gift from my parents before they passed.

Dad knew he wouldn't last long without Mom. After she died last year, he gave me the chair and said, "We made this in the hopes that we'd get to meet our grandkids one day."

Tears welled at the thought of my parents. The wound was still fresh, but having Mia helped with that.

While she drank her bottle, I sang "Can You Feel the Love Tonight" by Elton John. It was a song my mother used to sing to me when I was a child. I'd just seen *The Lion King* and was devastated by the scene when Mufasa was killed. I hadn't realized that my parents were capable of dying until then. I told her I wanted to die before she did. She hugged me and said, "Kids aren't supposed to die before their parents. But you don't have to worry about me. I'm not going anywhere for a long, long time." She sang that song every night until I fell asleep.

Now it was my turn to sing it to my child.

"I'll never let anything happen to you," I whispered to Mia. "I'm going to protect you and take care of you. And I'm not going anywhere for a long, long time."

TWENTY-SIX

COLE

THE SOUND of laughter greets me as I step through the gate.

So much for slipping into the pool house unnoticed.

The sun is making its descent, casting blinding rays through the swaying trees. It's still early, but I'm ready for bed. I've been working overtime all week, needing the distraction to keep me from my thoughts.

To keep me from *her*.

When I agreed to move in with Josie, my plan was to exist. Work, sleep, repeat. Self-isolate until I could save up enough money to disappear somewhere else. Somewhere far away from family, and love, and happiness.

Callie Kingston was never part of the plan.

Kissing her the other night wrecked everything, yet I feel revitalized. Like she kick-started my dead heart, and now I can't turn it off. My head knows better. I know I have nothing to give her.

But she looks at me like I handed her the world, and God do I want to try. I want to give her the kind of love I was once filled with, back before my life was pulled out from under me. I know I can treat her better than Paul did, but that's not saying much. Callie deserves more. She deserves all of me.

And what's left of me just isn't enough.

"Uncle Cole, come night-swimming with us!" Miles shouts.

"I'm exhausted, buddy. Maybe another night."

Josie rests her hand on her hip. "You're not swimming in the Olympics, Cole. The water will feel good after a long day. Hang out with us for a while."

I glance at the house over my shoulder, my eyes like magnets to Callie's bedroom window. A dim light glows through the sheer curtains.

What's she doing?

How is she?

Why isn't she out here?

Is she angry with me?

"She's not coming down, if that's what you're worried about."

My attention snaps back to Josie. "I'm not worried."

She rolls her eyes. "I don't know how you operate heavy machinery at work all day with your head stuffed so far up your own ass."

Brandon snorts, but quickly slips under the water when I glare at him.

"She told me about the kiss." Josie plops Serenity down on the grass beside Lucas, amidst a plethora of toys. "I don't understand why you pushed her away. You obviously feel something for her."

"You don't know what I feel."

She laughs softly. "Sometimes I think I know you better than you know yourself."

"Maybe you used to." I gaze out over the tops of the tall palm trees framed by the orange swirls in the sky. "I'll never be that person again."

"You're still that same person." Josie runs her fingers through Lucas's thick hair. "Your mistakes don't define you. They teach you, sure. But they don't change who you are. They don't dictate your future. Not unless you let it."

I smirk. "Do you get these quotes from an inspirational calendar?"

She flips her middle finger up at me, but smiles. "I've made a lot of mistakes in my lifetime. Not as devastating as yours, but they add up. Being a mom means I'm guaranteed to fuck up at least once a day."

I lower myself onto the lush grass beside her. "Your kids are alive. You're doing fine."

She leans over and covers my hand with hers. "I'm so sorry, Cole. I'm sorry you experienced that. I can't ... I can't imagine."

I nod, averting my eyes to the boys playing basketball in the pool. "Sometimes I forget that it's real. I'll have a dream that I'm holding her in my arms, that everything's okay." I shrug and turn my head to face Josie. "How am I supposed to go on like this? How does life get better?"

Josie points her index finger up at Callie's window. "You start by finding someone who understands. Someone you care about. And you let her in."

I press the heels of my hands against my eyes, as if I can rub the image of Callie right out of my mind.

But I know I can't.

She's implanted herself in there, and she's growing roots.

"I know you care about her, Cole. You can't deny it. It's written all over your face."

I shake my head. "I don't deserve someone like her. She needs someone who can give her what she wants."

Josie lifts an eyebrow. "She wants *you*."

My heart twists in my chest. "Why?"

"You should ask yourself that question." She cups her mouth with her hand and calls to the boys. "Come out and dry off, guys. You need to be showered, in bed, and reading by eight."

Then she stands and holds out her hands for the twins. "Maybe you're right. You don't deserve her. Not until you can forgive yourself, and recognize the good person that's inside of you."

I watch her as she walks toward the house, with the twins wobbling in their puffy diapers on either side of her.

Brandon and Miles take Josie's spot beside me on the grass, wrapped in their towels.

"What're you guys talking about?" Miles asks.

I scratch the back of my neck. "Ah, just some grown-up stuff."

"Do you like Callie?" Brandon blurts.

This kid hears everything. "Why do you ask?"

He shrugs, plucking out blades of grass and tossing them. "She's sad, and you're sad. But when you're together, you're not sad."

The corners of my mouth tip upward. "You're an observant little shit."

Brandon grins. "Adults always think kids don't know what's going on."

"But we do," Miles says.

"Yeah, you probably know more than us grown-ups. Everything is simple when you're little. We mess it up as we get older."

Brandon fiddles with the edge of his towel. "Uncle Cole, can I ask you something, even though Mom told me not to?"

My spine straightens and I inhale a deep breath, bracing myself for the importance of this conversation. "Sure, kid. What's up?"

Miles chews his thumbnail, watching his older brother with wide eyes.

"Why did your baby die?"

Tightness constricts my lungs, and I want to get up and walk away. Avoid this conversation. Retreat like I always do. But this is a child, and he's asking to understand. I can't push him away.

I clear my throat. "I don't know. I ask myself that question every day. Sometimes things happen in life that we can't explain. We can't make sense of it."

"But she was just a baby." Miles' freckled nose scrunches, pushing his black-rimmed glasses up. "Was she sick?"

I shake my head. "No."

"That's really sad." Brandon hugs the towel tighter around his midsection. "Did you cry?"

I nod, swallowing around the lump in my throat. "Still do."

"Callie was gonna have a baby once," Miles says. "But now she doesn't have one. Does that mean her baby died too?"

"Yeah."

"Wow." He leans back on his elbows, staring up at the twilight sky, undoubtedly trying to wrap his head around the tragic mysteries of life.

"I think you should be Callie's boyfriend, Uncle Cole."

I lift an eyebrow at Brandon. "Oh, yeah?"

He nods. "She's a really nice person. And she doesn't treat us like all the other adults treat us. She's different."

Miles holds up his index finger. "And she always smells really good."

A chuckle bursts from my chest. "She does, doesn't she?"

"I'm serious," Brandon says. His dark eyebrows dip down. "You're not so angry when you're around her."

I don't think anybody could be angry around Callie.

"It's more complicated than that, little man." I reach over and ruffle his hair. "I'm sorry I haven't been the best uncle. I'm working on it."

"That's okay, Uncle Cole." Miles grins. "We still love you."

Warmth surges in my chest, rolling over me like a warm blanket. "I love you too."

Josie calls the boys inside, and they scramble to their feet.

Before he leaves, Brandon stands over me, gazing down with pensive eyes. "If you can work on being a better uncle, then you can work on being better with Callie too. I think you should try."

He's gone before I can respond, though I'm not sure I would've had anything to say to that.

The kid rendered me speechless.

Maybe he's right.

TWENTY-SEVEN

CALLIE

COLE HASN'T COME to the diner for lunch all week.

So I'm surprised to see him waiting with his back against the glass outside the diner when I arrive on Friday morning.

I feel foolish for going to the pool house the night we kissed, as if I were desperate and threw myself at him. I've tried to blame it on the wine I drank or the talk I had with Josie beforehand, but I know that, deep down, part of me *wanted* something to happen with Cole.

I can't deny it.

It's more than his handsome face. It goes deeper than his sexy, muscular body. Paul has all that on the outside too, and it proved meaningless in the end.

My attraction to Cole is because of our connection. It's in the way he sees who I truly am and doesn't want to stifle me. He encourages and supports me. He's helped me along my journey as I've come to the realization that I am capable and strong.

And as much as he hates to admit it, he's given me hope. Hope that there's life after loss. That I can find happiness after tragedy. That Paul hasn't destroyed my heart and that I can learn to love again.

Whatever happens between me and Cole, I'll always be grateful for him.

Now if only I could stop my brain from replaying the earth-shattering kiss every two seconds.

"It's a little early for lunch." I stop in front of him and slip my hands into my back pockets.

"This couldn't wait until lunch. I've been thinking about what you said all week. You're right. I'm scared. I'm scared of feeling this way about you. I shouldn't want you, but I can't stay away."

I swallow around the lump in my throat. "Why shouldn't you want me? Why is it so wrong to feel happy?"

He squeezes his eyes closed as if he can shut out my words. "Because I don't deserve it. I know I don't."

"Why don't you let me be the judge of that? I'm a grown woman, Cole. And I'm scared too. I've been through hell. But I want to give this a chance. I want to enjoy what we have and see where it goes. We can live in the moment—together."

He hums, touching his forehead to mine. "I want to try. You make me want to try."

Then he presses his lips to mine.

My hands fist in his ratty, stained T-shirt, and I lift onto the balls of my feet to gain better access to his mouth. We kiss as if we haven't seen each other in months, urgent and insistent.

Someone passes us on the sidewalk and clears their throat. Cole and I break apart, smiling, our cheeks tinged with pink.

I don't say anything more because I don't want to spoil the moment.

But whether he wants to admit it or not, Cole has found hope.

"Hello. Anybody home?"

My shoulders jerk at the sound of Gertie's voice.

She clicks her tongue and pushes me aside, snatching the spatula from my hand. "You're burning the eggs, sugar."

I glance down at the griddle, and sure enough, the over-easy eggs are over-charred.

"I'm sorry, Gertie."

"Don't be sorry. Just tell me what's going on in that pretty little head of yours that has you in a fog all week."

I lean against the stainless-steel countertop and toss my hairnet into the garbage can. "I'm fine, Gertie. I'm just in my head a lot lately. Wondering if I'll ever find love again. Wondering when it's okay to start dating."

"And does this *wondering* have anything to do with why Cole hasn't been here these past few days?"

I close my eyes and roll my lips together before blurting out the words, "I kissed Cole last Saturday."

Her eyes go wide, and she clutches her chest.

"I know, I know. I'm just as shocked as you are. But—" My words are cut off when I realize that Gertie isn't holding herself in surprise.

She's gripping herself in pain.

I rush toward her as she slumps forward. "Gertie, oh my God. What's wrong? What's happening?"

She lets out constricted gasps of pain, and it's then that I realize she's touching the left side of her chest.

"Help!" I yell as loud as I can, hoping one of the waiters hears me from the dining room.

I lower Gertie to the floor, propping her against the oven door as I dig my hand into my apron for my cell.

Please be okay, Gertie.

Two of the waiters burst through the kitchen door.

"Oh my God!" Ashley drops to her knees beside us. "What happened?"

"I think she's having a heart attack. I'm calling for an ambulance." I press my phone to my ear. "Do either of you have aspirin?"

Ashley shakes her head, eyes frantic.

"I'll go ask the customers if they have anything," Sarah says, running out of the kitchen.

I hold Gertie in my arms while we wait for an ambulance. Sarah quickly returns with a small white pill and a glass of water.

I slip the pill into Gertie's mouth and tip her head back so the water doesn't spill out. "Try to swallow this. It's going to help."

She chokes and sputters, but the water washes the pill down her throat.

"It's going to be okay, Gertie," I whisper. "I've got you. You're going to be okay."

I just wish I knew that for a fact.

IN THE WAITING ROOM, I attempt to fill out paperwork to keep myself occupied, but I don't know any of Gertie's information. The only people she has are the people who come to her diner.

Tears continue to spill down my cheeks while I wait, imagining the worst-case scenarios.

What if she dies?

What if she doesn't die but has severe brain damage?

What if she's a vegetable for the rest of her life?

What if I wasn't quick enough to call for help?

"Callie!"

I spin around to find Cole running through the sliding glass door. Scrambling to my feet, I meet him halfway and collapse in his arms.

"Are you okay?" He buries his nose in my hair and breathes in deep.

"Gertie had a heart attack. What if she dies, Cole? I don't want her to die."

Cole's arms tighten around me. "Shh, it's okay. We don't know that Gertie's going to die."

"I don't know her social security number. I don't know if she has health insurance. I don't even know if she has family. Isn't that awful? I should know these things."

He cups my face and tilts it up. "None of that is important right now. We'll figure it all out later. Let's just wait and see what the doctor says."

I nod, my chin trembling as I fight to stop crying.

Cole's thumb brushes my tears away. "When I got your message to meet you at the hospital, I thought something happened to *you*. For that split second, my heart stopped, and all I could think about was you not being here." He swallows, struggling to push the words out. "On this earth."

My chest aches, and I touch my palm to his cheek.

"I panicked," he continues. "And even though I knew it was Gertie, I kept imagining it was you. It felt like I was rushing here to find *you* in that hospital bed. It threw me for a loop. Made me realize that I'm in this a lot deeper than I thought I was."

What does that mean?

I want to ask, but I know it's not the right time or place. "I'm sorry you thought it was me, Cole. I'm here. I'm not going anywhere."

His eyes plead with me to understand. "But you can be gone in an instant."

He's right. But does that mean it isn't worth it to try? To have something great for a little while rather than have nothing at all?

I'm about to speak when a doctor emerges from the double doors and calls my name. "Mrs. Kingston?"

"Yes." I turn and reach for Cole's hand.

The doctor gestures to the chairs nearby. "Please have a seat."

My stomach churns, and Cole's hand squeezes mine tighter as we walk across the room.

Please let her be all right.

"I'm Dr. Fuller," he says once we're seated. "Miss May is stable."

"Oh, thank God." A relieved breath rushes out of me. "Will she be okay?"

"She suffered a heart attack, so it's a good thing you got her here as soon as you did. This will take a toll on her physically, due to her age, but with a change in diet and some medications, she should make a full recovery."

I bury my face in my hands as the tears overflow.

"Is she awake?" Cole asks. "Can we see her?"

"She's resting now. I can have one of the nurses inform you when she wakes up."

I shake the doctor's outstretched hand as he stands. "Thank you so much."

After he walks away, Cole snakes his arm around me and rubs my back in soothing circles. "She's going to be so happy to see you here."

"I should call the girls at the diner and let them know. They'll be so relieved. We should have a *Welcome Back* party for Gertie when she gets home."

"That's a great idea. Is there anything I can get for you while you're on the phone? Coffee or snacks? You're probably starving."

"Sure. I'll eat anything."

He pushes to his feet, but my hand shoots out for his before he can walk away. "Thank you for coming."

Cole smiles, and it's the most beautiful thing I've ever seen. "I'll always be here when you need me, Callie."

Warmth pools in my chest at his words.

Is that a promise? Or is that just one of those things people say to make you feel better?

I guess it doesn't matter how he meant it because I know the way I *want* him to mean it.

I guess I'm in deeper than I realized, too.

After I make a few calls, Josie arrives. "I'm here! Sorry it took me so long. How's Gertie? Any word yet?"

"She had a heart attack, but she's okay. We're waiting for her to wake up so we can see her."

"That's great!" She glances around. "Did Cole get here yet?"

I nod. "He went to get some food."

"He almost shit a brick when he thought you were in the hospital."

I grimace. "He told me."

"He cares about you, Cal. He's just so damn scared to lose you. He thinks that if he keeps his distance, nothing bad will happen."

I lean forward. "Josie, what happened to him? He won't tell me, and I feel like I'd understand this whole puzzle if someone filled in the missing pieces."

She blows a stream of air through her lips. "I can't tell you if he isn't ready for you to know. Just be patient with him." She covers my hand with hers. "My mom used to say, *'When someone pushes you away, you need to find the strength to hold on tighter.'* I think that's what Cole needs you to do. Don't let him push you away. You're the only one who can get through to him."

My lips tug downward. "I'm sorry I asked. I shouldn't put you in the middle like that."

"It's okay," she says. "You're my best friend. I want to tell you. But I think you need to hear it from him. It'll mean more."

I agree.

But will Cole ever fully open up to me?

Cole comes back with snacks, and the three of us chat while we wait. A little while later, a nurse comes out to tell us that Gertie is awake. Cole stays with Josie so she isn't alone while I go back first.

As soon as I lay my eyes on her in the hospital bed, I start crying all over again.

"Come here, sugar," she says. "Don't waste those tears on me. I'm all right."

I drag a chair to the bedside and clasp her hand in mine. "You scared me, Gertie! Don't ever do that to me again."

She gives my hand a weak squeeze. "I'm not ready to go just yet. Don't you worry."

I lift an eyebrow. "Oh, no? What are you waiting for then?"

"Well, first, I have to tell you everything I have planned for you."

"Me? What are you talking about?"

"I want to give you the diner."

My head jerks back. "What? No. You can't do that. The diner is yours. That's crazy."

She waves a feeble hand over her body. "Look at me. Does it look like I'm in any shape to run a business?"

"But you'll get better. The doctor said he'll give you medicine that will help, and you'll change your diet. You'll be good as new before you know it."

She shakes her head. "You're not hearing me, sugar. I've been thinking about this for a while now. Since you started working for me. The heart attack just proved my point."

"You could sell the diner to someone. You'd probably make a lot of money."

"Callie, look at me and hear me when I tell you: I want to give the diner to you. There's no one else I'd want to run it, and I know you'll take good care of it when I'm gone."

A pang stabs through my heart. "Don't say that."

"It's true."

I smooth my hand over her wiry hair. "Fine. Let's just focus on getting you healthy first."

She scoffs. "If these quacks think I'm eating kale, they can kiss my ass."

I bite back a smile. "You don't have to eat kale, Gertie. But you need to lower your cholesterol. I did some research while I was in the waiting room, and I have a plan. I'm going to take care of you."

"You're always so busy taking care of everyone else." She touches her hand to my cheek. "Who's going to take care of you?"

"I am."

My head snaps up to the doorway where Cole is standing.

Gertie smiles. "I knew you would."

He smirks as he walks into the room. "You gave us quite the scare, Gertie."

"I'm old. Why is everyone so surprised that I had a heart attack? It's what old people do."

"Not if you're healthy, it doesn't," Cole says.

Gertie crosses her arms over her chest. "Well, I'm not eating kale."

I look up at Cole with a smile. "The doctor told her she needs to eat healthier, so she thinks we're going to make her eat kale."

He leans his hands onto the back of my chair. "You're going to eat whatever it takes to make sure you stick around for a lot longer. You have people here who love you, and we're not ready for you to leave us. So do what the doctor says."

Gertie's eyes suddenly well. "I never had kids, you know. Always wanted them, but it never happened. Wasn't in the cards, I suppose. It used to scare me to think about what would happen to me when I got older. Didn't think I'd have anybody by my side in the end."

I swipe a fallen tear from her cheek. "You'll never be alone. You have us, Gertie."

She reaches for my hand, then Cole's. She places one on top of the other and wraps hers around ours. "And you two have each other. Love is the most important thing. Nothing else matters in this world. Don't let any other bullshit get in your way. Do you understand?"

Cole and I nod.

"Now, I'm tired. You two go home and get some rest. Just don't forget to come and get me out of this place in the morning."

We say goodbye, and then Cole, Josie, and I drive home.

After showering the day off of me, I curl up in bed. Everything Gertie said consumes my thoughts as I stare up at the ceiling.

My phone buzzes on the nightstand beside me.

Cole: You up?
    Me: Yes. Can't sleep.
    Cole: Me either. Wishing you were lying here with me.

MY HEART SKIPS A BEAT.
    Is he asking me to go over there?

Cole: Yes, I'm asking you to come here.

A SMILE BREAKS across my face, and I make my way out to the pool house.

Cole's waiting by the open door when I walk in. "Hi."

"Hi." I fidget with the hem of my tank top, doing my best not to gawk at his bare upper body.

He inches toward me, and my heart thumps faster with every step. "Been thinking about you all day."

"So have I."

"Oh, yeah? What about?"

"Why do you keep saying that you don't deserve me, Cole?" I need an explanation. Need more than what he's willing to give me.

His eyes tighten. "I did something unforgivable, and I have to suffer the consequences."

Every word he chokes out looks like it causes him physical pain, as if his words are acid on his tongue.

I edge closer. "What is it you think you did, Cole?"

He shakes his head. "You wouldn't look at me the same if you knew. You wouldn't be here right now."

"That's my choice to make. And whatever you've done, you've clearly paid the price. You've suffered enough."

He barks out a bitter laugh. "I'll never be done paying that price. It doesn't just go away."

I place my palms on his chest, my eyes begging him to open up to me. "Please, Cole. I want to know you. The good and the bad. You've seen my ugly. Let me see yours."

He trails his fingers down my arms. "I'm not ready to lose you to my ghosts yet. Can't we just pretend for a little longer?"

So close, yet so far.

"If you're not ready to tell me, then I can't force you. But you're the one who told me that every moment in life is fleeting. So, why should we spend it agonizing over the what-ifs? I've been crippled with anxiety for way too long, and I don't want to worry anymore. I don't want to waste any more time. I want to *live*. We can forgive ourselves for our mistakes, and we can move forward. We have the power. It's up to us. We can enjoy however much life we have left. Don't you think it's time?"

Cole's eyes glisten with adoration as he gazes down at me. "My Courageous Callie."

He brushes his thumb over my lips, and goosebumps skate along my skin.

Then he takes my hand and leads me to his bed. His sheets smell like him, clean and masculine, and I breathe him in.

We spend the night curled around each other, arms and legs entwined, blanketed by silence.

And my ears strain to hear the things Cole isn't telling me.

TWENTY-EIGHT

COLE

I WAKE up as the sun's rays peek through the windows.

Though it's mid-October, I can't tell by the weather. It's like I'm stuck in some dimension of *Pleasantville* with perfect weather, where it's always sunny. It makes me miss New York. The change of season always brought vibrant colors to the trees and a crisp breeze to the air. It smelled like football and pumpkin spice. Autumn, real and true.

I came to California because it's New York's polar opposite, in distance and in spirit. Plus, I had a free place to stay at my sister's. It was supposed to be temporary. I never imagined I'd want to stay.

But watching Callie Kingston as she sleeps mere inches from me —the rise and fall of her chest as she breathes, the little contented sounds that escape her parted lips, her golden hair fanned out on the pillow—it gives me a reason to stay.

She gives me a reason.

To stay, to live, to dream, to hope.

And it terrifies me.

It feels like I'm torn in two. Half of me is still in New York, still stuck inside Mia's nursery on that tragic night. I'm in hell, and this is my punishment to suffer for all of eternity, Callie dangled above me like my salvation, close enough I can almost taste it but just out of reach. Like she was sent to me as a reminder of what I can never have.

Or maybe she truly *is* my salvation. Maybe I'm getting a second chance. The other half of me wants to freefall into this feeling, to believe that Callie and I can actually be together, that two lost souls can start over and heal each other. I want to give Callie the love she deserves. Show her how she should be treated so that she'll never accept anything less ever again.

I just don't know what's left of me to give.

Callie's eyes flutter open. Her hand slides across the mattress and slips into my hair. "How long have you been up?"

"Just a few minutes."

"How did you sleep?"

"It's the first time I've slept through the night in a long time."

She hums and scoots closer to me, pressing her lips to my chest.

"I wish we could stay here all day," I whisper against her hair.

"Me too."

I glance at the cable box across the room. "I have to leave for work in twenty minutes. What time are you going to visit Gertie?"

She stifles a yawn. "I'll leave when you do. Not sure when they'll discharge her, but I want to be there before that."

"If you're still there at noon, I can stop by on my lunch break."

I feel her smile against my skin. "She'd love that."

"And maybe once Gertie is settled and everything calms down in a few days, I can take you out to dinner."

She peers up at me from under sleepy lids. "Like on a date?"

My heart beats like a bass drum. "Yes. If you'd like to."

She nods and places a gentle kiss on my cheek. "I'd love that."

Then I feel it zing through me.

Something I haven't felt in years.

Something I never expected to feel again.

Excitement.

Anticipation.

The start of something new.

THE DAYS LEADING up to our date, I don't see much of Callie.

She's been running the diner in Gertie's absence. She's also been staying with Gertie, cooking for her, keeping her company, and helping her get back on her feet. And she does it all with a smile on her face, like it's her mission in life to help everyone she can.

That's just Callie.

She's good and pure. An angel without the wings.

And I'm the dumb bastard who's foolish enough to think he could ever be worthy of her.

On Friday evening, Josie catches me in the backyard as I'm leaving.

She whistles as she surveys me. "You clean up nice. Got a hot date?"

I chuckle as I look down at my pale-blue polo shirt and dark jeans. "I do. Is this outfit acceptable for a date out on the town in California?"

"Depends where you're taking her."

"The Lakefront Tap Room?"

An approving smile spreads across her face. "Yes. Your outfit is perfect. She's going to love that lakefront view."

I nod. "Good."

"Wait." She puts her hands on her hips. "You are talking about Callie, right? Because if you're taking some other chick on a date, I will stab you with this steak knife."

The little brother in me wants to fuck with her, but I don't want to show up to my date with blood stains on my clothes.

"Of course it's Callie." I shake my head. "Who else would it be?"

She holds her hands up on either side of her head. "Just check-ing." Then she smiles. "I'm proud of you, baby brother."

I smirk and wave goodbye as I continue through the yard.

I stop at the florist, and then I'm on my way to Gertie's.

When I arrive, Gertie greets me at the door. "Well, look at you. Aren't you a sight for sore eyes?"

I bend down and wrap her in a hug. "I was about to say the same thing to you."

She swats me away. "Callie, get your ass out here. Your date is trying to hit on me."

I grin as I take a seat on the edge of her worn couch. "How've you been feeling?"

"I'm fine." She scoots closer to me and leans in. "But I want to talk about you. How are *you* feeling?"

My eyebrows draw together. "I'm fine. Did you hear that I was sick or something?"

"No, no. I'm asking how you feel about tonight. About Callie."

"Ah." I set the flowers gently on the floor and rest my elbows on my knees. "I don't know, Gertie. Don't know what I'm doing."

She nods like she understands. "You've convinced yourself that you don't deserve to be happy. It's hard to believe in the realization that you do. But you've been in your own living hell for a while now. It's time to move outta there."

"I think hell is where I belong. I don't deserve an angel like Callie."

"Nonsense," she spits. "Let me tell you something. If you believe in heaven and hell, then you have to believe in purgatory. Do you know anything about that?"

"Isn't that where people go after they die?"

She points her index finger at me. "It's where souls go to get purified before they enter heaven. We're washed of our sins, and then God accepts us with forgiveness."

I lift an eyebrow. "So then how do you know who goes to heaven and who goes to hell?"

"That's up to the sinner, whether he's truly sorry for his sins. And I can tell you're truly sorry, Cole. I can see the shame and sorrow. You wear it like a backpack full of bricks, letting it weigh you down. But you don't belong in hell. God knows that. That's why you're in purgatory. You're finding your way out of the darkness, preparing to be cleansed of your sins. Callie is your angel."

Something I once heard in my religious instruction class as a kid comes to the forefront of my mind. "Hey, Gertie. Can I ask you something?"

"Of course, sugar."

"Where do babies go when they die ... if they aren't old enough to be baptized?"

Her jaw goes slack for a moment, recognition flashing in her eyes. "Oh, Cole. Is that what happened to you?"

My jaw clenches. "Where do they go, Gertie?"

"Do you honestly believe your baby could go anywhere but heaven?"

I stare down at the floor so I don't have to see the pity in her eyes. "None of us knows what happens when we die."

"No, we don't, sugar." She glances into the hallway when she hears a door creak open. "Does Callie know what you've lost?"

I shake my head.

"Tell her, Cole." She grasps my hand and squeezes it tight. "Let that angel cleanse you. Follow her out of the darkness and find peace."

Callie's heels clack against the wood floor, and my heart stalls out when she steps into the living room.

For the past week, I've been asking God for a sign. Something that would tell me what I should do—be with Callie or leave this town and never look back. And now, after all this talk of heaven and hell, angels and demons, Callie stands before me in a white strapless dress. Form-fitting with a slit that hits mid-thigh, the soft material hugs her curves and flows out at the bottom around her ankles. Her blond hair shimmers as it falls in loose waves around her shoulders. She radiates natural beauty and kindness.

She is the embodiment of an ethereal being. An angel. And she just might be the sign I've been looking for.

"Look at him," Gertie says with a cackle. "You've stunned him into silence."

Redness creeps into Callie's cheeks. "I hope this is okay for where we're going. You know, since you refuse to tell me."

I lift the bouquet of blue irises from the floor and hand them to

Callie, searching for the right words to say. "I asked the florist which flowers symbolize hope."

Her lips part in surprise. "I love them. Thank you."

"You two have fun," Gertie says. "And I'm locking your ass out tonight, so don't even try coming back here after."

Callie's eyes widen. "Gertie!"

She shrugs. "I'm living vicariously through you, sugar. So, go out and get me some."

Callie's hand clamps over her mouth, and I throw my head back and laugh. I shoot her a wink. "I got you, Gertie."

"I cannot believe she said that," Callie says as we make our way out the door.

Her feet freeze, and she points to the shiny silver Jeep parked out front. "Is that yours?"

"Did you think I was going to take you on a date in my landscaper truck?"

She laughs. "I honestly didn't think about it. I was happy just to be going out to dinner with you."

I spin her around and pull her against me. "You look beautiful, Callie. You stole the breath right from my chest when you walked into the room."

"You look incredibly handsome." Her gaze drops to my lips. "Please don't make me wait until the end of the night to kiss you."

"I was going to be a gentleman."

She fists my collar and yanks me down toward her mouth. "Just be you, Cole."

I capture her lips, and we both let out sighs of relief. Her pouty, glossed lips taste like vanilla, and they feel like silk. The woman is a decadent dessert that I want to devour before we've had the first course.

With the way she's kissing me, we might not even make it to the damn restaurant.

I ease back and brush the pad of my thumb across her cheekbone. "What are the odds that Gertie's watching us from the window?"

Callie cranes her neck to look over my shoulder. "Yup. Just saw the curtains move."

I chuckle. "All right. Time to go."

On the drive to the restaurant, Callie tells me stories about what her week was like staying with Gertie. We laugh, and I keep her hand in mine for the entire ride. The mood is light and relaxed, and lightyears away from any of the horrors we've been through.

This is exactly the kind of night I want to give Callie.

Even if it's just for tonight.

Callie gasps when I pull into the parking lot. "I've always wanted to try this place! It's so beautiful and serene on the water."

"I figured you'd like it."

Her head tilts. "How do you know me so well?"

I shrug. "I'm technically a genius. Just ask Josie."

She swings her door open. "Oh, this story I've gotta hear."

The hostess brings us to our reserved table outside under string lights, with the moonlight glistening off the lake as our backdrop. We order drinks and appetizers to start while we look over the menu.

"Okay, genius." Callie slaps her menu closed. "Let's hear it."

"When Josie and I were in high school, our parents wanted to have a yard sale to get rid of some junk in the attic. While we were going through everything, we found this paperwork from a doctor that I'd seen when I was a kid. Apparently, I had a lot of energy, so Mom wanted to have me tested for ADD. In his report, the doctor mentioned how my IQ was above average and that I was a genius."

I lean back and fold my arms over my chest. "It took us a few minutes to realize that the report was for a child named Alexander Spotswood."

Callie's mouth drops open. "Your parents had someone else's report?"

I nod with a laugh. "Yup. All those years, they'd assumed I was exceptionally smart. They even bragged about it to a few of their friends. So, I always teased Josie, saying that I was the genius in the family."

Callie hunches forward with laughter. "That's hilarious. I wonder if Alexander Spotswood has your report."

"He's a genius, so he probably figured it out long before we did."

"I love how close you were to your parents. I was like that with my mom."

I take a swig of beer. "But not your father?"

She shakes her head. "He wasn't the nicest dad. But he wasn't the worst either, I suppose."

I reach across the table for her hand. "You always see the good in everyone."

"It's a defect."

"No, it's not. It proves what a genuine soul you have."

She smiles, hitting me with those spectacular emerald irises. "It's what helped me see who you are, underneath your gruff exterior."

I shake my head. "I don't know why you spoke to me again after the way I exploded on you the first day we met."

"I could tell that you were hurting. I saw it in your eyes. I wondered what could've happened to you that was so bad."

My thumb sweeps over the top of her hand. "I'm glad you gave me a second chance."

"And I'm glad you're giving us a chance. Tonight."

Us.

I thought I was destined to be alone for the rest of my life. Thought it was the consequence for what I did.

Now I'm part of an *us.*

"I still don't know if I'm doing the right thing, Callie. I'm still not sure I can be what you need. But I'm willing to try. The alternative—staying away from you—just isn't possible."

A tear slips free, and she swipes it away. "That's all I can ask of you, Cole. I don't know what I'm doing, either. But we have each other, and that's all we need."

I hope she's right.

After dinner, we take our leftovers back to the Jeep.

Before she gets in on the passenger side, I cup her face and tilt it up. "Am I taking you back to Gertie's, or do you want to come back to the pool house with me? No pressure either way."

She lifts onto her toes and brings her lips to my ear. "Take me to your place."

A shiver runs down my spine.

There's a small voice in my head telling me to stop here, saying, *Once you do this, you can never go back.*

But I ignore it and try to remain in the moment.

One night. That's all I want is one night free of guilt and suffering.

As soon as we get to the pool house, Callie drops her purse to the floor, and we're a frenzy of hands and lips. She opens her mouth and tangles her tongue with mine. I swallow her breathy moans, and the rumble sends vibrations down through every nerve ending in my body.

Greed knots in the pit of my stomach, the mounting need about to overflow. It's a sin to corrupt an angel. I shouldn't, but desire takes over, and I throw caution to the wind.

Callie's hands dip under my shirt, and her touch scorches my skin as they trail up my torso. I tear my shirt up and over my head, letting it fall by our feet. She takes a step back and lets her eyes feast on me for a moment.

"You're so beautiful," she murmurs.

I spin her around and bring my lips to her neck while I pull on the zipper at her back. She shudders as the fabric pools at her feet, leaving her in nothing but a strapless bra and white G-string panties.

I run my fingertips down her arms, interlacing our fingers for a brief moment. "You're the beautiful one, Callie. A perfect angel who looks like sin and temptation."

"I want you, Cole." Her voice is a trembling whisper. "I want your hands on me. I want you to touch me. I want to feel you."

It's now that I remember how much pain this woman has endured. The swollen eyes, the broken skin, the purple marks. This flawless, magnificent body has never been fully appreciated or respected.

I turn her until she's facing me. "Show me where he hurt you."

Her eyebrows pinch together, and disbelief twists her features. "What?"

"I want you to show me all the places you've ever been hurt, Callie. I want to erase every mark he's ever left on you, and I'm going to replace the old memories with a new one."

Her eyes glisten, and she shakes her head. "You don't have to do that."

I grip the back of her neck and bring her lips to mine. "Show me, Callie. Let me heal you."

Her hand trembles as she points to her eye, and I press a kiss to her soft lid. Her finger moves to her cheek next, the one I saw bruised from the back of that monster's hand. I press my lips to her cheekbone, and a salty tear meets me there.

She directs me to her neck, where his fingers once wrapped around, and I kiss her delicate skin again and again.

Callie leads me to every inch of bare skin on her body, places I knew he'd hurt her and the places he hurt her before I knew her.

I sink to my knees, worshiping her the way a goddess like her deserves. I kiss the small scars from her fibroid surgery.

Then, finally, she brings her finger to the last spot, hovering over her panties.

I sit back on my heels, looking up at her with uncertainty in my gaze.

She nods, and another tear falls.

I swallow around the emotion lodged in my throat like a boulder, trying to stay focused on the here and now. I hook my fingers into the flimsy strings on either side of her hips, and I drag the material down her legs.

I press a gentle kiss to Callie's most sensitive spot, and her legs quiver. My hands snake around to her ass and grip two overflowing handfuls. I groan as I lean in for another kiss, and another. I shower her with tender affection until her hips jut forward to meet me.

She fists my hair in her hands, begging for me. "Please, Cole."

I drag my tongue up her seam, inhaling her sweet scent, and she releases another moan. My eyes lock with hers, and her gaze never wavers. She watches me while I work my tongue, lapping up her arousal, bringing her closer to bliss. I reach up and unsnap the clasp on her bra, releasing the most glorious breasts I've ever seen.

Full and round, I squeeze them as she arches her back, serving them up to me, and my thumb draws a circle around a rosy nipple.

She lifts her leg and drapes it over my shoulder, opening herself up wider for me, and I let out a deprived growl. I slip a finger inside of her, encircling her clit with my tongue at the same time.

"Oh God, Cole. Yes. Please, yes."

And then my beautiful Callie comes undone. She shivers as wave after wave consumes her, pressing my face against her core and holding me where she needs me.

Her body goes slack, and I stand to bear her weight, cradling her in my arms.

"Cole," she whimpers against my chest.

"I'm here, Callie. I've got you."

Her fingers snake between us to make quick work of my zipper, and she pushes my pants down to my ankles. She palms me through my boxer-briefs and pulls my mouth down to hers, kissing me passionately.

My manic heart hammers in my chest, and I'm unable to contain the excitement that's been pulsating between my legs. I shove my boxers down, and my dick springs free, straining for Callie like it knows where it belongs.

I relish the gasp that tears from her parted lips as she sets her hungry gaze on me. She takes me into her hand and gives me a few pumps before lowering herself onto the mattress behind her.

I stroke myself while I watch her lie back and spread her legs, certain that I've never seen anything sexier. I crawl on top of her, and we kiss while I rock back and forth over her wetness. Her legs wrap around my waist, and she claws at my back, moaning, begging me for nonsensical things.

I'm right there with her.

Totally gone for this woman who obliterated any semblance of control I'd clung to.

It's clear now; I lost control the second she walked into Josie's backyard.

Our eyes lock, and I try to convey everything I can't bring myself to let pass through my lips.

You, Callie.

It's you.

You're all I want.

I reach for the box of condoms I'd bought earlier today and roll one over my length. Callie aligns us, lifting her pelvis, and when I push myself inside her, the dam breaks.

Emotion gushes free, bringing with it the muck and sludge from the very bottom of my depths. The parts of me that I've kept hidden for so long, the parts I'm ashamed to allow to be seen, the guilt and the hatred and the rage.

Callie opens Pandora's box and sets my soul free.

She meets me thrust for lustdrunk thrust, and we kiss as if our lives depend on it.

Right now, it feels like they do.

She's warm and tight—so tight—around me, and I lose myself in the maddening rhythm as I drive into her over and over again.

"I've had it wrong, Callie. This whole time I thought you needed a savior, and I knew I couldn't be that man. But I see it so clearly now. You're *my* savior. My angel. My redemption."

"And you're my hope." She grips my face, and our gazes entangle. "Give me everything, Cole. I want all of you."

She grips onto my ass and pushes me deeper, begging for more. "Let go. Please. Let go."

I want to so badly, to release my hold on the past. To fall. To forget. To leave it all behind and start anew. Want it so badly I can taste it. My soul is tired, and I have no will left.

So, I take the advice of my wise, old friend, and I let this beautiful angel guide me out of the darkness.

I hike her legs up, pressing her knees to her chest, and I plunge deeper, harder, faster.

"Oh my God, yes," she whimpers.

Callie comes, crying out as the waves of pleasure rack her body, and I follow, holding her close as we go under. We become one, moaning and gasping, completely lost in the moment, lost in each other. I kiss her mad, and I can't tell if it's her tears or mine soaking our skin. Maybe it's both.

And the remaining pieces of my heart splinter off and wash away with the flood.

TWENTY-NINE

CALLIE

My body jolts awake.

My hands are frantic as they reach out across the sheets for fear he isn't here, that it was all just a dream.

But Cole's warm, smooth skin is at my fingertips, a mere breath away.

"You want more already?" he grunts, his voice hoarse from sleep. "You're insatiable, woman."

I smile. "Just checking to make sure you're still here."

"Told you I'm not going anywhere." He pulls me into him, and our legs interlock. "Is that what has you up so early?"

I hum as his feather-light fingertips trail down my back, leaving goosebumps in their wake. His presence comforts me, as do his words, but the questions still swarm my mind, anxiety circling like a shark who smells blood in the water.

What does this mean for us?

Am I moving too quickly?

Does he regret this?

When will he open up about his past?

Will he ever let me all the way in?

I don't want to be *that* woman who asks a man to define their relationship after one night together, yet I can't help but wonder.

"My head is spinning. Last night ... last night was ..."

"I know, Callie. I know."

"You felt it too?"

"I was right there with you." His lips brush against my forehead. "Still am."

I gaze into his steel eyes. "This doesn't feel real. Three months ago, I was living a different life."

"I'm so glad you're not in that life anymore."

I prop myself up onto my elbow. "What was your old life like? Back in New York, before everything went bad."

I feel him start to slink back inside himself, signaling for the guards to raise the drawbridge, preventing me from finding a way to reach him.

"It doesn't matter."

I press my palm to his chest, over his heart, as if I could reach in and cradle it in my hand like an injured bird. "It does matter, Cole. It's a part of you. I want to know you."

He shakes his head. "You don't want to know *that.*"

"What are you so afraid of? Why won't you just tell me?"

His thumb skates over my cheek, my jaw, my lips. "Don't you see, Callie? It's you who should be afraid. I'm not this wonderful man you think I am. I keep trying to tell you, but you won't listen."

"I won't listen to you because you're wrong." I swing my leg over him, straddling his waist until I'm hovering above him, my hair falling around his face so that I'm the only thing he can see. "Whatever you've done in your life, whatever mistakes you've made, it has led you to this very moment. It has turned you into the man I know."

I take his hand and place his palm to my cheek. "You're the man who sees me. Who hears me. Who believes in me."

I take his other hand and flatten it over my heartbeat. "You're the man who makes me feel."

I roll my hips against his hardening length. "You make me want."

Grief and anguish twist his features, mixing with adoration and desire emanating from his eyes. "You make me feel like I deserve a second chance," he whispers.

"You do. We all do. Even the worst of us. If you're truly sorry, and you want to make things right, then you can have that second chance."

His hand moves from my face to the back of my neck, and he draws me down to him, kissing me softly. "What if I can't make things right? What if I don't get a do-over after what I did?"

Dread tightens my stomach as I try to make sense of what that might mean.

"I didn't mean to, Callie. I didn't fucking mean for it to happen. But the responsibility was mine. The blame lies with me."

I pepper his beautiful face with kisses, desperate to heal him in any way I can. "If you didn't mean to, then it was an accident. And accidents happen, even the most tragic ones. You can't banish yourself to a life of misery and isolation. Whoever you hurt wouldn't want that for you."

A lone tear slides down over the contours of his face, dropping onto the pillow. "All she wanted was me. I let her down."

She.

Penny, his ex-wife?

Someone else?

A child?

"Who, Cole? Who did you let down?"

His eyes squeeze shut as he brings our foreheads together, and he whispers the softest sound. "My daughter."

I choke back a gasp, trying to keep the horror from flashing across my face. I don't press him for more. I won't. He's already given me more than he can handle.

Instead, I wrap my arms around him, burying my face in the crook of his neck, suctioning our bodies together. I hold onto him as tightly as I can, showing him that I'm here, I'm staying. That I'll hold all of his broken pieces and put him back together.

If only he'll let me.

~

THE FOLLOWING weeks all mesh together.

Long days on my feet in the diner, making sure everything's running smoothly.

Evenings at Gertie's, making sure she's taking her medications and eating the healthy foods I've been cooking for her.

Nights spent tangled in the sheets with Cole.

I'm exhausted, running on fumes from the lack of sleep. But I wouldn't trade these nights for the world.

Each night, I arrive at the pool house, our clothes come off, and we're reaching for each other. I wonder if it'll always be this way with Cole, and why it wasn't this way with anyone before him.

Maybe it's because I'm finally the person I want to be. I say what I feel, I do what makes me happy, and I'm surrounded by loving and supportive people.

I no longer live in fear.

I'm free.

The sadness of not being able to have a family of my own will always lurk in the dark corners of my mind. There will always be days when I'll see a woman and her baby and yearn for what I'll never have. There'll always be nights I cry into my pillow after playing with Josie's kids. Birthdays, and holidays, and gatherings of any kind will serve as reminders.

I may never be a mother, and I need to learn how to accept that.

Everyone's waiting for me when I walk into Josie's house.

Brandon and Miles jump on me when I enter the living room.

"Callie, you're on my team with Dad." Brandon takes my hand and drags me toward the couch.

I lift an eyebrow at Cole, who's grinning at me from the recliner. "The Luciano siblings on the same team? That doesn't sound very fair to me."

Dan chuckles. "I'm an expert at *Pictionary*. You're in good hands on my team."

Brandon covers his mouth so his father can't see his lips. "Dad is the worst artist in the history of mankind."

"Lower your voice next time," Josie says. "Your hand isn't soundproof."

Cole stands and wraps his arms around my waist. "Are you hungry? I can make you a plate."

I shake my head and stretch up onto my toes, pressing a chaste kiss on his lips. "I ate at the diner. How was your day?"

"Good. Missed you, though."

Gagging noises sound throughout the room, and my cheeks burn. I toss a pillow at Josie, hitting my target on the side of her head.

"You're kissing my brother, and it's making me nauseous."

I roll my eyes and lower myself onto the floor next to my teammates. "All right. Let's get this party started."

"Dad's up first," Miles says, handing him the deck of cards.

Dan selects a card from the top of the pile, stares at it for a moment, and then nods. "Set the timer. I'm ready."

I bite my lip to keep from laughing. These people take Family Fun Night to an extreme level.

Dan begins to draw, and it becomes evident that Brandon was right. Our heads tilt as we try to make out what Dan's drawing.

"Is it a skateboard?"

Dan shakes his head.

"A hot dog?"

"A worm?"

He keeps pointing to the log-like picture he drew, but it's not helping.

Brandon thrusts his hands through his hair. "Dad, stop tapping on the picture and draw something else!"

Buzz.

"Damnit!" Dan flings the marker across the room.

"Dan, what the heck was it?" I ask.

"A unicorn!"

A laugh bursts from my throat, and I clamp my hand over my mouth.

Josie's face is priceless. "A unicorn has four legs. What you drew looks like a slug."

"Whatever." He slumps onto the couch and crosses his arms over his chest.

I pat his knee. "It's okay. We'll get it next time."

"Yeah," Brandon mutters. "Just keep him away from the marker."

Cole is laughing so hard there are tears spilling out of his eyes. His smile lights up his entire face, and it's a sight I don't think I'll ever get used to.

Over the past few months, I've changed, but so has he. The angry, closed-off stranger gave way to the sweet man who's holding on to hope. Heartache and regret still haunt him, and I think they always will, but it doesn't hold him back anymore.

He catches me staring and leans down. "What?"

I thread my fingers through his hair and press my lips to his cheek. "You're beautiful when you smile."

"That's because I'm around you."

Warmth pools in my chest, slow yet overwhelming, like a molten river. I know I'm going under. Know where this is leading. And for once, I'm not scared. I don't care about timeframes or people's opinions or guilt.

For once, I just want to be.

Josie, Cole, and Miles win Family Fun Night by a landslide. Poor Dan may never recover. I help Josie clean up, say goodnight to the kids, and then follow Cole to the pool house.

"I cannot wait to shower the smell of grease and ketchup off of me," I say, hanging my jacket on the hook by the door.

Cole hoists me up and tosses me over his shoulder. "I'd love to do the honors."

I squeal and belly-laugh until he sets me down on the tile in the bathroom. With hooded eyes, he gazes at me, pulling the hem of my shirt up painfully slow. He drops it to the floor and falls to his knees, sliding my jeans down at the same maddening rate. He stays there after I step each leg out of my pants and pulls my panties to the side, dragging his tongue over my already drenched folds.

He inhales deep, letting his eyes close, and confessions begin tumbling from his lips like he's intoxicated.

"You're everything to me, Callie."

"Need you like the air I breathe."

"My angel."

"So goddamn sexy."

"Want to keep you."

I hum and moan while my legs tremble, unable to stand his soft, teasing licks a second longer. I yank him up by his hair and make quick work of his pants, shucking his boxers at the same time. He tears his T-shirt over his head, and finally, he's standing before me in all his naked glory.

Hard ridges and deep contours.

Strong and bold.

A dark intensity radiating from his eyes, looking at me as if I'm the only thing he can see.

My heart is a stampede, thundering in my chest as Cole takes my face in his strong hands.

"I love you, Callie," he whispers against my lips. "I've been falling since the day we met, and I don't know how to stop."

Please don't ever stop.

He engulfs me in his embrace, gripping me like I'll float away if he doesn't. "I'm terrified of this. Of us. You fill me with hope, with possibility. And I don't deserve it; I don't deserve *you*, but I can't let you go. I can't go back to a life without you. You make everything better."

Then, the storm that wrecked my heart for so many years finally lifts. The wind dies down. The ominous clouds clear and give way to bright, blue skies. The pain and suffering rolls back out to sea.

Amidst the rubble, my soul rebuilds.

Emotion strangles me. "I love you too, Cole."

Disbelief flashes across his face, as if he can't trust what his ears just heard, and then our lips collide. Fused together, we stumble into the shower. He twists the lever to hot, and steam fills the stall.

Cole takes his time, lathering me with soap, smoothing his hands over my skin in the most sensual way, with such care.

When we're both clean, he takes me to bed, and we make love into the late hours of the night.

And his words hammer into me with every thrust.

"I love you."

"I love you."

"I love you."

When dawn breaks, we lie together, blissfully sated.

And we are loved.

THIRTY

COLE

"AM I BORING YOU, SWEETHEART?" Billy asks.

Callie smiles. "I'm so sorry. I'm exhausted. Feels like I can barely keep my eyes open these days."

Billy elbows me in the ribs. "Bet I know who's keeping you up at night."

Her cheeks tinge with embarrassment, but she flashes me a devilish smirk before returning to the kitchen.

"Man, I never thought I'd see the day." Billy shakes his head and sits back against the stool.

"Neither did I."

He claps me on the back. "I'm happy for you. Jealous, but happy."

I chuckle, and my chest swells with pride.

The bell above the door jingles, and Gertie walks in. She stops and closes her eyes, raising her nose and inhaling deep. "Smells like home."

"There's my favorite girl," Billy says, standing. He wraps her in a hug and rocks her back and forth. "How are you feeling?"

"Like shit."

I wipe the corners of my mouth with my napkin and stand to give her a hug. "The place isn't the same without you here."

"Well, get used to it because it's not going to be mine for much longer. The lawyer is drawing up the business transfer paperwork as we speak."

"Callie is so excited to be taking over." I squeeze Gertie's frail hand. "This means the world to her."

"That girl is the only thing that keeps me going. Don't know what I'd do without her."

Me either, Gertie. Me either.

Love courses through me. I never expected I'd feel this way again. Never wanted to. I fought like hell against it, but some things are inevitable. Falling in love with Callie was impossible not to do.

Preordained.

Unavoidable.

Penny was my first love, and it was beautiful while it lasted. But life had other plans for us. Wretched, unfathomable plans that neither of us could've survived. I don't blame her for cheating on me. We were broken. Ripped to shreds by sorrow. She tried to replace the debilitating feeling with something else, while I looked to bury it.

Loving Callie doesn't erase what happened. It doesn't lessen the pain from the loss of my daughter.

My precious Mia.

She's a wound that'll never heal.

I'll never move on from her, but I'm learning to move forward with my life. One day at a time, little by little, the confines of guilt lessen their hold.

After work, Callie meets with her lawyer. The divorce is close to getting finalized, and I know how much she's looking forward to closing that chapter in her life. As long as Paul doesn't fight her for Maverick, it'll all be over soon. She misses that dog like crazy, and I'm not sure how she'd handle it if she lost him to that monster.

She's been mentally and physically drained lately, burning the candle at both ends. She bolts around, taking care of everyone like a damn superhero, and she forgets to take care of herself.

Which is why I've set up a homemade dinner with a bottle of her favorite wine. Candles and low music fill the pool house. I plan on rubbing her sore feet and letting her fall asleep on my chest so she can get a full night's rest.

If we can keep our hands off each other.

I head over to Josie's house while I wait for Callie to arrive. I promised the boys I'd toss the football around with them, so we play catch in the front yard.

"Uncle Cole, are you and Callie going to get married?" Miles asks.

I smirk. "Not sure, bud."

"If you do, can I be your best man?" Brandon asks.

Miles pouts. "No, I want to be your best man!"

"How about you can both be my best men?"

The boys jump into the air, pumping their fists overhead.

I shake my head, but a smile tugs at my lips. It's too soon to be talking about a wedding, but fuck if my heart doesn't skip a beat at the thought of Callie walking down the aisle toward me in a white dress.

And my heart races at the thought of ripping her out of it at the end of the night.

Ten minutes later, Callie pulls into the driveway. The boys bum-rush her as they often do, yelling about how they're going to be the best men at our wedding.

Callie's eyebrows shoot up in surprise. "We're getting married?"

I lift her into my arms and twirl. "Apparently."

She laughs and shoves out of my hold. "Interesting. Think I'll need to get divorced before I'm allowed to remarry."

As if Callie just summoned him from across the street, Paul walks out of his house with Maverick on his leash.

The smile falls from Callie's face, and her eyes go wide at the sight of her dog.

Paul ignores us, keeping his head down, but Maverick has other plans. His keen nose sniffs Callie out, and the second he spots her, he takes off. The leash slips out of Paul's unexpecting hand, and Maverick bolts into the street.

I should see it coming, should hear the engine rumbling louder from just up the block, barreling toward us. I'm not focused on it, and I don't realize before it's too late.

But Callie does, and she sprints into the street.

And my heart drops to the ground, my feet frozen where I stand.

"Callie, no!" Brandon's voice sounds muffled, and I don't hear much over the deafening sound of blood pounding in my ears.

Until the tires screech against the pavement.

Callie's body envelops Maverick, shielding him like the super-hero she is. A guardian angel sent to serve and protect.

My angel.

My angel.

The car swerves left and then right.

Terror clutches my throat, seizing my breath as I watch Callie heave Maverick out of harm's way—sacrificing herself instead.

A flash of blond hair tumbles up onto the hood of the offending car and then rolls off onto the ground in a heap.

My angel.

My angel.

Please don't leave me.

Please be okay.

THIRTY-ONE

COLE

One Year & Ten Months Ago

"Cole! Oh, my God. Something's wrong!"

I tore the covers off my legs and leapt out of bed. Still half-asleep and disoriented, my shoulder slammed into the wall as I sprinted into the hallway.

"Ow, fuck. Penny, where are you?"

"Cole, hurry! Oh my God."

I followed her voice into Mia's nursery, but something about the expression on Penny's face made my feet stop in their tracks. Standing beside the crib, horror twisted my wife's delicate features as tremors racked her body. Her eyes were wide as tears spilled down her cheeks.

"What's wrong?" I couldn't move, muscles tight, fear binding my ankles together. Afraid to go any closer, afraid to see what Penny saw.

Her hand shook violently as she reached out to point into the crib. "Mia," she whispered.

My stomach twisted, reeling from anticipation. Dread crawled up my spine as I made my way to Penny's side.

I peered down at Mia, and at first, nothing seemed wrong. "What—"

The words stilled on my tongue, disintegrating, turning to ash.

I placed my hand gently on her tiny belly, but it didn't rise and fall with her breaths.

I wiped away the froth bubbling at her tiny lips and stroked her cheek, giving her a gentle nudge, willing her to open her eyes and look up at me.

But she didn't.

Bile rushed into my throat, acid burning as I tried to swallow it down.

No, no, no, no!

I reached into the crib and scooped Mia into my arms. "Come on, baby. Wake up. Wake up for Daddy."

Her tiny head lolled to the side.

I placed my thumb in her tiny hand, but her fingers didn't latch on.

I tried to suck in jagged breaths, panic taking over any rational thoughts. "She needs CPR."

I kneeled down and laid Mia on her back.

Penny choked out a sob and then dropped to her knees beside us. "It's too late, Cole. It's too late."

"It's not too late!" I roared.

Using two fingers just like the doctor showed us, I pressed on Mia's tiny chest.

Thirty compressions.

Tilt the chin.

Two puffs of air.

Again and again, I tried to breathe life into my baby girl.

"Stop," Penny wailed, yanking on my arm. "Enough, Cole! Please! Enough!"

But I couldn't stop. Couldn't accept reality.

Thirty compressions.

Tilt the chin.

Two puffs of air.

Still, nothing.

Penny hunched over and vomited on the carpet.

I lifted Mia into my arms again, pressing my lips to the top of her tiny head.

How could this happen?

Guttural sounds ripped from my sternum, and I wept.

I wept over my angel baby.

THIRTY-TWO

CALLIE

"Ouch."

I groan as I shift my legs under the blanket.

The nurse grimaces, leaning onto the bed railing. "You'll feel sore for a while. The Tylenol should help." She glances up at the monitor. "Your vitals are good. You have a concussion but no internal bleeding. No broken bones. Just some bruising."

Bruises. I'd laugh at the irony of that if it didn't hurt so much to breathe. "The bruises will fade."

"They sure will. Many women in your condition aren't as lucky. It's like you had a guardian angel watching over you two."

My heart lurches. "I hope Maverick is okay. He was probably so scared."

"You've already picked out a name? Wow, you're good. What if it's a girl?"

My eyebrows collapse. "What?"

"You said Maverick." She makes a few checks with her pen on my chart. "What if the baby turns out to be a girl?"

Baby?

I scoot myself up to a seated position, grunting from the stabbing pain in my right side. "I'm sorry, but I don't understand what you're talking about. I didn't save a baby today. I saved my dog, Maverick."

The nurse's eyes widen. "Oh, I thought you were referring to your baby's name. I'm so sorry."

"That's all right." I hike a sore shoulder. "I don't have any children."

The nurse glances back down at my chart and then swallows.

The privacy curtain slides open, and a tall man in a white coat walks to the foot of my bed. "How are you feeling, Mrs. Kingston?"

"Like I've been hit by a car."

He chuckles and takes the chart from the nurse as she scurries away. "That's understandable. You did a very heroic thing, jumping in front of that car to save your dog. You're lucky you sustained only minor injuries."

"I wouldn't be able to live with myself if something happened to him."

He rolls his chair around to the side of the bed. "I'm Dr. Goodwin. I stitched up your head while you were unconscious."

I reach out to shake his hand. "Thank you, Dr. Goodwin. I'm Callie."

He sticks his stethoscope into his ears and motions for me to sit up. "Take a nice deep breath in for me, Callie."

He places the stethoscope on my back, and I wince as my chest expands.

"What kind of dog is he?" he asks.

"A Golden Retriever."

"They're very good dogs." He moves the stethoscope to the other side of my back. "They're excellent with babies."

Again with the baby talk?

"I can't have children, so he's all I have." I inhale again. "Maverick is like my baby."

Dr. Goodwin lowers his stethoscope and tilts his head. "What do you mean *you can't have children?*"

"I have submucosal fibroids. I've gotten pregnant a couple of times, but it never went further than the first trimester. Tried surgery, tried IVF. Nothing worked."

He clears his throat and lifts my chart, his eyes scanning the page. "Uh, Callie, are you aware that you're currently pregnant?"

My head jerks back. "I'm not pregnant."

He places the clipboard on my lap and points to the top of the page. "Your pregnancy test states otherwise."

I stare down at the results, disbelief jerking my head from left to right. "No. This isn't possible."

"When was your last period?"

"It was ... uh ... what's today's date?"

"November 25th."

I close my eyes, racking my brain, willing it to remember something helpful in my defense. "I can't remember when, exactly, but I know I got it in October. Let's say sometime around the beginning of the month."

"And it's now almost the end of November." He leans his elbows onto his knees. "Have you been sexually active?"

I blanch. "Yes, but we used condoms."

"Condoms are 98% effective. They break, sometimes without the couple even realizing it."

"It can't be. This doesn't make sense."

Dr. Goodwin smiles. "I know you're afraid to believe it with all the difficulties you've experienced in the past. But just because you've miscarried before doesn't mean you'll miscarry again. Try to stay positive. A positive mindset can only help you."

Am I dreaming?

Is this really happening?

How can I be pregnant?

He pushes to his feet, and my hand shoots out, gripping his arm. "Where are you going?"

"I have patients waiting to see me. If you feel up to it, you have some guests who're waiting to see you too." He lifts an eyebrow. "Pretty rowdy crew. They're raising hell in the waiting room because I wouldn't let them see you until you were done with all your tests."

Cole.

I flatten my palms over my stomach, and my heart rate gallops faster.

I'm pregnant.

I'm pregnant with Cole's baby.

Tears spill down my cheeks, and Dr. Goodwin hands me the tissue box. "Should I tell them to wait?"

I shake my head. "You can let them in."

"There's only one allowed back at a time. You want to see anyone in particular?"

"Cole."

"You got it." He winks. "Congratulations, Callie. Good luck with everything."

Good luck.

Because I'm pregnant.

There's a baby growing inside me.

Maybe this is it.

Maybe I'll get to be a mother after all.

I bury my face in my hands as a sob breaks free.

Several moments later, Cole flings open the curtain and rushes toward me. "Callie, oh thank God. How are you feeling? Are you okay? They wouldn't let me back sooner."

He crushes me against his chest, and a yelp slips out of me.

"Shit, I'm sorry." He pulls back, worry creasing his forehead. "Where are you hurt?"

"Everywhere." I offer him a gentle smile. "But I'm okay. Just a few bruised ribs."

And a baby.

He drags a chair over from the corner of the room and laces our fingers together. "I was so scared. I thought I lost you. That asshole drove away, but I gave the cops the make and model of the car."

I squeeze his hands. "I'm right here. I'm okay."

And I'm pregnant.

He drops his head and presses his lips to the top of my hand. "Don't ever jump out in front of a car again. You hear me, Wonder Woman?"

I laugh softly. "No, I definitely can't do that anymore."

Because I'm pregnant.

"Good." He cups my face, his thumb brushing over my cheekbone. "Because I can't lose you."

"You won't." My stomach clenches, and more tears brim over. "Cole, I have some news for you."

His eyebrows lift. "News?"

I chew my bottom lip and nod. "I just found out."

"Fuck." His spine stiffens. "Did the doctor find something wrong? Is that why they wouldn't let us back here sooner?"

"Nothing's wrong, but the doctor did find something."

His eyebrows pinch together as he gazes at me with resolute intensity. "Whatever it is, we'll get through it together."

A breath of relief rushes out of me. "I was hoping you'd say that." My heart feels like it's beating in my throat, and I swallow around the emotion. "Cole, I'm pregnant."

He blinks, looking stunned.

"The blood test came back positive," I continue. "I had no idea. Dr. Goodwin just told me."

Cole's hands slip out of mine as he leans back. "What are you talking about? We used a condom every time."

"The doctor said it must've broken. That's the only way it could've happened. But Cole, it happened. Me and you, we made a baby. And I know it's foolish to get excited for something that might not come to fruition, given my track record, but I can't help it. I'm excited." Tears careen down my face in salty rivers. "I might actually become a mother, and you are the reason it's happening."

He shoots to his feet, knocking over his chair. His eyes are wild, and he runs his fingers through his hair as he paces. "You can't be pregnant. We can't be having a baby. This isn't happening."

My head spins, whirling with confusion and fear. I reach out for him, but the IV in my hand catches and pulls. "Ouch! Cole, come here. Please, sit. Let's talk about this."

He vehemently shakes his head, licking his lips. "You're not hearing me. We can't have this baby!"

His words pierce me like bullets. "I don't understand."

"How could you not understand? You know what happened,

what I went through. I can't do this again." He jabs his finger toward the floor. "I won't."

"And you know what *I* went through, so you shouldn't be asking me to *not* have this baby!"

He huffs out a manic laugh. "It's not the same. You don't understand."

Anger flares in my gut. "How can I understand when you refuse to tell me? You never let me in, Cole. Not all the way. You keep me at arm's length, and I don't know how to help you."

"You can't help me. That's what I've been trying to tell you all along." He scrubs both of his hands over his face. "I knew this was a mistake. I never should've gotten involved with you."

And my heart, my full heart—the heart *he* filled up with so much love and hope and joy—plummets to the floor.

"Don't do this, Cole. Don't push me away. We can figure this out."

He shakes his head, his mind made up. He turns and walks back the way he came.

My chin quivers as I speak. "Please don't go."

But he's already gone.

THIRTY-THREE

COLE

My phone buzzes for the millionth time today.

Josie's name flashes across the screen. Gotta hand it to her, she's persistent. I haven't listened to any of her messages, but I'd bet they're ugly.

I deserve as much.

I hold my thumb over the power button, and the screen goes black.

A baby.

A baby.

A baby.

I still can't wrap my head around it.

Agony throbs in my temples, my stomach rolling with each new wave of nausea.

Why should I get another chance?

Why does a new baby get to live when Mia didn't?

Why, why, why?

The cab rolls to a stop, and the driver looks over his shoulder. "Where do you want me to drop you?"

"Here is fine." I slip his money through the partition and swing open the door.

The cold air slices through me when I step outside. Didn't think to bring a jacket with me when I left. Didn't think at all. Just followed the irrational need to get away and bought a ticket for the first flight out of California.

Ended up here.

The dead grass crunches under my shoes as I travel across the cemetery. Haven't been here since the day I watched them lower Mia's tiny casket into the earth.

I couldn't understand it then, and I still can't make sense of it now.

When I reach her headstone, my knees buckle, and I drop down. My fingers claw at the ground, wishing I could crawl inside and be there with her.

Instead of her.

Moans of misery wrench from my chest, my eyes soaked with sorrow. "I'm so sorry, Mia," I whisper. "Daddy's so sorry he wasn't there for you."

I succumb to the grief, no longer able to contain it, surrendering everything that's left inside me. And I weep. I weep for my angel baby.

"Please forgive me. Please. I never meant for this to happen. Never wanted to lose you. I loved you so much, Mia. Daddy loved you so much."

Sudden Infant Death Syndrome, the doctors told us.

The unexplained death of a baby in her sleep.

Cause unknown, they said.

Couldn't have been prevented, they said.

"But I should've gotten up. It was my night to get up and feed you. None of this would've happened if I wasn't so damn selfish."

"Is that really what you believe?"

I spin around to face the voice behind me.

Her curtain of dark hair whips across her face, billowing in the wind. Dark eyes that once gazed up at me in adoration are now filled with pity.

My once-lucky Penny, now tarnished and dull.

"Do you truly believe that you're at fault for Mia's death?" she asks again.

I throw my hands up and then let them fall. "If I would've gotten up when I was supposed to, maybe——"

"Maybe she would've died *after* you fed her. Or maybe you would've gotten to her too late. You can't know what would've happened, Cole. You can't live the rest of your life stuck in that kind of torture."

I scoff. "I should be like you then? Move on and forget about it as if it never happened?"

She flinches. "I haven't forgotten about it. About her. I never will." She rubs her palm up and down her stomach. "But I have other things to think about too."

My jaw goes slack when I spot the roundness of her belly, the small swell under the buttons of her peacoat.

"How ... how could you ..." My words trail off, too many questions fighting for attention.

"How could I not?" she asks. "I don't want to let that solitary, tragic event rule the rest of my life. I have to believe in more. I have to believe there can be good again. Otherwise, I might as well be in that grave with her."

I shake my head, refusing to see any logic in her conviction.

Penny lowers herself to the ground beside me. "Your sister called me. She said you're having a baby too."

Bile churns while my heart thrashes in my chest like a caged beast. "No. I can't. I can't. I can't."

Penny's hand rubs circles on my back. "Yes, Cole. A baby. This is good. You can be a father again. The father you've always wanted to be. The father you *deserve* to be."

A baby.

A baby.

A baby.

Mine.

Mine and Callie's.

My sweet angel.

I bury my face in my hands as another sob strangles me.

"Cole, I'm so sorry for what I did to you. I was broken and just trying to feel something other than the crippling pain. I know it doesn't justify what I did, but I am sorry. You are a good man. You deserve to find happiness again. And it seems like you already have. You just need to let yourself accept it."

Then she smiles that smile I used to love so much. "I know you're a Cali guy now, but you'll always be a New Yorker at heart. And New Yorkers rebuild. We take the past with us as we move forward, and it makes us stronger. Smarter. You can do this, Cole. Don't let that woman go through this without you."

I squeeze my forehead with my fingertips. "I fucking left her, Penny. I yelled at her, and then I left her."

Stupid and selfish.

"She'll forgive you. She'll understand. Help her understand." She winks. "And thank your sister for calling me to come help your stubborn ass."

I gaze down at Mia's name etched onto the stone and trace it with my index finger. "I miss her so much."

Penny presses her fingertips to her lips and then places them onto the top of the headstone. "Me too. But our baby girl was loved."

Yes, she was loved.

CALLIE DOESN'T ANSWER any of my calls.

I've called and texted to let her know that I'm on my way home.

That I'm coming for her.

That I'm sorry I left.

That I love her.

It was a bitch getting a flight out with Thanksgiving only a few days away, but I didn't care. I would've done it if I had to fly the damn plane myself.

I need to make this right.

My sister and her husband are watching TV with the boys when

I get to her house. Not one of them looks up at me when I walk into the living room.

"Is she here?"

Brandon crosses his arms, and Miles follows suit.

I smirk. The little shits are taking her side.

"Come on, Josie. Is she here?"

"No, asshole," she spits.

I look at Dan for help, but he knows better than to talk to me when his wife is pissed.

"I screwed up." I lift my hands and then let them smack against my legs. "I freaked out, and I ran."

"Ran like a little bitch," Josie mutters under her breath.

Fine, I deserve that.

"But luckily, my incredible sister helped me out. Josie, I'm so thankful for you and for all you've done for me. You opened your home to me when we weren't on the best of terms, you let me stay here for free, and you never gave up on me."

"Even when you were being a total dick," she adds.

I smile. "Yes. Even when I was being a total dick."

Josie rises from the couch and comes to stand in front of me. "I know things haven't been perfect between us in our adult years. But you're still my brother, and I still love the shit out of you. It kills me to see you so broken. It kills me to watch you push Callie away like she isn't the best damn thing that's ever happened to you."

She is.

"Help me make things right," I say. "Where is she? At Gertie's?"

Josie huffs out a sigh. "She's in the pool house."

My eyebrows collapse. "She's at *my* place?"

She nods. "She wanted to be there for you when you got back. She knew this would be difficult for you."

My angel.

Always worried about everyone else.

"Hey, Uncle Cole?"

"Yeah, Brandon?"

His lips flatten into a hard line. "Don't break her heart."

Pride swells in my chest. "I won't, kid. Promise."

And I bolt through the house, out the back door, and sprint across the lawn.

Callie startles when I burst into the pool house. She winces, clutching her ribs. "Ow."

I cringe. "Shit, sorry."

She's in my bed, propped up by pillows, with a bandage sitting just above her left eye. The memory of her tiny body rolling over the hood of that car flashes through my mind.

Everything could've been gone in an instant.

Callie ... and the life I didn't even know was inside her.

My world.

"You're back." Her voice is soft, but her expressive eyes are wide, so much confusion and worry swirling around inside.

"Came back for you."

She nods. "I got your texts."

"Meant every word."

She nods again.

I edge onto the bed beside her, careful to not upset her injuries. "How are you feeling?"

She shrugs. "Better now that you're home."

I take her face into my hands, resting my forehead against hers, inhaling her sweet scent. "I'm so sorry I left you. I'm sorry I said the things I said. I didn't mean any of them."

"I know," she whispers.

I lean back just enough to look into her eyes. "Callie, I love you so much. I want this baby. I want us to be a family. I'm just so damn afraid. Scared to feel excited. Scared to feel hopeful. I don't know how to do this. But I want to."

A tear trickles down her cheek, and I sweep it away with my thumb.

"I know you're scared," she says. "I am too. I keep wondering if I'm going to lose this baby like all the rest. But it feels different this time, and I know that's because of you. *Everything* is different.

"I was hurt when you left, but I knew you'd come back. I knew you had to figure it out on your own, just like I figured my life out on my own. You were patient with me, and you were there when I needed you most." She glances around the pool house. "That's why I waited here for you. Not because I'm weak or a doormat for abuse. But because I know you've going through something horrific, and you need time. I want to be here for you, Cole. I just wish you'd let me."

I lift her hand to my lips, placing a kiss onto her soft skin, and I prepare to give Callie what she needs. What she deserves.

To be let in, all the way.

"I had a daughter. Mia. She was beautiful. Perfect in every way. I hadn't felt love like that before. An all-consuming kind of love when you know you're changed forever. That's what it felt like. When I held her, and I looked down into those big, innocent eyes, I felt the happiest I'd ever been. I saw my future in her eyes. I saw myself doing everything with her, teaching her, helping her."

I huff out a laugh. "I even imagined what it'd be like when she grew up and wore an outfit I didn't approve of. What our first fight would be like. If she'd be sassy like her mother, or if she'd be stubborn like me. For two months, I held her and planned out how our lives would be."

Callie swallows a sob and strokes my jaw as if she's coaxing me to continue, comforting me as I get closer to the end of my story.

"Having a newborn was exhausting. I'd work all day, long hours. Penny's father was my boss, and I knew he didn't approve of me. I didn't come from money, so I felt like I had a lot to prove. But I still wanted to help Penny with the nighttime feedings. That was my favorite time with Mia. We'd sit in the rocking chair while she drank her bottle, and I'd sing to her. Same song my mother sang to me as a child. It was a special time, no matter how tired I was."

My chin drops, sorrow gripping my throat. "Mia was underweight, so we had a strict feeding schedule mapped out from the doctor. We'd set our alarms and take turns throughout the night. It was my turn. I was supposed to get up with her that night. I was so tired when my alarm went off. I remember shutting it off, but I don't know what happened after that. I must've fallen back to sleep. Mia wasn't crying. And then the next thing I knew, Penny was screaming for me."

My body shudders, and I squeeze Callie's hand. "It was SIDS. Happens to infants, and no one knows why. The doctor said she didn't suffer, that she went peacefully in her sleep. He said there was nothing we could've done to prevent it, but I can't help thinking that it wouldn't have happened if I would've gotten up when I was supposed to. Maybe I could've stopped it."

Callie shakes her head furiously. "No, Cole. You don't know that. You can't beat yourself up for what might've been if you did this or if you did that. I know what it's like to blame yourself for the loss of your child. I might never have held my babies in my arms, but I've still lost them. I've beaten myself up thinking there was something I did that caused it. But that's not reality."

She smooths her palm down my cheek. "I'm so sorry that you lost your baby girl. I can't imagine what that must've been like for you and Penny. I wish I could take your pain away."

I smile, blinking through my watery vision. "You do take my pain away. You make it better. You make *me* better." I tip her chin up and press my lips against hers. "You're my angel. My second chance. The hope I stopped believing existed."

I kiss her again. "I visited Mia's grave when I went to New York. I needed to feel close to her. To remember her. I think I felt that having another baby would somehow replace her, and that scared me. But I realized something. The scar from losing Mia will always be there, just like the scars from your surgery will always be on your skin. But that doesn't mean I won't ever heal. I can heal and take Mia's memory with me. At the same time. You healed me, Callie. You … and this baby growing inside of you."

She buries her face in my shirt, muffling her cries, and I wrap my arms around her, holding us both together with our love.

With our hope.

Callie sniffles. "What if we lose this baby, Cole? What if the same thing keeps happening to me, and my body just can't do it?"

"Then we'll apply for adoption."

She jerks back to look up at me. "What?"

I nod, caressing her beautiful face. "I want to have a family with you, even if our children don't have our DNA. They'll have our love, and that's the most important thing."

Another sob bursts from her throat, and she flings her arms around my neck. "I love you so much, Cole."

I grin. "And I love you."

My angel.

Forever.

THREE MONTHS LATER

THIRTY-FOUR

CALLIE

"WE HAVE a new member joining us at group tonight. Ladies, this is Camille."

A chorus of *hellos* sound around the circle.

Camille tucks a strand of light-brown hair behind her ear and gives us a tentative smile. "Hi, everyone."

The bruise under her eye is visible but fading. I'd say she got hit a little over a week ago. The deep-purple marks that line her arms, though ... those are fresh.

Melissa gestures to me. "Callie, why don't you start tonight?"

I nod, understanding why she's calling on me. "Six months ago today, I left my abusive ex-husband. He'd found a journal I was writing in as an exercise for therapy, and he didn't like what he read. He put his hands around my neck, and he strangled me. I managed to get away, and I ran out the door. Ran right in front of my neighbor's truck in my bathrobe."

I laugh a soft chuckle as I look down at my protruding belly. "It's funny how life works out. You stay in bad situations for so long, convincing yourself that it's the right thing to do. You lie to the people you love in order to hide the truth from them, but you hide the truth from yourself too. I don't know why. I don't know what

260

makes us think we deserve to be in those messed-up situations. Maybe it's the way we were raised. Maybe we don't have enough self-worth. Or maybe we need to go through those tough times in order to get to the good that's coming."

I hike a shoulder and look straight into Camille's eyes. "A wise, old friend once told me: Losing yourself in a relationship is never an option. I lost myself for a long time. But six months ago, I decided it was time to find myself. It wasn't easy. It was the most terrifying thing I've ever done. But I did it anyway."

"How?" Camille's voice is soft.

Scared.

The way mine used to sound before I found it.

"How did you do it?" she asks.

"I leaned on my friends. I found a job that makes me happy. I kept going to therapy. And I had hope. The most important thing to remember is that you're not alone, Camille. You have us now. You don't have to go through this alone."

Janae leans over. "I have room at my house if you need a place to stay."

Carrie raises her hand. "My job is hiring."

One by one, women chime in with ways to help our new friend.

And that's my favorite thing about coming to group. No matter how low you feel, no matter how scary the world seems, these incredible women keep showing up and sharing their love. It's an incredible reminder of how powerful women can be when we support each other.

We listen to several stories, and when group ends, I pull Jasmine to the side. I've been meaning to get together with her, but between doctor's visits and running the diner, there hasn't been much time.

"Hey, Jasmine. Do you have a minute?"

She smiles. "Sure. What's up?"

"Getting hit by a car was one of the best things that ever happened to me. I know it sounds crazy, but it's true. It's the day that changed my life forever. I found out that I was pregnant, and it pushed Cole to finally face his demons and start healing."

I clasp her hand in mine. "And now, the accident is about to change your life too."

Her eyes bounce between mine. "What are you talking about?"

"The police found the man who hit me based on Cole's description of his car. He agreed to settle if I dropped the charges, so I'll be getting a large sum of money. I want to help you, Jasmine. You and your husband. You'll be able to afford the adoption fee, and you can finally have the baby you've always wanted."

Jasmine covers her mouth with her trembling hand. "I couldn't accept that kind of money, Callie."

"Yes, you can."

She shakes her head. "But what about you? Surely you could use the money for something."

I rub my palm over my stomach. "I already have everything I need. Plus, I'm receiving money from my divorce."

Paul agreed to give me everything I'm entitled to.

"Oh, my God. I don't know what to say, Callie."

"Say yes."

Her eyes well, and she nods. "Yes! Thank you so much. Yes!"

I hold Jasmine while she weeps, and I cry with her. "You deserve to have what you want most in life," I whisper.

"So do you, Callie. And I'm so happy that you're getting it."

Me too.

The journey was difficult, but I'd go through it all again if it meant I'd end up exactly where I am today.

I say goodbye and head home. Our temporary home is at the pool house while our house is being built. Cole is building us a small house on the water in Lake Arrowhead with the help of Billy and some friends.

He claims it'll be done by the time the baby is here.

I'm not so sure, but I don't tell him that.

Before I pull into Josie's driveway, a text from Cole flashes on my screen:

COLE: Come to Josie's. She said she wants to show us something.

. . .

I SHAKE my head and grin. Probably another piece of furniture for the nursery. She is *so* ready to get rid of all things baby.

Dan should really think about getting a vasectomy.

When I arrive, I knock before walking inside.

"Surprise!"

My head whips around. Cole, Josie, Dan, the kids, and Gertie are huddled in the foyer. Pink and blue streamers are draped from the corners of the ceiling.

My eyebrows press together. "Uh, guys ... what's going on?"

Cole snakes his arm around my waist. "We made it past the first trimester, so everyone wanted to celebrate."

I close my eyes as a grin pulls my lips. "You didn't need to do all this."

"Of course we did." Josie steps forward. "Every part of your journey should be celebrated."

Life is precious.

"Come on. The party is out back." Josie links her elbow with mine. "We can't leave Maverick out there too long or else he'll start eating his own turds."

I scoff. "He doesn't do that anymore!"

"Once a shit-eater, always a shit-eater."

I give her a playful shove as we step out onto the patio. Maverick charges at me but stops about a foot away. Then he gets down and army-crawls the rest of the way—something we've been teaching him as my stomach grows.

"Good boy, my Mav man." I scratch behind his ears, and he flops over, giving me his belly.

"Callie, can we give Maverick a bath tomorrow?" Miles asks.

"Of course."

"Yes!" He pumps his fist in the air and then takes off running. "Brandon, she said yes!"

Cole grins. "The things that excite them."

I push to stand, something that's getting more difficult each week. "How was therapy today?"

He presses a kiss to the top of my head. "It went well. Had to take a nap after."

I laugh. "Yeah, it can be exhausting sometimes."

"We talked about making a worry box. Have you ever heard of something like that?"

My head tilts. "No. What is it?"

"You write down whatever's on your mind. Whatever's making you anxious, or whatever you're scared of. Then, you fold it up and slip it into the box. It's supposed to help get the negative thoughts out of your head, and it serves as a visual, like you're physically putting the thought away." He shrugs. "He said we could read it together if we wanted to. Or not."

I dab at the corners of my watery eyes. "I love that idea. I think we should do it."

Cole wraps his arms around me and pulls me in close. "Pregnancy tears again?"

I shake my head. "I'm just so proud of you, Cole. You've come so far in such a short amount of time."

"Couldn't have done it without you." He leans down and presses his lips to mine. "My angel."

"My hope."

"Get a room," Gertie barks.

I laugh. "Way to ruin the moment, Gertie."

"Ah." She waves her hand. "You'll have another moment in two minutes."

Josie throws her head back and laughs. "Those hormones are really doing a number on your sex drive."

I cross my arms over my chest. "I don't know what you're talking about."

"You two can barely keep your hands off each other," Gertie says. "You should see them at the diner. It's unsanitary."

Cole tosses a wadded-up napkin at her. "You were the one who pushed us together. You only have yourself to blame."

"This is true. And you are giving me a great-grandbaby, so I guess it's not all bad."

"We should start taking bets on the gender," Josie says.

Dan raises his hand. "I say girl."

"Boy!" Brandon and Miles shout at the same time.

Gertie shakes her head. "Definitely a girl."

I lift an eyebrow at Josie. "Well? What's your guess?"

"You're going to have twins. One boy and one girl."

I glance at Cole, who's beaming. "You think you put twins in me?"

"It is possible." He brushes an imaginary speck of lint off his shoulder. "I do have super sperm, you know."

"Gross!" Brandon scrunches his nose.

"What do you think, Callie?" Miles asks.

I rub circles around my belly and shrug. "I'll be happy with whatever comes out."

Girl or boy, one or two.

Either way, I'm grateful for this miracle.

"Oh!" I snap my fingers. "Gertie, I almost forgot. I have the paperwork from the lawyer. He wants you to look it over before everything is finalized."

"You're going to be the owner of the diner?" Brandon asks.

"Yeah, B. Pretty cool, huh?"

"Maybe I can work there when I'm old enough."

I wrap my arm around him and squeeze his shoulder. "You've got a spot waiting for you."

"Can he start now?" Dan asks with a chuckle.

"Then we can start charging him rent!" Josie holds out her fist, and Dan bumps his knuckles against hers.

Brandon buries his face in his hands. "You guys aren't cool just because you fist bump."

This sends Josie into a ten-minute rant about all the reasons why she thinks she's a cool mom.

"I'm going to run to my car," I whisper in Cole's ear. "I want to get the paperwork for Gertie before I forget."

"Want me to grab it?" he asks.

"I've got it." I pull him in for a kiss. "Be right back."

After I take the file out of my car, I stop and glance across the street at the house where I once lived.

In the life that was once mine.

With the secrets that were my own.

And I choose to smile, because life is all about the choices we make.

We choose to see things one way or the other.

We choose to accept or to hate.

We choose to be happy or sad.

Bitter or grateful.

To forgive or blame.

To hold on or let go.

When I look back on that former life, I don't resent it. It's a part of me. Part of my journey. So, I carry those scars with me, and I choose to wear them like a badge of honor. Like a warrior.

Because that's who I am.

That's who I choose to be.

Callie the Courageous.

EPILOGUE

COLE

Five Years Later

"From the moment you called me the landscaper, I knew that we'd be together."

Callie's head tilts back and her eyes squeeze closed as a full belly laugh bursts from her throat. "You are so full of shit."

I grin. "Okay, maybe I didn't know we'd be together just then. But I think I somehow knew that you were important. Special."

Callie's expression softens, and she leans in to brush her lips against mine. Then she whispers, "I thought you were an asshole."

I give her shoulder a playful shove, and she laughs again.

Callie's laughter is one of my favorite sounds in the world.

"Daddy! Daddy!"

My son calling me *Daddy* is another.

"Whoa there." Callie intercepts Nicholas, scooping him up before he can fling himself into my arms like he often does. "Remember what we talked about, little man?"

His dark brows pull together as his steel-blue eyes roam over the small bundle in my arms. "Be careful so I don't hurt Layla."

"Good job." Callie threads her fingers through his brown curls. "Want to help feed her?"

His eyes turn to saucers. "Yes!"

I bite back a smile at the sound of his lisp. "Come sit next to me, and I'll hand her to you."

He climbs up beside me on the couch, and Callie wedges a decorative pillow under his elbow. "You have to hold her head up."

"I know, I know."

I transfer my daughter to my son's arms, and my heart swells with immense pride.

My babies.

Callie dabs at the corner of her eye as Nicholas strokes Layla's cheek.

"Her skin is so much darker than mines," he says.

I smooth my palm over the crown of Layla's head. "It is."

"Why do you call her black when her skin is brown?"

Callie smiles as she adjusts the angle of the bottle in his hand. "That's a good question. I don't know. We're peach-colored, yet we're called white."

Nicholas nods. "That's weird."

Callie met a young woman named Cynthia at group last year. Cynthia had just found out that she was pregnant, and was contemplating getting an abortion. She'd never wanted to get pregnant, but she'd been raped, and therefore didn't want to keep the baby. After spending time in both therapy and group, Cynthia changed her mind. She decided that she wanted to put her baby up for adoption instead.

Callie and I had applied for adoption earlier that year. We'd enjoyed the one-on-one time with Nicholas, and with him going off to kindergarten in the fall, we thought it'd be the perfect time to expand our family.

Sometimes, you can't fathom why awful things happen in life. People say there's a reason for everything, and maybe they're right, but I still haven't been able to understand why Mia had to die. I'm not sure I ever will.

Yet I *have* been able to appreciate the good that came after those bad times.

Cynthia may never know why she had to go through something so heinous, but she knows that her daughter will always be loved. She knows that a miracle arose from the ashes.

We adopted Cynthia's daughter two months ago.

"I love you, Layla Mia." Nicholas leans in and nuzzles the tip of his nose against hers. "I'm going to be the bestest big brother."

My vision blurs, and I swipe a tear away with my thumb. "Yes, you are, bud."

Glancing down at Nicholas and Layla, I know in my heart that this was always supposed to be the way my life ended up. Maybe I didn't see it when Callie Kingston—now Callie *Luciano*—mistook me for the landscaper, but I see it so clearly now.

After Nicholas finishes feeding Layla, Callie takes her to the bedroom to burp her and get her ready for bed.

Nicholas latches onto my hand when I stand, and I lead him to his bedroom.

"Daddy, can you sing that lion song to me tonight?" He jumps on top of his Spiderman comforter and scoots underneath the sheets. "The one you sing to Layla?"

"Of course." I lower myself onto the edge of his bed. "You like that song?"

He nods emphatically. "I want to learn the words so I can sing it to Layla."

My heart squeezes. "I think she'd love that."

I sing the first few lines, and Nicholas repeats after me. We practice them until he has them down, and then I tell him we'll learn the next verse tomorrow night. He pouts, of course.

So, I end up teaching him half the song.

The kid's a little con artist. He knows how to crumble my resolve.

After he falls asleep, I tiptoe into the hallway and gently close his door. My next stop is Layla's room. She's sound asleep in her milk coma, so I kiss my fingertips and touch them to her head.

When I step into our bedroom, she's sitting up against the cream-colored quilted headboard, eyes closed and mouth open.

I let out a soft chuckle, and click off the lamp on her nightstand. Her eyes flutter open as I press a kiss to her forehead.

"Are they asleep?" she mumbles.

"For now."

I climb in beside her, and curl around her body, inhaling her sweet floral scent.

A small moan vibrates in her throat, and she reaches back to run her fingers through my hair. "We should have sex now before one of them wakes up."

I chuckle. "You're exhausted, angel. Sleep."

She mutters something incomprehensible that sounds like a protest, but her arm drops back onto the mattress, and she's out cold.

I lie awake for a short while, listening to the sound of her steady breaths.

Fear still grips me in the middle of the night. I'll wake up in a cold sweat once in a while, and rush from room to room, checking on my kids. Therapy has helped, but I don't think anything can take away the worry of a parent—especially one who's suffered the loss of a child.

Callie understands. She's patient with me, and validates my neuroses. I don't think I could love her more for all the ways she's helped me. She came into my life when I was at my lowest, drowning in the depths of despair, and somehow, she brought me to higher ground.

My angel.

For a long time, I wasn't sure what was left of me after everything I'd endured.

Now, I am filled with an endless amount of love.

Now, I am complete.

When you're sure you've lost everything, there's one thing that always remains deep down inside yourself.

Hope.

THE END

Thank you for reading *What's Left of Me.*
Want more emotion & angst?
Keep reading for a sneak peek of Inevitable

New to me?
I always recommend starting with Collision
Book 1 in The Collision Series

Need something funny and light?
Check out my Amazon Top 30 Best Seller Hating the Boss

Want to gain access to FREE books, exclusive news, & giveaways?
Sign up for my monthly newsletter!

Come stalk me:
Facebook
Instagram
Twitter
GoodReads

Want to be part of my KREW?
Join Kristen's Reading Emotional Warriors
A group where we can discuss my books, books you're reading, &
where friends will remind you what a badass warrior you are.

Love bookish shirts, mugs, & accessories?
Shop my book merch shop!

All titles by Kristen are FREE on KU

The Collision Series Box Set
Collision (Book 1)
Avoidance (Book 2)
The Other Brother (Book3 – standalone)
Fighting the Odds (Book 4 – standalone)

Hating the Boss – RomCom standalone
Back to You – RomCom standalone

Inevitable – Contemporary standalone

INEVITABLE

KRISTEN GRANATA

1

GRAHAM

No.

Two letters. One syllable. Such a simple word.

It's one of the first words we learn as babies. How easily it flies from our mouths, without even a second thought. We say it because we mean it, we feel it. We don't know enough about the pain it can cause, the guilt that follows, the magnitude of what it symbolizes.

Our parents become angry when we say it. It's a demonstration of defiance, us against them. They have the power, and we're standing up to them, threatening to take that power.

But they always win.

And at that age, parents *should* win. Otherwise, most of us would've been dead from sticking our fingers in sockets, or crawling into the pools in our backyards. Our parents set rules and boundaries to keep us safe. And we trust them. So, we listen. We obey.

People often say family is everything. They're not wrong. Our parents make us into who we are. They sew together the fabric of our lives, weaving our realities, carefully stitching our mindsets. What we think, what we know, what we do and say, all stems from our families.

But there are parents who abuse that power they wield.

Their warped version of love forces us to do things, awful things, while binding you in guilt. Because they know we're loyal. Because they know how desperate we are to make them proud. Because they know we'll do anything for them.

They prey on it.

On us.

And we let them.

Family *is* everything. But I don't say that with the same warm and fuzzy sentiment you think of when you see that phrase on a Hallmark card.

Family can destroy your life.

Just ask Romeo and Juliet.

The Montagues and the Capulets led their children to their deaths. A fight amongst adults was responsible for terrible tragedy. I can't even remember what the hell they were fighting about, but we all remember the result. Shakespeare wrote about dozens of twisted families because he knew.

He knew how a dysfunctional family can play a direct part in one's demise.

My life could've been a lot different than it is. I had the talent, the drive, the opportunities. But family got in the way. I lost everything I'd worked for. Or as Dad would say, I threw it all away.

Now, at twenty-four with no college education, I'm stuck working for my father's private investigation company. I'm the best P.I. he's got, which means about as much as being the best fry cook at McDonald's. Sure, I bring in the most money. But after Dad takes his cut, and I give a chunk of it to my sister, I'm not left with much. Had I not given up on my dream, I could've provided for my family. Could've given them anything they needed.

And Dad reminds me of it every chance he gets.

I despise my father. He's a narcissistic asshole. If he dropped dead today, the only thing I'd feel is relief. I don't stick by his side because I want to. It's guilt that keeps me where I am, and Dad yanks me around by it like a leash.

"What do you say, son?" My father clasps his hands and rests them on his stomach as he leans back in his worn leather chair. There isn't an ounce of fear or worry in his cold eyes.

He knows he has me by the balls.

"Why do you even bother asking?" I fold my arms over my chest. "Do you get off on it, pretending like I have a choice?"

His green eyes narrow, the corners of his thin lips tipping upward. "You always have a choice, son. You know that. If you don't want to do it, just say the word. Of course, you'll have to explain that to your sister come payday."

I rise from my chair in front of his desk. "When do I start?"

His mouth spreads into a full-blown evil grin. "Tonight." He slides a manila envelope across his desk toward me. "Everything you need to know is in this file."

I reach out to take the envelope, but his hand clamps over mine, his smile gone. Soulless sapphire eyes glare up at me. "Don't fuck this up, son. This is it. The moment I've been waiting for."

I lean forward, pressing my knuckles onto his desk, and bring my face down to his. Disgust pulses through my veins, but I stamp down the urge to ram his teeth down his throat. "I won't fuck this up. You'll get your money."

"This is about more than money. I'm going to take back what's mine. I'm going to take his empire and build my own, right on top of his grave."

I shudder at how psychotic he sounds. I suppose years of obsessing over something will do that to a man.

Without another word, I take the envelope from him and stalk out of his office, making sure to slam the door closed behind me.

He hates it when I do that.

I walk back to my apartment, hoping the crisp autumn air will soothe the years of pent-up frustration and resentment boiling inside my gut.

I used to love living in Brooklyn. It's like living in Manhattan without the expensive price tag. Then Dad moved his office less than a mile away, because God forbid I have anything that's truly mine.

When I arrive home, I swipe the bottle of Jack Daniels from my kitchen counter before collapsing onto the couch, and flip open the file in my lap.

The headshot captures my attention in an instant, a photo paper-clipped to the inside cover.

Long, raven-colored hair frames her perfect heart-shaped face. With porcelain skin and plump pink lips, she's a natural beauty. She's covered up in a cap and gown, the picture taken from her high school graduation last year. To the untrained eye, she looks like any other pretty face.

But I've been trained to look deeper.

Her dark eyes stare up at me, and I spot a playfulness in them. Coupled with the way her lips are curved into a smirk, it's almost as if she's daring you to do something. There's an edge to her, trouble brewing just beneath the surface. And the longer I stare at her picture, the more I want to know.

Evangeline Montalbano.

Pretty name. Nineteen years-old. Born and raised in Manhattan, a New York native like me. I peruse the rest of the information in her file and then I groan. She's involved in multiple charities, and spends her free time shopping and partying with her elite friends.

I tip the bottle back, letting the whiskey slide down my throat. Rich bitches like Evangeline are all the same. They use charity work to hide the fact that they're stuck-up and self-absorbed. Can't blame them, I suppose. They've had everything handed to them. This Park Avenue princess wouldn't know a hard-days' work if it bit her on her undoubtedly perfect Pilates-formed ass. Her greatest hardship in life was probably a hangnail.

But this job isn't about her.

Evangeline's daddy owns a multi-million-dollar corporation. Anthony Montalbano is one of the richest men in the city. He also used to be my father's best friend.

According to Dad, Anthony unexpectedly pulled his money out of the business they'd started after college, and ran off with Dad's girlfriend. It was a lifetime ago, but you'd better believe my father held onto it. He holds a grudge like a Pitbull in a tug-of-war match.

All Dad talks about is how he was betrayed, how it should've been him with the million-dollar company instead of bill collectors and a dead wife.

To him, this isn't just a job. It's personal.

This is revenge.

My instructions in Dad's plan are clear: Pose as Evangeline's bodyguard. Tail her, night and day, and infiltrate her home. Collect any and all information about Anthony Montalbano and his company. Dig up dirt, uncover skeletons in the closet. Anything my father can use for blackmail.

Sounds simple enough. But I'm left with one question as I dial my father's number and press my phone to my ear.

"Graham," he answers. "I take it you've looked over the girl's file."

"How are we going to convince her father to hire me as her bodyguard?"

My father snickers, and a chill runs through me. "Oh, we're going to be *very* convincing."

I CAN'T BELIEVE I'm doing this.

I sigh, pulling the wool ski mask down over my face. This is a new low for me.

"You ready?" Tommy asks.

"As if I have a choice."

Tommy's gloved-hand pats my shoulder. "Don't worry, G-man. Clemmons and I will do all the work. You're just along for the ride."

"Why, exactly? Why does my father want me here?"

He shrugs and tugs his mask into place. "I don't get paid enough to ask questions."

And he's not smart enough to ask the right ones.

Dad pays these guys to do his dirty work. His lackeys. All brawn and no brains.

Clemmons glares at me in the rearview mirror. "Just don't speak. The girl can't recognize your voice. Your father will have our asses if we fuck this up."

I'm well-aware. "Let's just get this over with."

As if on cue, the glass door swings open and Evangeline Montalbano steps out of the bar. I do a double-take as she pulls a set of keys from her back pocket and struts over to the red and black Kawasaki motorcycle parked in front of our van.

Yes, we're in a blacked-out pedophile van with ski masks on.

Not the point.

Evangeline tugs a helmet on over her hair, which is streaked with deep red highlights unlike the picture I saw. A cropped black tank top fits snugly around her chest, revealing her tiny midsection and gleaming belly ring. What surprises me most is the tattoo on her left arm: A warrior woman's face, marked with war paint under her eyes, inside the head of a lion. She swings a leg over the bike, her ripped jeans tucked inside black combat boots, and leans over to grip the handles, giving us a glorious view of her plump, round ass.

"Wow," I say on an exhale.

There's that edge I caught in her headshot.

Tommy chuckles from the passenger seat. "Fucking hot, right?"

Hot isn't the word. It's too generic. Evangeline is stunning. Gorgeous. She's a gravitational force pulling me in. And she looks nothing like a Park Avenue princess.

More like Biker Barbie.

"Here we go, boys." Clemmons turns the key in the ignition and waits a few seconds before pulling out behind Evangeline's motorcycle. He stays behind her for several minutes, following her every turn. She weaves in and out of traffic, changing lanes without signaling, making it difficult for us to keep up.

Then she makes an abrupt swerve down a side street.

"Where's she going?" I ask, leaning forward.

"Fuck if I know," Tommy says.

Clemmons shrugs. "Let's see where this princess is headed."

We come to a construction site and hit a dead end blocked off with orange cones. Evangeline skids to a stop, props her bike up, rips her helmet off, and stomps toward the bumper of our van.

"I know you're following me!" she yells.

Shit.

Clemmons and Tommy fling their doors open, and Evangeline's eyes go wide as realization sets in: Two men in ski masks are charging toward her in a deserted alley.

Tommy gets to her first and grips her bicep, dragging her toward the van. To my surprise, Evangeline yanks her arm back and kicks Tommy in his kneecap. Clemmons runs up behind her and wraps his arms around her waist, lifting her off the pavement. Tommy lunges forward to grab her ankles, but she kicks him in the face. Then she rams her head back into Clemmons' nose.

This isn't good.

Tommy spits a mouthful of blood over his shoulder and swings his fist.

"No!" I shout, as he punches Evangeline in her face.

Her head hangs forward and her body goes limp.

Fuck.

Tommy and Clemmons shuffle toward the back of the van, my cue to open the doors. When I do, they toss Evangeline's lifeless body in beside me.

Clemmons zip-ties her ankles together, and then her wrists.

"Maybe I'll take this pretty little Power Ranger for my own ride when she wakes up." Tommy's hand slides up her leg.

I twist his hand backward before he can go any further. "Touch her again and you'll lose your hand."

The sick bastard laughs and closes the doors.

My stomach twists when I see the purple, swollen lump already forming on Evangeline's cheek.

Tommy hoists himself into the passenger seat. "That bitch can fight."

"Yeah, well, that *bitch* almost took you out," Clemmons says.

"Fuck you. We got her, didn't we?"

The two continue to bicker, but I can't tear my eyes away from Evangeline's face. I brush her hair back, staring down at her bruise. "We need to get her some ice."

"Shut the fuck up, man!" Clemmons yells.

"Screw my father's orders. She needs ice!"

"Yeah, hold on. Let me take this van with a kidnapped girl through the McDonald's drive-thru and ask for a cup of ice." Clemmons shakes his head, glaring at me in the rearview mirror.

"She'll be fine," Tommy says. "I didn't hit her that hard."

Spoken like a true piece of shit.

When we reach Park Avenue, Clemmons pulls down on a side street near Evangeline's building. The van jerks to a stop, and Evangeline stirs beside me. With heavy lids, she blinks up at me, looking confused and disoriented.

I lean down and whisper, "Don't worry. You're home now. Everything's going to be okay."

I push open the back doors and Tommy yanks Evangeline out of the van. He and Clemmons carry her to the sidewalk and toss her onto the pavement.

Then we drive away and ditch the van, parting ways as if nothing ever happened.

We just scared the shit out of a young, innocent girl. All so my father can fulfill his twisted, lifelong dream. No doubt, he'll sleep like a baby tonight, while I'm haunted by the image of Evangeline's bruised face.

They weren't supposed to hurt her. That wasn't part of the plan. But the men working for my father are thugs. Mindless yet dangerous men following orders.

I guess this makes me one of them.

2

EVA

"No!"

Two letters. One syllable. Such a powerful word.

Too bad it doesn't mean shit to my father.

Dad sighs, pinching the bridge of his nose. "This is not up for debate, Evangeline. You were attacked the other night. You need protection."

I'm seconds away from stomping my foot. "I will *not* have an overgrown babysitter following me around!"

"Yes, you will, because I say you will. You are my daughter and—"

"And I am nineteen fucking-years-old."

He flinches. "Language."

"You can't tell me what to do anymore!"

"Watch me." He looks to his assistant, Jerry, motioning for him to open the door.

Because God forbid my father ever opens a damn door on his own.

"This man doesn't just wield a gun," Dad says. "He knows how to fight. Plus, he grew up here so he knows the area well. He was the best candidate we could find on such short notice."

I roll my eyes. "Lucky me."

I *should* feel lucky. I come from a wealthy family. I live in a luxurious, residential skyscraper in the greatest city in the world. Cars, clothes, accessories, trips on a private jet. On the outside, it looks like I have it all. What more could I want, right? Money can buy almost anything.

But it doesn't buy happiness.

It doesn't buy love.

It doesn't diminish the pain or heartache.

All money does is mask reality. That's why rich people live in huge-ass houses. They build fortresses to shield themselves from the harsh truth, convincing themselves that they're important; that they deserve what they have; that they're worth a damn. They fake kindness, fake having humanity. Empty words and meaningless gestures. There's no real love. No passion. They cling to money because it's the only thing that makes them feel *something*.

And I'm stuck here with them, a human amongst robots.

Jerry returns with a large man towering behind him. Large might be an understatement. Muscles bulge under the snug, black T-shirt he's wearing, and strong thighs strain against his dark jeans. He's also wearing scuffed-up Timberland boots with the laces untied. He's dressed nothing like the rich men in this room. My world is filled with suits and ties and shiny shoes. I'm surprised Dad even looked twice at this guy. He looks more like the type of man a father would want to *protect* his daughter from, not pay him an exorbitant amount of money to follow her around. Then again, maybe that's why Dad hired him.

He looks dangerous.

Scruff peppers his jawline, which is defined and chiseled like his body. His dark hair is messy, and not the on-purpose messy that preppy dudes use pomade to achieve. No, this guy legit towel-dried his hair after his shower and called it good—if he even showered. He looks like the type that would roll out of bed, sniff the armpits of a T-shirt plucked from the floor, and decide it's wearable. Everything about him screams *zero fucks given*.

It's a damn shame his aviators block his eyes from me. I'd bet they're as dark as his eyebrows, which are dipped down, pinched together in a perma-scowl.

My gaze follows him as he strides toward my father and engulfs his hand in a firm shake. He moves with a natural, physical dominance, the kind that commands your attention.

He's certainly got mine.

The man is beautiful.

Wait, no. What I meant to say was, "Are you fucking kidding me, Dad? You want *this guy* to follow me around all day?"

Dad rubs his temples in small circles. "Language, Evangeline. And yes, I do want *this guy* to follow you around. Mr. Carter is going to protect you."

"I don't need protection!"

"Have you seen your face?"

I roll my eyes. "It's Manhattan. People get mugged all the time."

"You're not *people*. You're my daughter. And you didn't get mugged. They took you, hurt you, and left you right outside our building. They had another purpose, and I don't intend on giving them a second chance to find out what that is."

A frustrated growl rumbles in my throat. It's no use arguing with him. I yank my leather jacket off the back of my chair, and stomp past my father like a toddler.

He hired me a babysitter—I might as well act the part.

"Where are you going?" Dad pushes to his feet.

"What does it matter? I've got Thor here to watch over me now. I'll be safe and fucking sound." I don't wait for him to respond as I spin around and barrel through the doorway.

Heavy footsteps clunk behind me in the hall.

I stop.

He stops.

I walk.

He walks.

I turn the corner.

He turns the corner.

I speed up.

He speeds up.

This is irritating me already.

I make an abrupt about-face and slam into the body guard's steel chest. "Do you have to walk so close to me?"

"That's kind of how my job works." His voice is deep, matching his burly size.

"Well, it's obnoxious."

He pops an unapologetic shoulder.

I prop my hands on my hips. "Look, you can go back to wherever it is you came from. You're not needed here."

"I only take orders from your father."

"And I don't. I'm a smart, capable girl, and I can take care of myself."

"If you're so smart, then why'd you drive down a dark alley and try to confront the thugs who were following you?"

I lift my chin, ignoring the fact that he's right. "I had a bad night and I made a dumb decision. It won't happen again."

"Lucky for you, I'll be right by your side to make sure of that."

Lucky. Ha!

Another growl makes its way up my throat.

His thick lips twitch. "I'm starting to understand why you got that lion tattoo on your shoulder there."

"Oh, you haven't even begun to understand me, Big Guy." I step into his space and poke his chest with each word. "Now back. The fuck. Off."

My hair whips around my shoulders as I turn and storm toward the elevator. When I step inside, I expect him to follow me, but he doesn't. He just stands there like a statue with that stoic expression on his ruggedly handsome face.

Did I say *ruggedly handsome*?

I meant annoying. Who wears sunglasses indoors?

When I reach the lobby, he's nowhere in sight. I slip my arms into my jacket sleeves with a smug smile and push through the revolving door, inhaling a lungful of New York air.

It smells like hot garbage, but still. This is my city. My home.

Was getting kidnapped the single most terrifying moment in my life? Yes. But I refuse to let that stop me.

I won't let fear control me.

I force myself to walk the few blocks to Starbucks, clutching my pepper spray in my palm, ignoring the drumline in my chest. The muscles in my body tense each time someone gets too close—which happens literally every step of the way. New Yorkers don't know the meaning of personal space. With over 1.6 billion people crammed onto an island that's only 13.4 miles long, we're bumbling into each other like mass-produced cattle.

Only when I step inside the coffee shop do my shoulders lower and my breaths come easier. My best friend Deanna waves as I approach our usual table by the window, but her smile vanishes when her pale-blue eyes drop to the obvious purple splotch on my cheek.

"What the hell happened to you?"

I plop into the chair across from her. "I'm fine."

She leans forward, her blond curls bouncing around her shoulders. "You have a giant bruise on your face."

"I got jumped the other night. No big deal."

Her eyebrows hit her hairline. "No big deal? Eva, what happened?"

I sigh, raking a hand through my hair. "Two dudes in a van tried to follow me home after I left you with Will at the bar. So, I drove down by the construction site and asked them why they were following me."

"Why would you do that? Are you crazy?" Her hand flies up, palm facing me. "Never mind. Don't answer that. I already know the answer."

I stick my tongue out at her like a brat. "Anyway, they hopped out of the creeper van wearing ski masks and I tried to fight them off. One held me back while the other knocked me out cold, hence the bruise."

I rub my wrist under the table, still able to feel the unforgiving plastic ties that bound my limbs together. "Then they dumped me on the sidewalk near my building."

Deanna's hand clamps over her mouth.

I shrug and take a sip of the latte she ordered for me before I arrived, skipping over the part of the story when Dad insisted his doctor examine me using a rape kit. *I just want to be thorough,* he'd said. Little does he know, a rape kit is almost as invasive and humiliating as a rape itself.

But I'd be lying if I said the thought hadn't crossed my mind. It sickened me to wake up, confused, unsure if my body was abused while I was unconscious.

"Why would someone want to do that to you?" Deanna asks.

Because people are sick. "No clue."

"Does your Dad know?"

"Oh, he knows." I'm about to tell her about his ridiculous idea to have me tailed by security when a large shadow casts over our table. Someone's standing right outside the window, blocking the light from the setting sun.

I don't even have to look up to see who it is.

I already know.

I keep my eyes fixed on Deanna, hoping she won't notice. "So, how are things with Will?"

"Uh, do you know this guy?" Her eyes dart up to the window.

"What guy?" I take another swig of my latte, feigning ignorance.

She jerks her thumb to the left. "The giant man who's staring at you like a serial killer through the window right now."

A low growl settles in my chest as I shove my chair back and stand. "Unfortunately, yes. I'll be right back."

Outside, I whip around the corner of the building and give his shoulder a hard shove. He doesn't budge—instead I stumble backwards, which only angers me more.

"Why are you here?"

He heaves a sigh as if I'm the oversized gnat that won't go away. "I thought we went over this. I'm your bodyguard. Wherever you go, I go."

My jaw clenches. "I don't need a bodyguard."

"Did we not just have this conversation five minutes ago? Maybe you should go to the doctor and get your head checked."

My face heats and I move into his space until I'm craning my neck to look up at him. "Maybe the doctors should check your hearing instead, because I already told you that I don't need you."

"Your face says otherwise."

"Bruises heal."

"Not if you're dead."

We stand there, locked in a glaring match, until a bubbly voice perks up beside us. "Hi, I'm Deanna. I'm Eva's best friend."

Big Guy doesn't flinch, so I keep on staring a hole through his sunglasses when I say, "Go inside, Dee."

"I'd love to. Why don't you both join me? What does your friend like to drink?"

"He's not my friend."

His head turns toward Deanna. "I'm Eva's bodyguard."

Her jaw drops open. "Oh, wow. I didn't know you had a body-guard, Eva."

"I don't. Dad thinks I need one after the other night."

"He's right," they say in unison.

My hand smacks against my thigh as I look up at the sky and groan. "Not you too, Dee. I don't need anybody to follow me around all day. Come on, this is crazy."

She scoffs. "Eva, you got attacked. You're the daughter of one of the richest men in the city. Why is it so bad to have someone watching your back?" She leans toward me, twisting her lips to one side. "Especially someone who looks like him."

I don't miss the smirk tick on Big Guy's face.

Cocky bastard.

Rolling my eyes, I turn to face Deanna. "You know, just because you talk out of the side of your mouth doesn't mean he can't hear you."

She shrugs, giving him a sly smile.

I step in front of her. "Stop that. Don't smile at him. You're supposed to be on *my* side."

"I *am* on your side," she says. "That's why I want you to be safe. So what, you have a body guard? I don't see what the big deal is."

"Because it's just another way for my father to control me!" I shout, scattering several nearby pigeons. "He thinks he can track my every move. He thinks he can tell me where to go, how to dress, what to do. I just want to be a normal girl, Dee. I want freedom. This is just one more thing he's trying to take from me."

Deanna looks at me with pity reflecting in her eyes. "He just doesn't want you to end up like Eric."

I hate when she looks at me that way, and even more so when she mentions Eric's name. Plenty of people have it worse off than me in this world. I don't deserve anyone's pity.

I snap my sardonic armor back into place as I glare up at the giant-sized thorn in my side. "You want to stand here looking like a psycho-stalker while I enjoy my latte? Knock yourself out."

I stomp back inside with Deanna in tow. I swipe our cups off the table we were previously sitting at and press my middle finger against the window in front of his face. Then I move to another table across the room, the one farthest from the windows.

Deanna is just about frothing at the mouth when we drop into our seats. "Holy mother of God, that man is beautiful! You're so lucky!"

I groan and drop my forehead onto the table.

Yeah, that's me.

Lucky.

Continue reading Inevitable
Free with Kindle Unlimited!

ACKNOWLEDGMENTS

To Stacy, my beautiful wife, thank you for being so patient with me while I wrote this. It means the world to me when you get as excited as I do about my books. You always push me to believe in myself, and to keep going. Because of that—I do. I love you & appreciate you beyond words.

TayTay! Thank you for making this cover look as good as it does. But more importantly, thank you for being my friend. I've spent many nights laughing at our wacked-out texts, and I always feel better after we have a vent session. I hope we never have to show our tits to a sugar daddy on Instagram, and I hope your children enjoy college after I changed my covers 472982 times—tell them I said you're welcome (SJ: send erase the word send.)

Mary, thank you for going back and forth with me every time I sent you snippets of this story. You're always such an important part of my writing process because you kick my inner demon's ass!

Becca, your comments on each and every chapter are so helpful. I know quarantine life hasn't been easy, but you made time for me anyway, and I appreciate the shit out of you!

Chloe, your thoughtful insight on these characters helped make me a stronger writer and look at this story in a different light. I am so grateful for your help, and your friendship.

Jasmine, Carrie, Jennifer, Janae, & Chelsea: I don't have the right words to express how much I appreciate you allowing me to include your voices into this story. I hope you know that your words are going to help someone else out there who's struggling. You ladies will forever be a part of my warrior tribe.

Jenn Lockwood, thank you for polishing my book to perfection. I'm so happy I found you in the Insta world. You are awesome!

To all the bloggers & bookstagrammers, I appreciate you more than you will ever know! It's because of you that my books get read, and I am forever grateful.